THE EXILE

By Richard S. Wheeler
from Tom Doherty Associates

Aftershocks
Badlands
The Buffalo Commons
Cashbox
Eclipse
The Exile
Fool's Coach
Goldfield
Masterson
Montana Hitch
Second Lives
Sierra
Sun Mountain
Where the River Runs

SAM FLINT
Flint's Gift
Flint's Truth
Flint's Honor

SKYE'S WEST
Sun River
Bannack
The Far Tribes
Yellowstone
Bitterroot
Sundance
Wind River
Santa Fe
Rendezvous
Dark Passage
Going Home
Downriver
Deliverance

THE EXILE

RICHARD S. WHEELER

A TOM DOHERTY ASSOCIATES BOOK
NEW YORK

For Kathleen, Mary, Michael, and Margaret.

THE EXILE

Copyright © 2003 by Richard S. Wheeler

This book is printed on acid-free paper.

A Forge Book
Published by Tom Doherty Associates, LLC
175 Fifth Avenue
New York, NY 10010

www.tor.com

Forge® is a registered trademark of Tom Doherty Associates, LLC.

Library of Congress Cataloging-in-Publication Data

Wheeler, Richard S.
    The exile / Richard S. Wheeler.— 1st ed.
        p. cm.
    "A Forge book"—T.p. verso.
    ISBN 0-312-87847-8
    1. Meagher, Thomas Francis, 1823–1867—Fiction. 2. United States—History—
Civil War, 1861–1865—Fiction. 3. Irish Americans—Fiction. 4. Revolutionaries—
Fiction. 5. Politicians—Fiction. 6. Soldiers—Fiction. 7. Exiles—Fiction. I. Title.

PS3573.H4345E95 2003
813'.54—dc21
                                                                    2003049144

First Edition: December 2003

Printed in the United States of America

0 9 8 7 6 5 4 3 2 1

PROLOGUE

Each spring, the snows that whiten the backbone of the continent melt and find their way to the seas. Across the northern Rockies, the icewater drains from alpine cirques and collects into runnels and rivulets and creeks, which harvest the winter's work and funnel it toward the three great streams that form the Missouri River, the Jefferson, Madison, and Gallatin.

At the Three Forks in central Montana they become the Missouri and begin a majestic race across much of the continent. They plunge through the Gates of the Mountains, the canyon named by Lewis and Clark where the Missouri breaks out of the Rockies and pierces the high plains. The waters tumble over the great falls and into a bleak trench that carries them ever east.

At Fort Benton, once the head of navigation on the mighty river, not far below the Canadian border, the rolling river traverses a flat where an old adobe fur trading post once rose. There, in the 1860s, river boats that had fought upstream clear from Independence or even St. Louis discharged their passengers and cargo, and swiftly returned on the spring flood carrying men and gold back to the States. The water is clear and runs fast there.

The river sweeps eastward through fantastic crenellated

canyons, past scores of islands, oxbowing through a silent wilderness until its great tributary, the Yellowstone, conjoins it. From there it winds into the Dakota country on its long, lonely way to the sea over two thousand river miles distant. It collects the murky waters of prairie streams, bisects the historic dominions of the Mandan, Arikara, and Sioux, flows past one and another old fur trading post—relics of empire—and through lush tallgrass prairie where buffalo grazed in countless numbers.

It gathers to itself the waters of the Platte, and passes into the central plains, rolls past Independence, curves through the wooded riverbanks of Missouri, and at last debouches into the Mississippi near St. Louis, its icy waters from the Rockies mingling with waters from the north.

At Fort Benton, on the night of July 1st, 1867, the icy Missouri received into its bosom the body and spirit of Thomas Francis Meagher, Irish exile. The fate of Meagher's mortal coil is unknown. The fate of his spirit is perfectly known. The river cupped that spirit into itself and gently carried it toward home.

Then the Mississippi carried the lost heart of the exile past New Orleans and into the Gulf of Mexico, and out to the gulf current, which bore him north and east, across the lonely Atlantic, ceaselessly taking him to the place of his birth, and at long last washed him ashore upon the stony strands of Ireland, where he found the peace that had eluded him all his years of exile.

PART I

Escape

1

I beseeched the winds to has-
ten the *Elizabeth Thompson*. But her white sails didn't rise from
the haze of Bass Strait, and I feared I might perish. Of traffic in
that narrows there was a plenty, and time and again I built a
signal fire, only to watch the cloud of canvas slide past and sink
over the horizon along with my heart.

With each passage, and every hour, my peril increased. I
was a wanted man, yea, a celebrated and wanted man, and I
knew that Governor Denison would stop at nothing to thwart
my escape. Behind me, Van Diemen's Land crawled with the
Queen's constables and spies, all determined to catch
O'Meagher and put him in the lockup for life.

But the merchant vessel didn't rise. And all through those
fierce summer days of January, in the third year of my exile, I
sweated and roasted, thirsted and hungered on that barren
strand. I saw vessels bloom out of the haze when there were
none, spotted sails that proved to be only a shimmer of light,
scoured the empty seas with sun-blasted eyes, and all the while
looked over my shoulder, fearful of the royal constables rowing
out to Waterhouse Island.

It was a botched job. Something had gone wrong. I'd either
die or spend my life in chains at Port Arthur, regretting my
rashness. I didn't think much about Catherine, and sometimes

wondered why not. I should have pined for her, but I didn't, and I had no trouble consoling myself about our separation.

She was safe, and would join me in the American Republic by and by, along with our child who would soon come into this world. I was not running from her, and a curse upon any man who said I was! I comforted myself by remembering my larger purpose, which was to lift the chains of oppression from Ireland. I was not escaping for my own sake, but for Ireland's.

The Barrett brothers, true friends of Ireland, had sailed me to this place in their rude boat. They fished the strait and knew every cove. They brought food enough for two days, and from the ruins of wrecked ships and rotted sails we built a hut and feasted on smoked herring, cheese, and ship biscuit until time ran out, and they had to return lest their absence awaken suspicions. We had spotted vessels rising over the main, built smoky signal fires, danced and flagged and waved on the beach, but no bark had paused, and each ship posed the chance of betrayal. We were seen and ignored.

Then I was alone, with little enough to eat, no way to escape, and the clock of fate was ticking. What was left? Gnawing doubt, miserable meals of boiled beach crabs and shellfish, and lurking regrets which I manfully banished from my mind.

So many had helped me. I was oath-bound not to escape unless I revoked my parole, my promise to the penal authorities not to attempt to escape, but that did not prevent me from laying plans, or recruiting the assistance I needed. I was honor-bound not to escape, but I had never given my oath that I would make no plans. I am sure some will accuse me otherwise. I am a man of honor and I will personally flog the man who says I am not.

But it was a fine line, the one that separates planning from doing, and I pride myself that I drew it carefully, and adhered to that code of conduct that befalls all civilized men. The means by which I arrived on this desolate beach were impeccable, and I suffer no shame for it. I will escape this accursed prison island, this desolating countryside that harbors the human sewage of England and Ireland, transported here for decades and prevented from leaving by their conditional paroles—and the forbidding sea.

They sent me here in eighteen and forty-nine, after first sentencing me to death by hanging, drawing and quartering, for rising against Queen Victoria. They caught almost all of Young Ireland, we who had fomented revolution, and tried us, and the packed juries found us guilty not of sedition but of treason. It was in Clonmel, in the county of Tipperary, they sentenced me, but the sentence was commuted to transportation after a great uproar among the civilized nations, and I was brought here, along with the rest of Young Ireland, including my friends George Mitchel, Kevin O'Doherty, Smith O'Brien (that direct descendent of Irish kings), and Terence MacManus: those of us who dreamed of justice and sought liberty.

We were offered a ticket of leave, limited freedom to live outside of prison walls, upon giving our parole that we would not escape, and I took it, though O'Brien did not, and for his stubbornness he was sentenced to solitary confinement in a miserable cottage on Maria Island, one of the Queen's special hellholes for the intractable, and there he starved nearly to his doom in solitude until good men intervened.

And so began our sojourn at the bottom of the world. I was confined to the Campbell Town district, where I was free to roam. I disliked that stolid little crossroads, found Ross more to my liking, and finally settled in a cottage on Lake Sorel, in the uplands, where I lived freely and in comfort, along with a vast boredom, which is the true affliction of the exiled. At least I could ride and hunt, but that didn't quiet my restlessness. I hired a convict named Egan to look after me, and there I whiled away my dull days.

It was there, by and by, that I met Catherine Bennett, a comely young woman of nineteen, shy and mannered. One thing led to another. Her father, Byran, was an Irish highwayman, long since emancipated and settled as a rural burgher. She was the governess for the children of my friend Doctor Hall, and I found her fetching, though of course her station was very different from my own, and I had received as well a good schooling at Clongowes Wood, the Jesuit-run college in County Kildare. Some would have said we were unsuited, but I did not see it that way and pursued the match. It suited me to take a wife. And Bennett was pleased to see his daughter receive my attentions.

She knew exactly who I was, Meagher of the Sword, and was flustered by our first meeting, though I rather enjoyed it. The name had been hung on me for a speech I had made, calling for Ireland to make use of the sword to free itself. Well, I married her. Bishop Willson performed the rite. It was a good wedding, and some of my exile friends attended in disguise, looking like bushmen, illegally crossing the penal district lines to be with us.

My Young Ireland friend John Martin asked me searching questions about suitability; he obviously disapproved the union, but I claimed my Kate, and she soon joined me at the lake cottage. She was a perfect whirl of domesticity, attending to the little things that mattered to her, and sharing with me a disdain for the English. I don't suppose I can ever change matters, because marriage is eternal, and so I find myself wedded to this bucolic woman who fawns upon me. At times I found it oppressive, and fled to the amusements of Ross, but there is no shame in it that I can admit to; these are simply the differences of rank and station.

But I was made for larger things, and I say this without shame. When I proposed escape, she snugged me tight in her arms and said, "Go! I'll join you in America." She is subdued by nature and always accedes at once to my plans. She does not share politics, for those are quite beyond her, but is the perfect mate for an active man. There was, and is, nothing to stay her here, she's a freewoman, and once the child is born and she can travel, I will make sure she has funds to take ship. I won't be there for the birthing, and that troubles me, but she will be in good hands, with her solid parents and Doctor Hall attending. So why not? Ireland perishes, and I am trapped in exile.

My father will help; he has always helped, whether or not he approves of all I do. He was a partisan of the great liberator, Daniel O'Connell, and is also a man of means, lord mayor of Waterford, and an M.P. The only divide between us is method. He is content to fight for Ireland in parliament; I believe in strong measures. He will be proud of Kate, and the child, no matter that she comes from simpler and more rural stock. Her father robbed a mail coach, but that too was a revolutionary act, and he got caught soon enough and shipped to Van Diemen's Land. I applaud the old gentleman pirate.

Now I pace the shore restlessly, hunting food, wrestling with the deepening prospect that I might become a castaway here; might slowly starve and die. For all those who might have helped me will be watched. How little they know: it was not only the Irish, but good Scots and Englishmen with great hearts who supplied me with horses and havens as I worked my way westward, riding horses through silver moonlight, to the estuary of the Tamar River, where the Barretts rowed me ever west, toward the sea and my liberty.

On the morning of January 3rd, I sent a note to the constabulary at Ross, by my trusty servant Egan, and he handed it to the police magistrate, Mr. Mason. It said, simply, that I would revoke my parole in twenty-four hours, but would revoke it immediately if I was pursued.

By then of course I was packed and ready. We waited, two or three of us, at my cottage on Lake Sorel, and sure enough, about eight in the evening the constables showed up to arrest me. Mason had sent them immediately. I sat on my horse in some brush, within hailing distance of the cottage where my friends were gathered. I knew one of them, a man named Durieu. He and his fellow officer put up their horses in my little stable, and I sent Egan to let Durieu know I was willing to talk outside the stable, but the constable remained within, looking after his horse.

I thought to myself, O'Meagher, this man's staying in there for a purpose. The fellow's willing to avoid a meeting, so I emerged from my shelter of brush, and hailed the man, and took off at a good clip. There was no shame in it; I did the right and honorable thing, and let no man say I broke my parole, having revoked it before fleeing. The matter is not on my conscience, and never will be, and my witnesses were there to attest that it was done right.

So I galloped off into that fading light of a long summer's day, rounding the shore of the lake, and stopping at the cabin of an old timer to shave off my moustache. It would profit me to change my appearance whilst I could, and the quickest way was with the razor. Then I made my way westward through the high country, sheltered by sturdy families whose admiration for Meagher of the Sword bound them to help me.

So here I am, pacing the lonely strand, hiking the confines of this barren isle, waiting for my salvation from the sea, and always watching its landward side for the thing I dread most, a vessel bearing the constabulary.

In my solitude, I realized that there was one thing I had not properly thought through in the preceding weeks. If I surrendered my parole and escaped, I could never go home again for as long as I lived. O'Brien was determined to stick it out and win a pardon and go back to his beloved estate in Ireland. I had chosen a different and more fateful course. Never, as long as the British ruled my island, could I see my ancestral home, or Waterford, or walk upon the soil of my birth. I might escape this penal colony, but not exile. The die was cast, and that made my choices all the more painful. I had said good-bye to Ireland forever.

Then, one awful morning, I beheld an eight-oared boat with half a dozen men in it bobbing my way, the four men on the oars pulling hard against the ocean swells. There could be only one explanation: they knew I was here, and they were coming for me.

2

I searched frantically for a place to hide, a cliffside niche, a hole, a hidden glade, but it was all futile. This windswept sea-girt island was little more than naked rock. The evidence of my presence was everywhere: the hut fashioned from oars, mast, and sail, the cookpot, the ashes, the kitchen debris. They would root me out before the sun set. But maybe, if I hid myself well, I could commandeer their big boat, row away and strand them. Ah! But one man straining at the oars of a craft that size would be a bull's-eye.

So this was the fate of O'Meagher. I sighed. I was not used to hard labour but I would soon get used to it. And my shins would soon chafe from the irons around my ankles.

The craft headed for a sandy cove and rode a breaker into the beach, while I peered narrowly at these minions of the Queen from a nearby ridge. Small dark figures, six of them, spread out on the beach, studying the rockpile of an island that harbored me. There was no escaping them, so I rose and started down the long rough slope to where they stood. They were as startled to see me in this desolate place as I was to see them. And I was all the more amazed to discover that they wore ordinary sackcloth and canvas attire, not uniforms.

"Welcome," I said, taking their measure. They were hauling rough sacks of goods out of their vessel, which was a home-made jolly-boat of hand-sawn plank, big and clumsy but sea-worthy. My spirits rose. I often could and did talk myself out of trouble and now I would try.

I walked gingerly down the rocky slope to the water's edge while they stared.

Convicts, the whole lot.

"What you here for?" one asked. I surveyed his beefy face, his low brow, his gap-toothed mouth, and his slightly smirky smile.

"Looking for gold," I said. "Prospecting. Not any luck so far."

They wheezed, and the tension drained away. "Nice Irish bloke like you, looking for gold," one said.

I smiled. We stood there, grinning.

"You wouldn't be one of them Irish politicals, get tickets of leave as soon as they step on shore here?" asked another, a thin, bag-eyed scarecrow with buck teeth. "Like maybe the treasonous Meagher, him what rebelled against Her Majesty? The one they're hunting for like the world got turned upside down?"

There was no hiding from this bunch. "Sure and I'll tell you who I am, gentlemen, if you'll pull the shirts off your backs and let me see who you are."

The whole lot hooted. Those shirts hid the tracks of the cat-o'-nine-tails, no doubt about it.

"As fate would 'ave it, matey, we're off to the goldfields our bloomin' selves. Port Phillip first, then Ophir or Turon River, or Gawd 'elp us, Ballarat."

"Two hundred miles across the strait?"

He licked thick lips. "Gold for the picking. Lying on the ground. Big nuggets, fat as a finger, pluck 'em up. Better than California. Beats Van Diemen's Land, don't it?"

I had to agree that it did. And their plight was my own, and that would be my ticket among these cutthroats.

"I'm Meagher," I said, dropping the "O" that I had attached to my name here just because it emphasized the Ireland within me, and my ancient race, and set me apart.

"We're Her Majesty's loyal pickpockets," one replied. "Would you be heading for the diggings?"

For the moment I chose not to say where I was heading. "No, not there."

They studied me a moment, respecting my evasion, and grinned. Then they set to work, surveying the rocky domain, pitching a tent and making a camp in a sheltered cove. I showed them how to catch crabs and shellfish, and soon we had a pot of seafood, potatoes, and leeks boiling. They eyed me curiously, even as I eyed them.

There we were, refugees from the penal system, but we had nothing else in common, and barely even a common tongue. But my fugitive status was all the passport I needed to their world. They shared their meal heartily, and made swift easy alliance. Beneath our camaraderie lay the misery of the whole weight of British penal life, and the hunger we all shared to escape somewhere, anywhere, from this sullen island in the southern antipodes.

They were frankly curious about me, the rebel gentleman in their midst, and I made use of it. After we had supped heartily and then doused the fire so that it would not be seen at night, I laid a proposition before them:

"My friends, I need your help. I'm waiting here to rendezvous with a Yankee merchant ship that's days late. I'm worried that something's amiss. I'm stranded here, unable to return to Van Diemen's Land, or go elsewhere. You have a boat. I have a few shillings and the means of getting more to you for your help if my ship doesn't come."

That whetted their interest.

"How late is she?" one asked. I didn't know his name. We had slid past names. They knew mine, but I knew only that one was called Bill and another Emmet.

"So late I fear I missed her. She's a week overdue."

"You're in a bloody squeeze."

"Stay here a few days. I'll make it up to you. And give you what I have here. My camp's over on the sea-side of the island. Maybe I'll go with you to the mainland if help doesn't come."

To my surprise, they agreed to it at once, and again I fathomed the solidarity of the convicts. I was one of them; they would help. We were in this together. Never had I felt so beholden to a gang of cutthroats and brigands, pickpockets, pimps, purse cutters, and thugs.

But in fact they were hoping to redeem themselves in their own way: gold in their britches would transform them into other things, give them means less desperate than the miserable options open to the lowest classes of England. These men dreamed: gold might enable them to whip the whole system, thwart the Crown, vanish into the interior of Australia far from the eyes of the Crown, buy passage to distant shores, find women, live again. Perhaps they didn't see it that way; saw only easy pickings and a continent of bush and wilderness to hide in. And the easy pickings might come from murder rather than prospecting.

We waited together for my vessel, but no vessels paused, and I began to doubt that I would ever see my rescuers. We traded stories: I told them of the misery and famine in Ireland, the deaths and disease that scythed down my people, the cruel landlords, the halfhearted relief provided by the Crown, the injustices, the persecution of Catholics. I told them of Young Ireland, my bold speeches, of stirring an uprising among the peasants, writing and publishing seditious tracts, my capture and trial and the sentence to be hanged, drawn and quartered, and then the banishment.

They said little about themselves, which worried me.

By day we watched the empty sea, until at last, one afternoon, a three-masted ship rose out of the haze and began lowering sail, one sheet after another. My pulse lifted. We saw a puff, and that was immediately followed by a sharp crack; another puff and crack; and all the while we danced and waved as the vessel hove to and slid to a halt under the tether of a sea-anchor. High on the mizzenpeak flew the stars of the Australian League.

My ruffian friends got their leaky boat around, and we set out across the frothy sea, the convicts rowing their hearts out, dragging that lumbering cockleshell across the great breakers and into Bass Strait. Then at last we pulled up alongside, while the polyglot crew watched, bemused.

"My friends, thank you, thank you," I cried to my convict saviors. "Here, take this!"

I tossed them a leathern sack that contained my whole wealth, several pounds and a few shillings.

"Farewell and good fortune in the goldfields!" I cried.

And then I leapt from the careening boat and clambered up a jacob's ladder, and before I knew it I was standing on the quarter deck of the *Elizabeth Thompson* and shaking the hand of the ruddy little captain, named Betts, the selfsame man who had rescued my Young Ireland colleague Terence Bellew Mac-Manus and carried him to San Francisco.

I watched this odd crew, the handful that hadn't deserted in Melbourne for the goldfields, reel in the sea anchor and raise sail, even as my erstwhile colleagues in their tossing cockleshell drifted apart, waving cheerfully to me as they retreated back to Waterhouse Island.

I was a free man. The crew raised sail. I felt the ship heel under the wind, and saw a bubbling wake behind us.

"Captain Betts, sir, never was a man more welcome."

"Little late, Meagher, but we made it. . . . You had some company on that island."

"Good honest crooks, captain. Off to the goldfields."

"Ah! I lost half my crew. I'm undermanned, and these polynesian rascals scarcely know a mainsail from a bilge pump, but I'll make it. We're carrying a cargo of wool, fine Aussie wool, and bound for London, and I imagine you'll want to change ships, eh?"

I laughed, needing to give him no more answer.

"Recife, then," he said. "Catch a New York or Boston-bound vessel there."

"You've rescued me. You rescued MacManus."

Betts shrugged. "I was well rewarded."

"Did they search you before you left?"

"They always search us for stowaways, and right thorough they are, too, poking and probing, bayonets into bales, every cabinet opened, every crate studied. Nasty bunch. But they don't catch castaways."

I was suddenly anxious to know how he felt about Ireland. "Only for money?" I asked.

For a moment I thought he would not reply. "Not right, putting you down here, a criminal, for a little agitation."

"It wasn't little. It was an effort to incite armed rebellion."

"I'm a Yank, a New Englander. Let's just say I like to needle John Bull."

They stowed me, Meagher of the Sword, in a comfortable quarterdeck cabin, and then I retreated to the taffrail to watch Van Diemen's Land, my prison for two bleak and idle years, quarter away and diminish to a blurred gray line and then disappear. Now only the boundless green sea surrounded me, and my world was reduced to the creak of ship's timbers, the snap and chatter of a sail, the whine of wind in the rigging, the salt smell I knew so well, and the roll of this wool-filled Yankee bark.

Behind me, caught in that prison, was my wife Catherine, her belly filling with my child, living now in the bosom of her parents' home, safe with her father, the stagecoach robber Bryan Bennett.

She was haunting me, and her ghostly presence tempered my joy.

3

America at last. The *Acorn*, its sails reefed, slipped gently up the Hudson, carrying me to a new land, and a freedom I had never known. The New York harbor was beyond my fathoming, but the pilot of this Yankee bottom seemed to know every twist, while I watched anxiously. I cannot say why my heart ached so, with my liberty at hand and life so promising. Yet I was still the exile, the displaced Irishman three years removed from my hearth and home, and this New World exile could not be so different from that one in the antipodes.

I studied the city, perched on an island but spreading in all directions, wondering what sort of reception I might find. Everything looked hopeful. This Republic had an extradition treaty with England, but in the case of MacManus it had informed Her Majesty's government that the treaty didn't apply to political prisoners. And I had heard that a senate resolution had condemned the penal treatment of Young Ireland, and expressed the hope that we might be freed. The new president, Millard Fillmore, had urged his secretary of state, Daniel Webster, to approach the British government about its exiles, promising us a haven in these free states. So it was that I approached this sprawling city, not with trepidation but with an anxious joy.

Captain Betts had carried me across the Pacific without difficulty, and I spent my days reading, watching the moody sea, and visiting with him during his free moments. By the time we rounded the tempestuous Horn, I had acquired a fine tan and a blooming health. Letters of credit awaiting me on board, the thoughtful work of those Irish patriots who were seeing to my liberty, enabled me to purchase a suit of clothes and other necessaries, which Captain Betts supplied out of ship's stores.

I could never dissuade him from calling me *Meegur* instead of *Marr*, as it is correctly pronounced. Or better still, *Maa-er*, as the Irish pronounce it. But he had rescued me, true to his word, and whether he mangled my name was of no account.

At Pernambuco, in easternmost Brazil, I left the good captain and found passage on this Yankee bottom bound for New York. There I bought a good panama against the tropic sun, and we set sail for New York, three thousand six hundred eighty nautical miles northwest. I scarcely explored the Brazilian port. The polyglot Brazilians had absorbed me but little because my restless mind was on larger things. What would become of the exile, Thomas Francis Meagher?

I had friends in New York; indeed, some of Young Ireland had escaped to the city that was now rising before me. Michael Doheny, who was with us at Slievenamon, and John Blake Dillon, and my Clongowes school friend Pat Smyth. They would help; I could count on them. Dillon and Smyth had escaped the Queen's men on the same ship from Galway, Dillon disguised as a priest so successfully that Smyth wondered why the clergyman kept staring at him.

And I knew that a quarter of the population of the city was Irish, newly arrived and living in miserable tenements on the Lower East Side, or working farms north of the city, toiling in the humblest and meanest professions. And yet they were fed and housed, which is more than many were in Ireland, where they wandered and starved until they died. Slowly, slowly, the *Acorn* and a pilot boat drifted toward a berth at a depot called Castle Garden upon what I was told was Lower Manhattan, though I scarcely knew one precinct from another.

And so I stepped onto American soil on this warm 27th day of May, 1852, after four and a half months at sea and three years of exile from my beloved homeland. A new continent, a new life, but how I ached to go home. They bade me good-bye on the *Acorn*, those cheerful Yanks, and I made my way along the riverfront until I found an immigrant aid office, just as they had described, the sort that offers a bit of information while trying to recruit wretches like me for menial service somewhere.

"Where," I inquired of a string-bean clerk, "might the residence of John Blake Dillon be?"

The dough-faced fellow perused a hand-kept list. "The lawyer? Houston Street, I believe."

"And where is that?"

The clerk led me to a rude wall map, and pointed at a street running east and west, a good hike north. He supplied me with an address, and I set out, carrying my small satchel, which contained my entire worldly possessions, to find the man who might harbor me. Ah, what delight I took to walk in perfect liberty through this old and new city! I was weak from the long trip and a poor diet, and my legs kept expecting the land to roll beneath my feet as I treaded solid earth and cobbled streets instead of a teak deck.

But in time I paced easily, an ordinary man like the other ordinary men here, except that the sea-sun had bronzed me. I cherished my obscurity. I found Houston easily enough, but when I made inquiry at the address, I found that Dillon had moved to Brooklyn. It was already dusk, and I needed a haven, food, and rest, so I made my way back to the United States Hotel, booked a room, and spent my first night in the Republic in perfect anonymity.

The next morning, following instructions, I walked south to the offices of Dillon and O'Gorman, at 39 William Street. There, I knew, I would find welcome. Richard O'Gorman was one of ours as well, having led the rebels in Limerick.

This law office was easy to find, near Fulton Street and Wall Street, in the heart of the city's commercial area. I passed through busy crowds until I happened on the place, entered a corridor, found an oak door marked with the firm's name, and entered.

I was greeted by a young clerk.

"Mister Dillon, please."

"And who shall I say—"

"Tom Meagher!" The roar of that voice boiling from within an adjacent office could have shattered glass. John Dillon rushed out, pumped my hand, clapped me around my shoulders, and next I knew, the whole firm was crowding about, beaming, touching, patting, shaking hands. O'Gorman joined us. I knew him less well, but now he was treating me as a long-lost friend, as perhaps I was.

What a hubbub!

Next I knew, Irish from the whole area were jamming into that office, disrupting the day, treating me as if I was a hero and I could not imagine why. What had I done except give voice to the passions of my people? Yet here they were, beaming at me, shaking my hand until I thought my arm would lose the company of my body.

The other thing that mystified me was that I seem to have been expected.

"How is that?" I finally asked O'Gorman.

"Boston paper, the *Pilot*, published word of your escape," he said. "Oh, a week ago. It said you were expected here. Word must have come by Panama. And ever since, the whole of Ireland's been waiting."

"For Meagher?" I could not grasp why anyone would be waiting for me.

"For you, Tom Meagher," he said, tenderly.

There was no time to visit; waves of men, and not a few women, from Cork and Limerick and Clare and Tipperary and Waterford and Wicklow and Kildare crowded in, and I embraced them all. The partners all but declared a holiday, and shut down ordinary business.

I saw something in those faces: these immigrants weren't well, and I meant to ask O'Gorman about it. They were pale and sick and I heard the rattle of consumption in their lungs. The New World wasn't giving them much, but it was more than oppressed Ireland was giving them. And beyond their pallor was a simple joy in my presence. If it took an Irish rebel to lift them up, then Meagher was lifting them.

I embraced people I didn't know. Some just wanted to touch me. The women offered curtsies. Exhaustion overtook me; the partners noticed, and O'Gorman took me to his brownstone house not far distant, with the crowd trailing behind as if I were some legend.

"You'll stay here this night or I'll know the reason why," O'Gorman said, and I nodded at once. "We'll have dinner."

I know not what happened during the next hours, but when I peered from my upstairs windows I beheld a great crowd: work-worn men in dungarees and soiled shirts, with black cloth caps; gaunt women holding children to their thighs; an occasional man in a black top hat and handsome suit. And all of them standing in the cobbled and narrow street, waiting for a glimpse of Meagher, as if I could somehow lead them out of their troubles, free Ireland, heal the sick, give them hope. Maybe I could give them some hope, but there was little else I could do, for I had no money and no weapons, save for the silver tongue that had made me a leader of Young Ireland.

Ah, what a dinner that was! We toasted Young Ireland, toasted my success, toasted those who were still in fetters, toasted independence.

I rose. "My friends, I wish to toast this Republic, which holds me safe, gives us hope, and harbors us in perfect liberty."

They cheered that toast in a different way, solemnly, nodding, agreeing beyond what I suspected. They were republicans, every one, and would have no part of monarchy. And belonged to the Democratic party, to a man. If that was their party, it would soon be mine.

"And now," said O'Gorman, "we have something to show our honored guest."

He led us from that table to a window overlooking the wet street, opened it, and I discovered a sea of faces, thousands of them, extending blocks in either direction. They had come to see Meagher. Meagher! I waved. A great throaty yell greeted me.

And a band struck up an air.

"Brooklyn Cornet Band," Dillon said.

And then, to my astonishment, I saw a parade.

"It's the New York Sixty-ninth Regiment, the militia here, come to give Meagher a serenade, old friend," said Dillon.

I could not fathom it.

"The eyes of Ireland are upon you," he said.

I was too tired to make sense of it, but I knew this much: during my years of exile, Meagher had become a celebrated figure. I enjoyed the greeting, the airs and band music, the marching men, and wondered why all this came to me. I waved and they cheered.

If anyone wants to know what makes me as I am, I have a simple reply: I am a man who feels pain. Let a cottager face an eviction, let the famine starve a child, it is all the same to me as a wound in myself. I hurt for Ireland as much as I hurt for myself. Call it tribal if you will. What afflicts any part of Ireland, afflicts me. If one humble Hibernian suffers, so do I, and that is how I am made, and that is why I felt in my bones, that evening, the tribute they were paying me, and the unfinished business before us all.

4

They never stopped celebrating Tom Meagher, and I began to think these balls and dinners and parades were for someone else. Who was I, and who was that other Meagher they invited to levees, toasted, honored, and promised political appointments? I was invited to several cities to address them. Governor Lowe, an old Clongowes schoolmate, even summoned me to Maryland.

It became a great fashion in New York to quote back to me my farewell to the world, uttered at Clonmel before my sentencing by that grim, periwigged judge, Chief Justice Blackburne, who was assiduously serving Her Majesty. Thus it was that one or another of my hosts would rise at a banquet, paper in hand:

"Having done what I felt to be my duty, having spoken what I felt to be the truth—as I have done on every other occasion of my short career—I now bid farewell to the country of my birth, my passion and my death; whose factions I have sought to still; whose intellect I have prompted to a lofty aim; whose freedom has been my fatal dream. I offer to that country, as proof of the love I bear her and the sincerity with which I sought and spoke and struggled for her freedom, the life of a young heart. . . . Pronounce then, my lord, the sentence which the laws direct, and I will be prepared to hear it. I trust I shall be prepared to meet its execution. I hope to be able, with a pure heart and perfect composure, to appear before a higher tribunal, a tribunal where a Judge of infinite goodness will preside, and where, my lord, many, many of the judgments of this world will be reversed."

And so I heard my words, usually conjoined with an important point of evidence: I was not at Ballingarry, where Young Ireland fomented armed rebellion, and I had not lifted the muzzle of a gun against the Queen's men, for I had been out recruiting when O'Brien and MacManus led the peasants to their fateful meeting with the Crown. And then it was customarily added that, nonetheless, for this I had been found guilty of high treason, and was sentenced to be *hanged, drawn and quartered.* And that was a thing that brought even more wetness to the eyes of these New Yorkers as they toasted me.

It was not only the elite who celebrated my arrival. Ofttimes I found the humble patiently waiting for me in the street outside my hotel, men in black cloth caps, the map of Ireland in their faces, gaunt women in their Sunday skirts with little children tugging their hands, waiting in twilight, or mist, or shadow.

"So it is you, bonny Thomas Meagher. Sure and we have come to see the one who would set Ireland free, so we might go back home some day," one might say. And they would shyly press around, if only to touch my sleeve or share a smile.

"See, lad," they would say to a half-terrified child tugged toward me, "here's the very one that faced the constables, faced the lords and judges. Here's the very one, Tom Meagher he is, who's come back from the dead, from the bottom of the world. Look well now, boy, for here's an Irish knight, bold as ever was made by God."

And I would clasp the cold hands of a ten-year-old consumptive boy, or a sniffling girl, and the parents would thank me for the simple act of blessing their children, and I feared that when I died they would want to put my saintly relics under their altar-stones.

And so they came to my hotel to serenade me, to shake my hand, to see the one who would sweep them home to a free Ireland, the one who would lead and inspire them, raise armies, slay British dragons, drive the vipers out of Erin, like some latter-day St. Patrick.

I basked in this, even while growing impatient, because there is life to be lived and good causes to be furbished. But I scarcely knew what to do. I was an exile in a strange nation, a bustling city whose precincts I didn't know, and whose people I barely fathomed. Was I truly welcome? Perhaps not. The Irish were shunned in many quarters, except perhaps as servants. Once, during a street serenade for me soon after my arrival, an old Yankee gent opened his windows and played "God Save the Queen" on his pianoforte.

Dillon's advice was to sit back, enjoy it, and see what opportunities the Republic might offer me. I certainly needed something; I had no means and a family to support. But everywhere I turned, people wanted me to talk. They wanted to learn about Ireland, the uprising, Australia, the British penal system, and Van Diemen's Land with its great monastic prisons. I thought there might be a living in it, at least until the novelty of listening to Tom Meagher wore thin.

I addressed various societies during the summer and found them enthusiastic about my cause, which was simple and powerful: free Ireland. Free her suffering people from the landlords both English and the Queen's privileged Protestants, the rent-takers, the hard men who put families out of their cottages, the absentee barons who ran cattle over a poor man's potato crop and never set eyes upon those they'd ruined and starved.

They feted me. I did not puzzle over this. Plainly I was a symbolic rebel, an icon of resistance to the crown, and if that mythical Tom Meagher didn't match the real one, I could not help it. I can bewitch a crowd, it is a gift, and I did so, drawing on my powers of persuasion to bring people to my point of view.

On May 29th the local politicians held still another reception for me, and invited me to speak. I talked about Australia, the convict system, and the struggles of its better classes to end transportation and bring that bounteous continent into respectability. The convicts, I said, were a low lot, but the freemen settling there were not, and deserved support.

But even as I lectured, I knew that these Americans would soon weary of me, and I could not continue forever. For the moment I was comfortably fixed; in the longer term, I needed a more substantial means. I did not neglect to write my father, Thomas, Senior, of my safe passage to the United States. He would rejoice in his restrained way. Though he never quite approved of my conduct when it came to Irish Independence, I could expect him to help.

And of course there was always Catherine, to whom I also penned a note or two detailing my successful hegira. I could suppose she had long since borne a child, and even now I awaited word from her about my new son or daughter. Sometime I would need to bring her and the child to these shores, but there was no rush: the child would need to grow, wax strong, in order to endure a long sea journey. In Kate's case, no news was good news, and I felt assured that all was well in Ross.

I received, at last, a letter from her, telling of the birth, in February, of a son, whom she named Henry Emmet Fitzgerald

Meagher, upon my instructions. I had a son! And he had a name that resonated with the liberty of Ireland! I wrote Kate at once, rejoicing, urging her to recover her health, which was fragile, and strengthen the little lad for the long ordeal at sea. I posted it, knowing it would be several months before the winds would carry it, in the bellies of several ships, to my wife. I had a son. I had a family. I had a wife. My friends celebrated with me.

In July, the Irish of New York held a grand parade in my honor. With Pat Smyth, I hiked down to the Battery, and there the whole of the Irish militia had gathered to march for me: the Emmet Guard, the 9th and 69th New York volunteer regiments, the Shields Guard, the Mitchel Light Guard. There they all were, parading for me before most of the Irish of New York. Doheny asked me to speak, and I was ready: The light glistening off those bayonets, I proclaimed, would shine off the clouds and illumine the glory of those regiments.

There was even a song published about me, an account of my escape and arrival in New York.

The moment young Meagher, in sight he did come,
Their hearts with joy bursting, all round him did run,
Sixteen thousand or more, was the friendship was shown,
You're welcome young Meagher, though an exile from home.
The New York brave heroes, will never forget,
That for Francis Meagher, in friendship they met,
It is plain to be seen, for Erin go bragh,
That the sons of New York they still have a graugh.

One day, while imbibing ale at Phelan's Tavern with O'Gorman, I posed the question: "What am I to do, Richard?"

He smiled. "Look about you," he said.

I did, seeing a warm, comfortable haunt of the Irish, where

men from half the counties of the old country were gathered to drink ale or stout, and cough—yes, cough, for the Irish were a coughing race, and the cough killed someone in every family. Some wore baggy wool suits that turned them into morticians or barristers or clerks; most wore rough workingmen's clothing, for these were dray men, muckers, street sweepers, butchers, hod carriers, laborers who worked by the sweat of their brow. There was not the slightest barrier between the poorest and those whose well-brushed derbies sat jauntily upon their locks.

"What do you see?"

"Irishmen, like a tight little club."

"Yes, and you're also seeing other things: politics and business . . . a little help for the desperate and loans to bring someone over, across the sea, sometimes a sack of spuds. And above all, jobs. Jobs are what's gotten here, and in a hundred other public saloons."

I waited for more, and O'Gorman swiftly led me into a new world.

"We have our ways. We're a quarter of the city, the poorest quarter, but we stick together, and we govern."

"What ways, Richard?"

"Law and office. We have our judges, our clerks, our inspectors, our constables. We have our party, the Democrats, and we have our city club, called Tammany, and these control the patronage, the funds, the licenses and permits, the way public money's spent. There's not a poor widow from Ireland that cannot get a little bit to get her by, just by applying right here. And here's where it starts, here in our saloons."

"What does this word Tammany mean?" I asked.

"Name of some red Indian chief. We didn't start this club. It's been around almost as long as New York. Aaron Burr, the man who shot one of the founders of the republic, Alexander

Hamilton, in a duel, was a Tammany man. It used to be a patriotic society; some Indian rituals, wigwams, all that. But it's always been Democrat. It fought against imprisonment for debt, and for other things, such as broad suffrage. And now it's helping all of us."

It was not so different from the old country, I thought, where the public house brought men together for a glass, and where we looked out for one another, and where we talked and talked because that is what we do.

"There's not a thing that happens in Ireland, or here, that doesn't pass through this saloon," O'Gorman said. "News! It's not the Irish papers, it's the saloon where we gather after a day's hard toil, to learn how the world goes. You've met dozens; here are thousands, and they all know the name of Tom Meagher."

"What are you saying, Richard?"

"A living's here. You're a college man. Read the law, pass the exams, become a lawyer, and help Tammany."

"Read the law? I'm not a citizen. How could I be licensed?"

"Leave that to the party," he said.

"I could be a licensed lawyer and not yet a citizen?"

But my friend only nodded. It was then that I suspected that these countrymen of mine had their ways. And I soon found out the truth of it. The courts were turning plenty of Irish into American citizens without much waiting, and fetching Tammany new voters and fierce loyalty with every naturalization.

"Law and politics," I said.

"Law, anyway. A competence for you, poor as it may seem because you'll have Irish clients, and a platform. . . . that is, if you wish to support Irish Independence."

I inhaled a great charge of that smoky air, exhaled, and smiled. "Is that the best way, in this Republic?"

O'Gorman simply smiled. "We're proud to have you here, Tom Meagher."

For an Irishman, it was the best way. Maybe some day I'd be practicing law with Dillon and O'Gorman.

I fell into a routine, setting up lectures, polishing several talks—the one on penal Australia was the most popular—and biding my time until I could better understand this country. I stayed in touch with Young Ireland. D'Arcy McGee came down from Boston. I met with the members of a new Meagher Club, who presented me with Bancroft's *History of the United States*, a book I intended to study. I ventured upstate, and spoke in Albany and Utica and Rome, always collecting a handsome sum from my fifty-cent lectures.

The summer passed without further word from Catherine, and then one September day, a letter did arrive, blown across the Pacific, carried over the equator, borne north and east to New York from that place of sorrow, Van Diemen's Land.

"Dear Mr. Meagher," Catherine wrote, using the formal address as she always did, though I had always urged her to call me Tom.

"I regret to inform you that our son, Henry Emmet Fitzgerald Meagher, died June 8 of sickliness. He is buried in Richmond, and we have put up a stone."

5

I walked down to the Battery under a leaden afternoon sky, wanting to be alone. I sat down there, before the waters. Haze obscured the sea, and I could barely make out the passage of vessels, which slid by me like ghosts.

Would I never escape Van Diemen's Land? Now flesh of my flesh lay buried there in exile, a wee boy four months on earth, but baptized and with God. The claws of imperial England seemed to pin me still. The sentence of exile was not lifted by my escape, and now it crushed me.

Catherine would be free to travel, and I would bring her to America. I wondered how a woman from the rural district of Ross would fare in urbane New York; whether she would be happy. She had expected to spend a lifetime with me down there in the other hemisphere. Now she was half a world away, and if she came here she would be the exile.

I knew I must write and comfort her. My father had sent her gifts and had welcomed her into the Meagher family, and for that I was grateful. She and I were wed forever; bound unto eternity by our troth and the sacred laws of the church. She was a Meagher. I sighed, knowing I would do what was required of me, get a living, support her, do my best, but my heart was tugging at me from other directions. I wanted to get back into the fight: free Ireland.

With that resolution, I headed into the bustling city again, heartened by it. I would need to prepare a place for a family, acquire a competence. For the moment I was solvent. I had been preparing formal speeches, no longer satisfied with remarks and notes, and now I would sing for my supper in a black frock coat and boiled white shirt.

This was an election year in the United States, and I followed the politics closely, knowing but little about my new country. A Whig, Millard Fillmore, held office, having ascended to the presidency upon the death of the Mexican War hero, Zachary Taylor. But he was not my man, not any Irishman's man. We were Democrats, supporting General Pierce, the New Englander who took a moderate view toward slavery, and welcomed the Irish into his ranks.

Fillmore sought support from those who had formed themselves into the Native American Party, and belonged to the Order of the Star-spangled Banner. These were the ones who put Help Wanted signs in the window, but with the proviso that Irish Need Not Apply. These were the ones who feared Catholics, tried to exclude Irish and Germans from citizenship, and advocated a *twenty-one year* residency before anyone could apply to become a citizen. That is to say, we could apply upon our death bed.

Pierce was our man. He drank too much, spent too little, and suffered a wife who abominated politics and Washington, but what did it matter? He welcomed us. I wasn't a citizen and couldn't vote, but I followed matters closely, taking my education from John Blake Dillon, who spent countless evenings while sitting in saloons making me aware of this nation's affairs. He couldn't even speak the name Fillmore without exuding contempt.

"What are the Know-Nothings?" I asked him one evening over some well-aged rye.

"The nativists. They started with secret lodges, and when anyone inquired what they were about, they always said they knew nothing."

"What is it they don't like?"

"Irish and Germans. We're dumb as stumps, we're drunks, we're papists. And the Germans don't speak English and many are Catholic."

"Is Fillmore one?"

Dillon nodded, and sipped his stout. "Not officially, but it's how he leans. Officially, he's a Whig, follows the Whig platform, supports compromise on the slavery issue, but he's lined up these Know-Nothings."

"Are they dangerous?"

"Are the British dangerous to Ireland?" he replied.

"How did this start?"

Dillon grunted. "Mostly immigration. We came here. We took the worst jobs. We're different. We're poor, and thanks to the English, we're uneducated. So they call us Paddy, and think we're fit to dig ditches. And we have our grievances, too, Tom. They use their King James Bible in the schools, making Protestants out of us. That's one grievance. Sounds a little like Ireland, don't it?"

I nodded. For generations, Catholic religion was all but driven underground in Ireland, while priests held secret masses in the hedges and dodged the law.

Dillon clapped me on the back. "We'll turn you into a good Tammany man yet, Tom. You know how to orate. You've got the tongue to melt hearts. You'll be good at politics."

The idea appealed to me, even though my whole being, my mind, heart, soul, and body, clung to Ireland. What had I fought for? What had I been sentenced to death, and exiled, for?

But Fillmore didn't win his party's renomination. Down in Baltimore they nominated General Winfield Scott after fifty-three ballots, defeating Daniel Webster in the process, and the election came down to Scott against Pierce. Fillmore was out, but some of the nativist parties were strong and dangerous.

I felt the withering Yankee winds sometimes in the lecture halls, especially when I headed toward upstate New York. Not everywhere was Tom Meagher a hero. There were hard questions: had I not violated my parole, my word of honor, when I fled Van Diemen's Land? What business had I, turning American citizens toward conflict with England? Who was I to arrive on these shores and begin lecturing people who had lived here all their lives?

I knew also that the whole of New York City, and especially its press, was watching, watching, watching me. One day a boy delivered a card: it was from Horace Greeley, editor of the *Tribune*. "Call on me," he had written on the obverse side. So I did.

I had known little about this fellow, but swiftly discovered that he was the wunderkind of American journalism, a somber Whig reformer, passionately opposed to black slavery, a proponent of the rights of labor and a hearty friend of working men. His paper was serious, avoided scandal and sensation, and oozed moral righteousness. Did the man never laugh?

I discovered an earnest man with a noble brow and long face and a withering stare, sitting like a slovenly king behind a dark desk in an ornate dark office. The man was a gloomy frog in a gloomy pond.

"Well, Meagher, do come in." He offered a firm hand. "I've been watching you. Following your career. Now, sir, you're here and I can learn what must be learned about the Irish Question."

"Ah, the question?"

"Who's right? Who's wrong? And why? How you stand. What you think of America. What the Irish are about over here. Why the Irish think as they do. Why they don't blend in. All that sort of thing."

"Those are broad issues, Mr. Greeley."

"Yes, yes, sir, indeed. Well, let's be about it."

There he was, vigilant, waiting, a pillar of Yankee rectitude, pen poised, treating me as a curiosity. I took a dislike to him, but held it in check, and began a steady description of life under British oppression, the famine, the cruelty of landlords, the evictions, the barefoot children, the religious afflictions imposed on my people, their desperate trips, mostly in steerage, to New York. But I had scarcely begun my discussion when he broke in:

"What I want to know is, Meagher, why are the Irish for the South? For slavery?"

"I think, sir, that you're mistaken."

"No, no, I see it in your Democrat press. You all favor the South. The thing you fear is abolition of black servitude."

"Ah . . ."

"Black slavery, Mister Meagher, is little different from what your people suffer in Ireland. Do they control their own lives? No, the British do, the landlords do. What's so different, then? Do black men not have rights?"

"The Irish in New York fear that their jobs will be taken if darkies are freed, Mr. Greeley."

"Ah! Is that it? A view so narrow? Not any consideration of other people, of the rights of all? The good of all mankind?"

This was becoming an ordeal, but I was getting my mettle up.

"Sir, when we solve our own problems, we'll have the leisure to look at other problems. Try living in a tenement, without employment, with six others jammed in a room or two, without piped water, and then tell me about the darkies."

"And meanwhile black men suffer, toil for no wage, cannot even keep a family together. Right here in this country! You favor the South, then?"

"I favor letting each region set its own course."

"I don't. We should crush slavery. Whip it, beat it, destroy it, drive the demon out."

"You're a man of bold schemes, then."

"Bold schemes? Ha! You know what Sam Houston called me? A man whose hair is white, whose skin is white, whose eyes are white, whose clothes are white, and whose liver in his opinion is the same color! Ah, there's a slaver I can appreciate." For once, he smiled.

I left a half hour later, scarcely knowing why I had been summoned to the great man's lair. He never permitted me to continue my dissertation on Irish matters, and expressed no further curiosity about the revolutionary Irishman sitting before him, but lectured me about his multitudinous reforms, chief of which was abolishing slavery.

I had the distinct feeling that he understood the Irish not at all, and that I understood these rock-ribbed Yankees even less. I left those chambers feeling a need to walk into the nearest church, bless myself with a quart of holy water, and receive the sacraments.

My first formal lecture, at Metropolitan Hall, was a great success. We packed the hall, and could have filled it several times over, charging fifty cents admission. Australia was my theme, and I told these New Yorkers every detail of my experience as an exile: how we were transported there, given tickets of leave on our parole not to escape, except for the noble Smith O'Brien, who refused parole and was treated as a common criminal thereafter; nearly starved to death, too.

I told them our business was not done. Some remained in bondage far across the silent seas. Patrick O'Donohoe, for one, William Smith O'Brien, John Mitchel, Kevin O'Doherty. But Terence MacManus had escaped, and lives now in San Francisco, and I in New York. The work was not done, I said. Young Ireland must be freed. Not only freed, but pardoned, their records expunged, for they were patriots, not criminals, and Ireland is our home and always will be.

And so I lectured for over two hours in that crowded hall, my voice carrying easily above the coughing of my audience, and my passion piercing them all. My lecture committee gave me a draft for $1,650, and I knew I could well support myself and family with that. Laboring men were lucky to get a dollar a day, six days a week, and here I was, collecting great sums upon an evening's work.

Now I set about lecturing wherever the committee sent me. I traveled to Utica and Schenectady, where the reception was cooler, and hard-eyed Yanks viewed the Irishman with skepticism and asked me the most painful questions they could conjure. But I had a cause, and a passion, and a gift for conveying my cause, and so they came, and I filled the halls wherever I went. There were those who just wanted to shake the hand of a man who defied the Queen, outwitted an empire, or, like their own Patrick Henry, risked death for the sake of liberty.

Franklin Pierce won the election, and I was heartened to have a Democratic-Republican in office and a sympathetic ear for the cares of the Irish. We did not neglect him, but voted en masse for our man, Protestant, Yankee, and New Hampshire-man though he was. The attacks on him were scabrous. During the Mexican war he had fallen from his horse in battle, and fainted from the pain, and this they took as a mark of cowardice and mocked his service to the republic.

I have heard that his strong-willed wife is depressed by it all. She had resisted his earlier career in Congress, despised Washington, and vowed she would not return. So the poor General will govern without his wife in the White House, and I pity him, for a wife who will not eagerly support her man in his great calling, nor afford him her company at a time so transcendent in their lives. He likes his whiskey, and that makes him one of us.

I spent that fall of 1852 traveling widely, lecturing about Ireland, Australia, and the plight of my friends still in fetters. My travels returned me to Schenectady, Utica, Albany, and other places upstate, and then to St. Louis and Cincinnati, where a Catholic paper chastised me because I had been critical of the Irish clergy, which had failed to raise the cross at that crucial moment when Young Ireland was laying siege to the English.

Then a man named O'Neill showed up at my door. He was, he explained, General Pierce's orderly during the Mexican War, and he bore a message from the president-elect: come visit the general at his home in Concord, New Hampshire.

I hastened there, pausing only to put together a lecture tour in the process. There, in crisp green Concord, I was welcomed by the handsome general, who shooed his aides away and conducted me into his private study, where he had libations ready.

"Mr. Meagher, I've wanted to meet you," he said warmly. "Your efforts on behalf of the Democracy have helped me. Your efforts to free Ireland have won my admiration."

THE EXILE

"I could do no other, sir, for Ireland bleeds."

He poured a generous dollop and handed it to me. "Tell me about the political prisoners in Australia," he said.

"Well, sir, if I have your absolute confidence, I will," I said. He nodded.

"A certain friend of ours, Pat Smyth, has been funded by a New York committee to free the rest of the prisoners over there, and even now he's in Melbourne making arrangements. We think he'll free Mitchel, O'Donohoe, O'Doherty and maybe Smith O'Brien, if he can persuade that stubborn man to leave."

"I'll certainly keep your confidence, Mister Meagher, and I'll see what my administration can do. Count on it. There are ways and means to assist your brave friends, promote Irish independence.

"I've asked you here because I need you. The country's being torn apart by these damned abolitionist radicals. I fear for the nation unless sanity prevails. Your eloquent rhetoric has reached countless ears. I would welcome any voice of moderation in this matter. I oppose slavery personally, but abolition of it is constitutionally up to the southern states themselves, not us. That's our party's philosophy; that's the message I want to foster, and you can help greatly."

"It's sound and honorable, General. You have my pledge."

"Good! There may be more in this for you soon," he said.

I liked Pierce. And I knew he liked me. We talked broadly, mostly about American politics, and North-South conflict, for half an afternoon before he bade me good-bye. And he made me promise to attend his inauguration, which I gladly did. I did not know what use the Pierce government would have for an escaped felon, who was not even a citizen, but I did not doubt that the support of the Irish would be useful to this shrewd

49

man. During the whole meeting I did not see his wife, who closeted herself from the likes of politicians and office-seekers.

My reputation seemed to march before me. In Fall River, Massachusetts, they gave me a thirty-two-gun salute. In Philadelphia I was met by an Irish militia unit called the Meagher Guard. I arrived in the capital on February 27th and spent the afternoon with Pierce at Willard's Hotel. We drank and smoked, and I knew I had a powerful friend in the White House, and he knew he had the Irish on all the North and South issues.

Even as we conferred, my bride Kate was at sea, or so I believed from her notes. At Hobart she had boarded the *Wellington*, bound for the British Isles, where my father, Thomas Meagher Senior, would welcome her to our ancestral home in Waterford, and then bring her across the Atlantic. I kept telling myself that I awaited her arrival with joy.

6

I could see Catherine Bennett Meagher, and my father, Thomas Francis Meagher Senior, standing midships of the *Thomas Pintlar* as the pilot boat eased the sea-stained merchant brig toward the gray Hudson River wharf.

Fetid, tropical heat smothered New York; it was so humid a man could change his shirt five times a day and not feel fresh. I marveled that my body could leak so much from so many pores.

I was expecting them. Word had reached me within the fortnight that Kate had arrived in Waterford, where an amazing crowd of *twenty thousand* had come to celebrate the arrival of the exile's wife. My father had taken her in hand, so the reports said, and would sail on the *Pintlar* for New York shortly, after Mrs. Thomas Meagher, Junior, had a chance to rest from her long voyage from Van Diemen's Land.

So my wife was in his capable hands. He and my brother Harry and all my clan had welcomed and embraced her. It would have been a most pleasant meeting, Kate and my brothers and father, it being my father's nature to gather his family close to his bosom.

And there she was, wearing a bottle-green affair with lace, no doubt Waterford lace, at the sleeves and neck. Her eyes were upon me; I could see that, and my father's hand was pointing me out from among the wet-browed crowd standing on that steaming pier.

A runner from the shipping company had come for me when the brig had been spotted, allowing me time to splash my face, change my shirt, tidy up my room at the Metropolitan Hotel, and then hike through the vile odors of compressed humanity toward the river. Behind me rose a great racket of carts and drays, snorting horses, and iron tires on paving stones. Before me, the vessel slipped toward its berth in eerie silence.

Kate waved, tentatively. I returned the wave.

I felt oddly detached from all this, almost as if it were someone else's wife, not mine. More eagerly did I scan the face of my graying father, Member of Parliament from Waterford, lord mayor, prominent merchant, supporter of Daniel O'Connell's great reforms that lifted Irish Catholics partly out of their oppression.

At last the sweating navvies made fast the brig with squeaking hempen rope and slid a grimy gangway to the stout wooden peer.

And then my wife and father crossed that last physical barrier between us, and she was there before me, filling my arms, a hesitant smile upon her face, and questions in her eyes.

"Kate? Are you well? Was it a good trip?"

"Oh, Mister Meagher, a long one and tiresome, and I only saw two porpoises. But oh, how good to see you."

I smiled, released her, and addressed my sire. "And you sir, welcome to the United States."

My father surveyed me, looking for the brands of convictry upon me that might reveal my past. There were none to see.

"Aye, boy, a good sail, and hotter than any in Ireland."

"Lord love a duck, what a jungle place this is!" she said.

I had planned to bring friends to this reunion, yet it had all happened too fast, and too early in the day. And now I was glad I hadn't.

I looked upon Kate with great attention, noting that she was thinner but still well rounded, and I felt a quickening of the pulse that came upon a tide of memories of our sweet hours alone on the shore of Lake Sorel, our cottage to ourselves.

"The boy, Kate, was he a sweet and bonny child?"

"Sure and he was stamped with you upon him, Mister Meagher, but he never took a strong breath. And fret he did, all the time."

"I will never get past it, Kate."

She fingered her dress and patted it. Around us the passengers bustled ashore, and teamsters and cartmen padded on board to collect trunks and valises. On the quarterdeck, an officer directed the seamen as they swung through the rigging.

"Word reached you we were coming, then," my father said. "I sent it ahead."

"It came, sir, Tuesday last."

"Well, have you a place for us?" he asked.

"It's a few blocks, the Metropolitan, fine modern hotel with private plumbing, or we could get a cabriolet."

My father deferred to Catherine, who looked small and enervated.

"A ride, Mister Meagher, if you will, sir."

I engaged a hansom from a toothless lout, and we took off at a good clip. It wasn't far, but the heat made it so, or at least it seemed to be the heat. The leather seats were clammy; the horse lathered and dripped.

My father studied the city sharply, his shrewd gray eyes taking in its bounty, the Irish laborers in their dungarees, the frock-coated men and stylish women, all mixed with the ragged poor, some of them begging.

But the Metropolitan was a marvel that raised his eyebrows. I paid the cabbie, led my wife and father into its wondrous interior, and offered them a libation with pond ice at the hotel saloon, but they declined. Kate had never been in such a place, with the flocked ruby wallpaper, fleur-de-lis, cream and gilded cornices, potted palms, servants in livery, and blue Brussels carpet. She gawked and clucked as we mounted two flights of stairs in foetid air.

"It's a palace, is what," she said. "They haven't thought of such as this, even in Hobart!"

"The draymen will have your trunks here directly," I said.

I had engaged a room down the hall for my father, and soon settled him in it. I escorted Kate to my own room, opened the door, and led her in.

"Oh, Mister Meagher, my oh my," she said, her gaze sweeping the room, the private bath and water closet and commode, the clutter of my foolscap and ink bottle and steel-nibbed pens on an escritoire, and at last, the tightly covered bed.

She folded into my arms, and again I felt a great quickening of pulse. I clasped her close, glad to embrace her, enjoying her solidness. She clutched me tight, kissed me, and I felt the stickiness of our sweat and the oiliness of her brow and the dampness of her hair.

"Oh, you cannot know how it's been since I buried our boy, Mister Meagher. How it's been, and how I ache for the little child we made. Oh, you wouldn't know that I have fresh flowers put on it once a week, Mister Meagher."

"I wish I had seen him," I said, breathing into her ear.

"Oh, he started so well, 'twas I all torn up, but I mended and had a hard time suckling him. Oh, how I wanted to present him to you, and now here we are, and I've not a child in my arm to give you, Mister Meagher, and it makes me weep."

I felt her convulse and the tears come, so I held her gently a while, feeling her sorrow. Finally the snuffling ceased, and she pressed herself quiet and clinging upon my bosom.

"I'll let you freshen up, Kate, after the long trip, and talk to my father for a while. Haven't seen him since 'forty-eight."

Her face crumpled, but she recovered swiftly, and smiled. "I'll be waiting for you, lovey," she said, and there was invitation in her voice.

I smiled, plucked up a brown bottle of rye, blew her a kiss, left her to her toilet, and padded quietly down the hall.

My father opened, a question on his face.

"She's done in, freshening up, and it's a good time to visit," I said.

"Is it so, now?" He eyed me sharply. "What are your plans?"

"To take you out to dinner if you're up to it."

I found two tumblers, and poured an inch into each. Good Hennessy Brothers whiskey, from Pennsylvania. He accepted the tumbler and nodded.

"Good to see you, and glad the passage was easy."

"Slow it was, and they swung south to pick up the trades, clear to the thirtieth latitude, they told me. Added ten days."

"And Kate stood it?"

My father nodded. "She's a plucky lady: you have a fine one, if you're asking. Got sick a few times, especially when it blew and we heeled hard, but she's aching to be with you."

There was a question in my father's eyes. Did he guess that Kate and I were ill suited? What worked in Van Diemen's Land would be more problematic here. I had known it, and my first meeting with her affirmed it.

"I'll be pleased to have her here."

He nodded and sipped. "When will you be pleased, Thomas?"

I sighed. "Getting a living isn't easy here, you know. I had hoped for more time to get established."

He simply grunted, and pointed at the fancy room that embraced us. "It's lecture money I am getting that pays it, father. They pay fifty cents to hear me, and flock in."

He pulled an old briar from his vest pocket, found a small pouch of tobacco, and soon had a pipe going, filling the room with its sweet fragrance. "You need a living, for sure, but you've an education. You'll wish to keep Kate comfortable. She's a Meagher, and will not want for anything. What is it you'll do?"

"They tell me to wait and see; why, 'twas just a few months ago the new president had me visit him, twice before the inauguration. He had kind words, and a hearty handshake. A good man, General Pierce, a friend of the Irish."

"What is that for a living?"

"A position, maybe."

"And you not a citizen?"

"Ah, I'll find a way, maybe in politics. I think he wants me in politics, not the government."

My father grunted. We talked a while more, and then he stared at me. "Sure and you don't suppose she's long since freshened up, do you?"

I startled, knocked back the sharp whiskey, and we headed down the hallway.

I knocked. "Kate, it's us."

She trilled something, and the door opened. She took my breath away. She wore white muslin now, almost filmy over her tall frame. Strands of her brown hair clung moistly to her washed face, shining in the gaslight.

"Ah, Mr. Meagher, see, I'm ready to see New York," she said.

Pretty thing. She'd turn many an Irish eye.

"And New York's eager to meet you, Kate," I said.

"My treat it'll be," said my father. "And a toast to the bride."

I wondered why it sounded like a question.

7

Kate lay beside me, sweated and content, the room dark save for the soft night-glow filtering through the windows. She was awake. I was drenched and hot. The Metropolitan might be a miracle of plumbing and hot water heat, but it was no proof against a humid July night in New York, which coated our bodies with beads of dampness. I could see that her hair was plastered to her head, and her forehead gleamed from the oils collected there.

But all that was the sweet part of our marriage, joyfully resurrected. I gazed tenderly upon her, and felt a great peace such as I hadn't felt earlier, introducing Kate Meagher to all those who had flocked to our table at Delmonico's, where six-lamp chandeliers added smoke and heat and a saturnine light to the aroma of steaks and wet armpits.

Wherever Thomas Meagher pauses in New York, he is soon surrounded by well-wishers, and so it was this sticky night when half of Ireland drifted by. One thing for sure; my father discovered how I stand in this Republic, and what others think, and I thought his view of me softened as he heard those honeyed compliments. But he was, if anything, a practical man, who knew how swiftly English steel had butchered the dreams of those who wished to free Ireland, and how deadly and well used was the queen's gallows in every county.

So it was that Richard O'Gorman had drifted to our booth, and I introduced Kate.

"Ah, the exile's lady, united at last!" he said.

"Sure and a long trip it was, too," she said. "But for my Mister Meagher, sir, I would take passage aboard a whaling boat up to the rails in blubber." She patted my hand.

O'Gorman laughed. "Tom Meagher, that's a pretty sentiment from a pretty lady," he said. He complimented my father, and drifted off, wreathed in smiles.

So Kate was in town, and my friends paraded by, and they festooned us in good wishes and compliments, until I grew restive.

Kate herself begged leave, pleading a headache and weariness after four weeks at sea. The night was young, so I escorted her across the paving blocks to the hotel, and returned to our booth, where a dozen crowded around my father, and we spun tales and poems for hours more. My father is a great listener, and as the evening wore, his face softened.

Then my father pulled a turnip watch from his waistcoat, and nodded to me.

I saw him to his chambers, and proceeded to mine, lit the lamp, and found my wife lying quietly under a sheet, her brown eyes upon me.

"You feeling better?"

"Wouldn't you know a little rest would do for me, Mister Meagher," she said, a tentative smile creasing her face.

I didn't need any more invitation.

Later she lay apart from me, the closeness of the air being too much even to touch one another.

"I'm Tom, not Mister Meagher," I said.

"Ah, my own, I cannot but pay respects as they are due," she said. "You are the soul of the Irish, and I heard it with my

own ears this night. But do you love me, I would call you whatever you wish, even if it rolls slow off my tongue. Whilst the
boy suckled, I would coo and give him his name, Henry, Emmet
for the great Emmet, and Fitzgerald Meagher. I would say to
him, take strength from my teat, grow up into a great Gael,
carry your father's sword, and soon we'll be together."

"Was he a fair boy?"

"Well, they darken, the hair, after a bit, leave their fairness
behind, and soon he would have been stamped like you, not
me. A good fine stamp of Meagher upon him, like your father,
but 'tis you that stamped him. And now he lies cold, Mister
Meagher."

I felt a premonitory shadow fall across me, and turned from
her. But she was up, padding to the table, scratching a lucifer
that blinded me, and then the coal-oil lamp glowed. The sheen
on her naked back glistened, stirring me.

"Mister Bennett sent you a gift," she said, rummaging in
her trunk. "See, here, now."

She handed me a light, tissue-wrapped object, and when I
pulled off the paper, I discovered a sepia-toned daguerreotype
within a soft brown matting, of the cottage at Lake Sorel, my
place of thorns. I glanced at it, not wanting to absorb the image
of my servitude, my exile.

"Why, I will write him," I said. "A good likeness."

"Sure and the place where you took me," she said, tenderly.
"There, in that little cottage, there was where we first loved."

"I will be sure and thank Bryan Bennett," I said, and then I
changed the subject by pulling her down beside me.

So it was in the flesh the first days passed. Kate was often
sick by day, and lusty at night, and I worried that the chronic
dysentery and typhoid that afflicted New Yorkers every summer
might strike a woman so fragile.

By day, we explored New York, my father curious about everything, especially its commerce, which drew its sustenance from the Hudson River, the Erie Canal and the New York and Harlem Railroad as well as the great port. We wandered through the poorest tenements around Five Points, where the Paddys and their Bridgets off the tall-masted ships collected and bred and coughed and died, and toiled as hod carriers and dustmen and sweepers, the jobs handed down somehow by the Tammany ward bosses in the grog shops.

More and more, Kate abandoned my father and me to tour the glove counters and milliners, and study fashion, whilst I took my father with me on my business, which was, is, and ever will be, freeing Ireland.

One afternoon, after Dillon and O'Gorman had shut their offices, we headed for a private room at Phelan's Tavern. I took my father with me, and introduced him to John O'Mahony and Michael Doheny. There, after we had been served our whiskey by a pug in a barkeep's apron, and lit up our briars, the lot of us got down to business whilst my father sat quietly, aware of the delicacy of this event.

"I will tell you now, Mister Meagher," O'Mahony said to my father, "that this is a private meeting of the New York Irish Directorate, a little society devoted to achieving certain ends, first of which is freeing Young Ireland, and what passes here is not for other ears, do you know?"

O'Mahony waited, his gaze steady on my sire.

My father nodded. He had guessed it would be something like that.

"We have heard from Pat," Dillon said, unfolding a letter. He turned again to my father. "We sent Pat Smyth to Australia with a large sum, in pounds, to forward the escape of the rest of Young Ireland. We've been receiving regular correspondence from him for months. He is posing as a *New York Times* correspondent. He crossed the Central American isthmus, across Nicaragua, and headed across the Pacific from there. Our money is well spent," he added.

I saw my father wanted to ask a question, but didn't, so I put his mind at ease.

"With honor, sir. No man among us will violate his parole. Smyth is spending his time looking at constables and police stations, and how to revoke a parole all good and proper, and yet escape."

My father, mayor of Waterford, Member of Parliament, sat tight-lipped while Dillon donned his spectacles and read:

"Pleasant time with JM and his family. We're going on a picnic soon, all arranged. No rain in sight."

Dillon paused. "That means, sir, that John Mitchel is ready and the whole business is proceeding without a hitch. It's a hard one, because his family's there. But leave it to Nicaragua."

"Nicaragua?"

"Smyth. He's so entranced by Central America, half his letters are stuffed with wild plans to colonize the place, build a coast-to-coast railroad, get rich. We've a small bet, Mister Meagher. Some of us say Smyth's next letter will not mention Nicaragua; some of us lay a dollar on the opposite." He smiled. "This time, lads, there is no 'Nicaragua' in the letter. He's obsessed with getting Mitchel out."

O'Mahony groaned. "A dollar into the directorate," he said, rummaging in his pocket.

I laughed and matched the dollar. My Clongowes schoolmate had gotten Nicaragua on the brain, and acquired a name out of it.

"We have three out," O'Gorman said, his harshness breaking off the humor. "MacManus in California, Meagher, and

63

now O'Donohoe. We have it that he landed in San Francisco a month ago."

"Is it so now?" asked O'Mahony. "How is it that you know?"

Dillon triumphantly unfolded an Independence paper and shoved it across the wet table. "Arrived on the American ship *Otranto* on June 27th, Tahiti to San Francisco. Got it this very day."

"It is so, then! Ah, what blessed news! We've another out of hell. Terrence is free from Governor Denison, at least."

The oblique remark puzzled my father.

I explained. "He's a prisoner of his habits, sir. He's been sipping. We hope that a free life in a free nation will set him right."

My father nodded. Whiskey was an old story in Ireland, and in Irish America.

We stepped into the evening, my father contemplative, for he had seen Ireland shaking its shackles.

"This is fair land," he said, "and you have the liberty to change the world. And you are busy doing this thing. But what of Kate?"

"What of her?"

"A man has a family, maybe it's time to support a wife . . . and children."

"I lecture."

"Ah, lecture, and how long will they pay coin to hear you?"

He was pressing me, and I felt uncomfortable.

"This place," he said. "It gives a man a chance to earn his way. There's no rents burdening a man, the way it is across the sea. Nothing stops you from starting a business. You're on an equal footing with the Protestants, and it's not held against you, your faith. You've an education. What does it get you? You could start a company, great port like this. Import Waterford glass. It's famous crystal, and these New Yorkers might covet it. Or good Irish linen. I could help you."

"They tell me I should wait for a position."

"And who'll give it to you?"

"The politicians. The Democrats. The Tammany Wigwam."

"But they haven't."

"It's just a matter of time, sir."

"Wait? And Kate lives in a hotel, where she isn't suited to be. Is there not a better place for her, now she's here? A little house or rooms in a neighborhood where families live?"

"I have to be in the heart of things, you know. I can't afford such a place."

He sighed. "I won't be telling you your business, Tom."

8

It was the fourth year of my exile and the fifteenth day of November. The next day I would sail for California. Kate and my father would sail for Ireland three days hence. We had an early Christmas at the Metropolitan, where my room was garlanded with boughs, and we managed to heap some gifts upon my escritoire.

The hotel was a wonder, its clanking radiators keeping the dank winter at bay and cheering our little festival, as much as it could be cheered, given Kate's tears.

When I learned that the California Steamship Company had offered me free passage to San Francisco, where I might lecture to wide audiences, I accepted at once. For lecturing is my business, and this promised to be a most lucrative way of filling my purse. California! How could I resist?

But Kate had received this news with a great sadness.

"You mean, without me?" she asked, as her face composed and discomposed.

"It's a hard journey by steamer and across the isthmus, where disease lurks, love. You aren't well enough, and you're carrying a child."

"Oh, Mister Meagher . . ."

"It'll only be a few months."

"But we've been together only four."

"Yes, four months, but a lifetime stretches before us, Kate my love."

"I will stay here, then?"

"It gives me unease. You need an escort in this city, and you are none too well."

"Do you have to go, Mister Meagher? And me with child?"

I took her in my arms and she settled comfortably there. "Love, I must sing for my supper. Money for the cause. Money to free Ireland."

She buried her head in my shoulder and I felt the wetness of her eyes. I didn't like all this a bit, and the more I saw her distress, the less happy I was about it.

"Have you told your father?"

"I have. And he and I agree that the Metropolitan is scarcely the place for you to reside."

She pulled free of me, to peer into my face. I saw fear in her eyes. "What then?" she asked.

"Kate, love, he'll take you to Waterford to await my return. There you'll have comfort, and he'll look after you just as if you were his own daughter. And some day, when I'm getting an income here, I'll send for you."

She stared out the window, upon the carriages and drays rattling below, and the restless sea of New Yorkers all in a hurry. "Will I see you again?" she asked, her voice so low I almost didn't hear the question.

"Ah, love, Kate, it's just a little while, and Ireland's your home. How I envy you, going to Ireland, where I can't follow."

"Yes, you can't follow me," she said, her eyes haunted.

They would be crossing by sail; I was embarking on my first steamship voyage. She would be crossing in winter, but would be comfortable in a stateroom, and my father as well. It was I who faced hard passage.

We pushed aside a Christmas dinner, ham, plum pudding, potatoes, that the hotel had delivered to us.

"Well then, Kate, it's time to open up the gifts," I said.

She seemed terribly uncertain, almost confused, by this turn of events, and fumbled about, as if she were running on clockwork instead of her own will.

"And what is this?" she asked, pulling one of my gifts out of its blue tissue wrapper with her pale, translucent fingers.

"It's my speeches, love, in a portfolio, all printed up. For you to read on board."

"Read?" she asked.

My father stared sternly at me. "Are they seditious?"

"Oh, a little."

"Sure and I'll try then," she said, mustering a shine in her face.

Kate warbled her delight at the rest: white kid leather gloves that set her cooing, a silver and jade rosary blessed by New York's Bishop Hughes, and an alpaca hand muff, lustrous as ivory.

"I'll pray to Our Lady for us, love," she said, pouring the beads through her fingers.

My father discovered the same collection of speeches, and smiled. "I'll read them, and we'll see whether they arrive in Ireland."

He meant that they might be consigned to the cold Atlantic, but I merely nodded.

The next morning they saw me off. Here was something modern: a great black hulk of a ship with side-wheels, coppered hull, white enamel above deck, three stacks, four masts that would carry sail only in the event of engine failure, a bunker filled with Pennsylvania coal, and comforts beyond imagining.

We gathered in my cabin, where I kissed my Kate farewell,

and she held back her tears to smile bravely at me through soft lips and smoky eyes. I shook hands with my gaunt and unsmiling father, wondering if I would ever see him again.

"Oh, Mister Meagher," she said, pushing away the tears in her smudged eyes. Her gloved hands touched my shoulder and sleeve, my own hands, my chest.

I wrestled with the turmoil I felt, and resolved that this was best: in time, there would be a place for her in New York, when I would get a living.

The whistle blew, summoning guests to shore, and we walked back to the gangway, where I hugged my Kate and watched them walk down to the wharf. The navvies rolled the gangway up, and the bridge between us was no more. Then, as the steam tugs pushed the ship away, they were diminished, small blurs down on the pier, and then beyond my vision.

I prayed God that she would be borne safely and comfortably to the old country and taken into the bosom of our family. She was three months along, she told me. There would be a child born there, in captive Ireland, to replace the one born in captive Van Diemen's Land. The claws of empire were still tearing at my flesh.

I took with me Hawthorne's *The Blithedale Romance*, and concluded that I would never understand New Englanders and their doomed social experiments. Harriet Beecher Stowe's *Uncle Tom's Cabin* was selling by the case-lot, a million copies I had heard, but I refused to endure literary propaganda whilst sailing the seas, and didn't like the inflammation of politics wrought by that book.

When we reached San Juan del Norte, Nicaragua, on the Mosquito Coast, and began the steam passage up the Rio San Juan to Lake Nicaragua, I saw at once what had captivated my friend Smyth. We were being transported through a leafy paradise of primeval forest, wealth beyond description. Rainfall blurred our vision of the foetid tropical shores, but there from the soaked deck I saw monkeys, gaudy parrots, a wild peccary.

But the air cleared as we headed into Lake Nicaragua, an inland sea that took us close to the Pacific. I stuck to bottled ale or spirits, and stayed healthy, though others more fastidious regularly succumbed to typhoid and other tropical plagues, and by the time we reached the Pacific, over a rugged and densely vegetated volcanic range to the west, half a dozen of us had taken ill, and one poor newspaperman was hastily buried on the shores of the great inland sea.

I reached cold and brooding San Francisco in early January, 1854, and explored the new city on the bay, which had exploded into a chaotic and filthy slum in the six years since the gold rush began. There I lectured, drawing large crowds, many of them Irish. The sons of Limerick and Clare and Tipperary had alighted here somehow, after steerage passage in the bilges of a thousand tubs, and were making their way, earning incredible sums even as laborers, their bellies filled and their eyes glowing. They cheered me, bought me whiskey, toasted me in every corner saloon. For the first time, I began to see the United States as more than a refuge for the exiled. Here was a land for my people, and here the freedom they needed to hold property, practice their faith, nurture a dream.

I took the riverboats inland, lecturing in Sacramento and in some of the mining camps, and filled many a leathern sack with dust, worth up to sixteen dollars the ounce. The place fascinated me: at every hand were humble men, digging, washing, tunneling, living with little shelter in that mild climate, yet enjoying themselves. They had made their own rules, and the camps were orderly places.

Were it not for the terrain, which I found sere and bleak, I might have enjoyed this bonanza state, but it is no place for an Irishman to put down roots, and 'twas at the end of the world, not unlike the penal colony from which I had escaped. So I tarried there only two months, and fat with profit, steamed back to New York, following the same route aboard Cornelius Vanderbilt's steamers, across Central America, and up the east coast. I knew, as I passed once again through Nicaragua, that I would return to that nation, where its upland cities boasted a mild climate and a languorous way of life that captivated me.

Back in New York in April, well tanned and momentarily affluent, I took up again at the Metropolitan, where my thoughts returned to the Irish difficulties. There had grown in me a new feeling: bring the wretched of that island here, where a better life awaited them. I did not wish to admit it, but the very thought was the first step away from the ideals that had impassioned me, condemned me to death and exile, and were still washing through me to that hour in April when I opened a letter from my sire:

I was the father of a boy, Thomas Francis Meagher III. A boy it was, and I rejoiced.

Then, late in May, came another letter: Kate, weakened by the birth, had died of typhus, the old, deadly famine disease of my home, and had been buried in the family vault.

9

A shame was the wake at Donaldson's, because we got into politics while my poor Kate lay cold in her grave, dead at twenty-two, and the little boy was an orphan whose father could not come to him.

John O'Mahony took offense when I said it was good that the Irish were sending a little coin back home, so the beggars might eat and the women might have a rag to wrap around them.

He did not think it so, and said if much Yankee coin went to the old country to make it bearable without throwing out the English, then the rebellion would die. Nothing would change, he said, the Protestants and landlords would fatten, and there was no good in that.

"It is a beautiful woman you're losing," said O'Mahony, and clamped an arm about my shoulder. "We loved her, and love you."

I was in a bitter mood, and drank hard from the spirits they were pouring, and stared sullenly at the rest, daring them to console me, for I could not be consoled. They left me to myself, which is what I wanted.

My father would raise the new boy. He had already gathered wet nurses and some women to coddle my son, and so the child prospered. But Kate lay cold in her grave, and I had sent her there to perish, and sealed her doom with my own decisions.

I left Donaldson's, off east Broadway, needing air to clear my head, and walked back to the Metropolitan. I would have to write Bennett. My father had, but I hadn't, and I kept putting it off.

It was a hard spring. I stopped lecturing. I attended the meetings of the Irish Directory, sitting silently even as they rejoiced that they had gotten John Mitchel out of Van Diemen's Land disguised as a priest. Now they were working on Smith O'Brien, who so far had resisted their every effort because he wanted a full pardon so he could return to his great estate at Cahirmoyle, County Limerick, and take up the old life, as if he'd never clenched his fist against the Crown.

My suffering never ceased. Increasingly, various Catholic newspapers were criticizing me for being too radical, maybe even apostate. Pox on them! My criticism of the Irish clergy plainly dealt with its timidity. Had the priests stirred the uprising, the suffering church would have been freed. Pox on them all.

And so among the very Irish I had set out to free from the heel of England, Meagher was abused. One of my worst critics was a nasty scribbler named James McMaster, who edited *The Freeman's Journal*. This ink-thrower took it upon himself to accuse me of fleeing Van Diemen's Land dishonorably. Oh, the shame of that! I had revoked my parole before departing, and waited for the constables to come arrest me before I fled, all proper. I had shouted to them before I put spurs to my horse. I wanted a retraction and headed at once for the offices of the paper, and confronted McMaster in his cluttered lair.

"You have blackened my name. I want you to retract!"

He didn't budge. "It is all true, and I'll not give an inch. You cast your honor to the winds."

"You have shamed a man who has no guilt in the matter, and I want it taken back!"

He pointed at the door. "Out! You're an oath-breaker, and a disgrace to the church."

I stared at him. "If you don't satisfy me with an apology, you'll take a whipping."

"Out!"

"A whipping then. Watch for me, because I'll be coming at you, and I'll cut the hide off your back. You will not call me an oath-breaker!"

I knew what to do, and I did it. I fetched a buggy whip and waited for him at his Sixth Street flat, and when he showed up I took after him, my whip cutting hard into the devil, over and over, my rage boundless. No man accuses me falsely and escapes.

It was a fine commotion, there on that street, and McMaster reeled back, pulled a revolver from his coat and fired. The shot seared my brow and forehead and burnt my face. My ears rang, and I tore into the man all the more, my fury unloosed. But a constable pulled us apart, took away McMaster's revolver and my whip, and I stared at the murderous devil, who was just as defiant as ever.

"All right you two, it's mayhem you're making, and that will cost you a good bit," the big flatfoot said. He hauled us off to the station house, where I soon learned that brawling on the streets of New York would cost me five hundred dollars, much of my California profit. My only consolation was that the editor was in just as deep. Of course *The New York Times* published a detailed and amused account of the whole affair.

I sulked the summer away on Long Island Sound, guest of the Devlins, weary of the city, of my critics, and of myself. I was alone, an exile, shamed, and humiliated. No position had come my way. I didn't know what to do. I was sick of the United States, sick of my exile. I was sure 1854, the fifth year of my exile, would be the worst of years.

My father wrote regularly, and reported that my son Tom had survived and was gaining. But even that good news left me sour and restless. I had, at least, a little public speaking to keep me going, and that took me out of New York State, even as far as Chicago and Michigan.

But with the fall, I had gained nothing, and sulked in my hotel hermitage, biding time. No position came. And to hurry one along, I began going to Democrat Party levees and Tammany rallies, and there I mingled with my own kind as well as all varieties of Americans who found common cause in our party.

And there, one warm September evening, I saw her.

She was slightly buxom, well curved, dark-haired, oval-faced, and handsome. But what caught my eye was her good humor. Even across a concert hall, she radiated that lively warmth that is the crown jewel in the diadem of a woman's gifts. I gauged her to be in her twenties, and judging by her nankeen dress—three strands of pearls and lace sleeves—well connected.

I found no ring upon her finger, and hoped that it meant she was free. She drifted widely, greeting people effusively, but always returned to the company of three well-dressed gentlemen who were deep in discussion at the punch bowl. Upon one of these, probably her father, she gazed fondly, casually filling his punch glass, and listening intently.

I felt a rare hesitation pour into me. She was rich. I lived by my wits on good days, and by borrowing on the bad, and my prospects had not improved.

I collared Antrim Stuyvesant, a man widely acquainted.

"Antrim, who is that? The fair lady with the shining eyes?"

"Libby Townsend."

"Is that her father?"

"Peter, yes. And her brother-in-law Sam Barlow."

"Ah, and what does Townsend do?"

"Owns Sterling Iron Works. Foundry."

"And Barlow?"

"Lawyer. You know the firm, Tom. Bowdoin, Larocque and Barlow. Railroad men."

"And is Elizabeth—"

"By God, Meagher, you're a fine one. See for yourself."

"Could you . . ."

Stuyvesant knocked ashes from his cheroot and dragged me over the lady. Close up, I saw she was the possessor of ravishing peaches flesh and great brown eyes that seemed to take me in with a glance.

"Tom Meagher, and so we meet," she said, trumping Stuyvesant.

"You know me."

"Of course. I've sat through several Meagher lectures."

Stuyvesant lingered a moment, nodded, and left me to my own devices.

"And you're Libby Townsend."

"You did your homework, no doubt while wandering around here, looking like you want to start a revolution."

"You were watching?"

She answered with a smile. "I've been circling you all night. I just wanted to see if you still have a crease on your forehead."

"You should see whether McMaster still has stripes on his back and arms."

"You like to fight, do you?"

"In Ireland, a man sips a little from a jar, and starts a fight with a good blackthorn shillelagh, and then we crack heads. And what do your people do?"

"Negotiate."

"Could I negotiate you into taking the air?"

"You could fight me, loser gets to be dragged away."

Never had a woman been so bold with me.

We stepped outside, into the warm, smoky New York night. The air was close. A sensuous joy filtered through me, and I knew that the same galvanizing attraction was besetting her. It felt so fine to have a handsome woman standing beside me, a quizzical smile lighting her face.

"Do you grieve?" she asked.

She had followed my affairs. "Yes, still. Kate is like a star in heaven now, shining there across such a sea of darkness. I look into the night skies and see her there, the mother of my sons, my memory a faded brown daguerreotype framed in pine boughs, and I think sadly of the noble mistress of my hearth, whom I knew so briefly, and who shared but a fleeting moment in my life. Rest assured, Miss Townsend, she remains a sacred vessel in my memory."

"That's sweet. I don't grieve anyone."

"Have you ever?"

"Oh, a few hundred beaux."

"You slayed them all."

"I think I'm going to like you," she said.

10

Winning Libby would not be easy. Her father had not taken to me, and squinted through question-mark eyes those first months of my courtship while I tried by every means to persuade him I was a worthy candidate for his daughter's hand.

At one point he handed me his card. "Come visit me, sir," he said.

I promptly did so, at his business chambers. He greeted me affably, handed me a Havana and a glass of Madeira, and settled into a quilted red leather wingchair opposite me.

"I have noted with great pleasure your interest in Libby," he said.

That seemed a good beginning. "She is the light of my life, sir."

He clipped the end of his cigar and licked it. "We're a family with means, and she's enjoyed a life of comfort. I take it as a paternal obligation rising from my fatherly affection for her, to assure myself and Mrs. Townsend of your intentions."

"I assure you, sir, my intentions are all that you would hope, and if you could but know what passes through my innermost mind in respect of her, you would be pleased."

He smiled. "I know by the signs; she's set her cap for you." He paused. "You were a part of the Rising of 1848, I take it.

Sentenced to death, too. Banished to Van Diemen's Land and paroled to the provinces."

"I could do no less for my suffering country, sir. I have no regrets."

"Ah! You took on the Queen; my grandfather took on the King; he was an American patriot, you know."

I felt Townsend's warmth, and knew this would progress well. "Yes, sir, Libby told me that he forged chains for the Continental Army to stretch across the Hudson and stop British men-o'-war."

"What did you do in exile, Mr. Meagher?"

"Lived in a lakeside cottage, sir, wrote, fished, hunted, rode horse, busied myself with matters of justice. And I am still in exile, sir."

"Normally, as I understand it, a prisoner's bound to a local farmer or merchant, and thus earns his keep while enduring his ticket of leave. Did you tend sheep?"

"It wasn't necessary, sir. My family was able to provide. My father was Lord Mayor of Waterford, an M. P., and a man of means. We are merchants."

"I see; well, that was a comfort for you, a stipend paying your way, giving you a luster in the eyes of your late wife." He eyed me closely as he lit his cigar with a lucifer.

"You are known as a great orator, Mister Meagher. In Ireland, you awakened the suffering people with the grace and power of your words. I have read your famous Sword oration, and found it most stirring."

"Yes, thank you, sir."

"And now you lecture, do you?"

"Yes, now and then, when I can book a hall."

"I, ah, am wondering. What calling might there be for an orator?"

"Sir?"

"Calling. A competence. I've puzzled it about in my head. How does an orator get a livelihood? Could you become a professor of rhetoric?"

Townsend's hospitality suddenly took a new turn, and I saw how this was playing out. I chose my words carefully.

"Well, sir, I haven't settled on a means, as yet. I've been absorbed in Irish questions; freeing my homeland is foremost among all my goals, and I've put off the humdrum, I'm afraid."

"Yes, a noble cause, Mr. Meagher. Ireland needs freeing from the yoke, and I support you and wish you all the best of it. But forgive an older man for worrying about the *humdrum*, such as wondering whether revolutionaries are paid for their efforts."

"No, Mr. Townsend, they're patriots, acting out of a vision of the public good."

"Ah! So it was with my grandfather Townsend! He lost money during the American Revolution, but never paused a moment to ask whether he ought to stop. He made a mighty contribution, and at great sacrifice. I admire your dedication."

Again my future father-in-law seemed benign, and the meeting little more than a pleasant exchange. I sipped his fine Madeira.

"Is this your *home* now, Mr. Meagher?"

"Home?"

"Is the United States your nation?"

"Sir, I'm an exile. Ireland is my childhood home, my sweet land, my birthplace. The Meaghers are rooted deep in County Waterford. I sojourn here. But of course, I cannot go home; not unless I am pardoned. So, rest assured, New York is as much a home as an exile can ever have."

"There is something that puzzles me, and perhaps you can enlighten me. I've noticed over many years that most who come to this nation want to put down roots. This is their new home. They take up land. Certainly that's true of the Dutch and Germans and English. There's no thought of going back to the old world. But the Irish . . ."

I saw his concern at once. "The Irish are driven here by cruel circumstance, sir, and cannot help their yearnings to return to their own land. We are all exiles. In the bosom of every son of Erin lies an ache for the dear old home, a hunger to go back to the green hills and the warm people, the neighbors in their cottages, in freedom, without persecutions."

"So it seems. And that explains the great agitations."

"There burns in the breast of every exiled Irishman a furious need to set his people free."

He nodded. "I'm sure you have plans to get a competence," he said, so suddenly that he surprised me.

"I've given it real thought, sir. The lecture circuit—"

He grimaced, ever so slightly, and peered at the cut-glass chandelier where three coal oil lamps burned. Cigar smoke coiled around them.

"I should like you to think about Libby's needs, Mr. Meagher." He smiled, rose, and extended a hand. I shook it warmly.

But as I was escorted out by one of his factotums, I knew there had been much more conveyed than reached my ear.

Things continued in that vein for weeks, and I sensed Libby was distressed. Peter Townsend was not persuaded that his family needed an indigent Irish revolutionary for a son-in-law, one yearning for home.

"Libby," I said one day as we strolled on Fifth Avenue, passing young matrons pushing perambulators, "is there something troubling you?"

"I think you know. He won't budge."

"Up to me, then."

"Yes, entirely. Oh, Tom, lecturing just won't do."

I had to do something, fast, to get a living. It had scarcely occurred to me that I might be reduced to that, but if I wished to enter the heaven that Libby promised me with her warm lips and open arms, I must do something.

I chose law, and announced to Townsend one day that I was reading to become a barrister.

"Ah! Then you've set upon a course! My son-in-law Sam Barlow's a good man at the law books, and he makes a competence. I employ him myself now and then. But remember this: Sam's a railroad man first, a lawyer only by vocation."

From then on, things improved, but Townsend had his cyclops eye on me, and I was still far from obtaining his consent.

Much changed in the space of year. I applied myself to the law books. My connection, however tenuous, with the powerful Townsend family was transforming my life. I spent days and weeks and months reading dry and dusty law with Judge Robert Emmet, and then with Judge Charles Daly, friend of the Townsends and Barlows. I drudged my way through Blackstone's Commentaries and American case law, applying myself to a task I cared little for but mastered quickly. At last my mentors deemed me fit to practice law, and Libby and I celebrated with a pheasant dinner at Delmonico's, and toasts to the future.

It took a special order of the New York supreme court for me to practice in the state because I was not yet an American citizen. But I had mastered law, was admitted to the bar and swiftly formed a partnership with my friend Malcolm Campbell, an attorney as impecunious as I was. We hung our shingle on Alice Street, near City Hall, and hoped some Tammany business would walk in, which it didn't. The old machine had its own counselors, and these were not ready to share the business with their own kind, and even less with Irish exiles.

I reported faithfully to my dusty desk at first, waiting in the great solitude of our bleak chambers for someone to walk in, some good soul wanting a will drafted or a contract reviewed. But such was our luck that we usually offered our services to destitute widows wanting a pension, or pickpockets wanting to get out of jail, or the swarms of easy girls who were regularly rounded up and needed writs. It added up to barely enough to keep our doors open.

I did better when I roamed, and got more business out of the pubs than sitting in those chambers, sharpening pencils and waiting to refill the burning coal oil lamps. Out in the saloons and restaurants I plied my trade, handed out cards, Thomas Meagher, Esquire, Attorney at Law, kept my ear peeled for cases and prospects. And sometimes I was lucky. Now and then an Irishman would walk into my chambers, and there would be a fee for a service rendered. I didn't do any trade with the others; my entire business was Irish, and it hinged on my reputation. If you wanted a will, the hero of 1848 would draft it.

I knew Peter Townsend was monitoring all this closely; he had a thousand mouths reporting to him. And Libby was growing restless. I lived in shabby circumstances, waiting for a competence that never materialized, and finally began lecturing again, even though the bloom was now fading and most of the city had heard whatever I wanted to say about Irish independence, Van Diemen's Land, the Australian League, and other shopworn Meagher lectures.

I was no less desperate after practicing law according to Peter Townsend's wishes, but then, miraculously, he relented. I know Libby had much to do with it. She could be as stubborn and iron-willed as her sire.

He invited me into their parlor one day:

"You have my blessings, Mr. Meagher," he said. "I know you'll keep her first and foremost in your bosom. She tells me you'll make a fine son-in-law."

"I can do no less than rise to your expectations, sir," I replied.

Odd how I was not exultant.

11

I lifted the veil from Libby's lustrous face, and kissed her. Thus did we seal the sacred vows we had just repeated in the parlor of Bishop Hughes's residence on Madison Avenue. It could not be a church wedding, this marriage of mine to a Protestant, but it was a liturgical one. I looked into her face and saw dreams and joy there, matching my own.

"My own, my love," she whispered.

Then we embraced the few friends and family we had gathered there, this November day of 1855. My new father-in-law, Peter Townsend, grasped my hand solemnly, and so did my new brother-in-law, Sam Barlow, and my sister-in-law, Alice.

We would be honeymooning out on the sound, but first there would be a small reception, toasts, celebration, and a night in the city. The only cloud on this most blessed of days was the silence from Waterford. But I knew that as soon as my family would meet Libby, they would be as smitten by her as I was.

The Townsends received our wedding guests in their spacious home, and I took it upon myself to introduce my friends, Dan Devlin, Michael Doheny, Richard O'Gorman, John Blake Dillon, John O'Mahony, Pat Smyth, and their watchful wives, as well as Bishop Hughes, to the Townsends and the Barlows and their friends.

But except for Sam Barlow, who gravitated back and forth, the Irish congregated in one corner, and the Townsends and their friends in another. Then Peter Townsend himself graciously stitched the guests together, heartily welcoming the Irish and introducing them all around.

After we had been properly toasted at our reception by Sam Barlow and then Richard O'Gorman, Libby and I slipped away to the Metropolitan for the night, raced up three flights of stairs, laughed our way into the Governor's Suite, and that was when I discovered twice as many stars in the heavens than I had ever seen before.

Libby was not shy, and was as enthused about the nuptial communion as everything else she had ever come across, and I have never experienced a sweeter night, nor a holier one, for I had suddenly come upon sacredness.

"Tom Meagher," she said dreamily, late in the velvet quiet. "I wish you had come along sooner. To think what I've missed. I was almost an old maid withering on the vine."

"Well, wither no longer!"

"Meagher of the Sword!" she whispered.

When we returned to the city and settled in an upstairs suite in Peter Townsend's manse at 129 Fifth Avenue, I stopped worrying about getting a competence. Libby was living in exactly the same comfort as before.

I started on a new project, *The Irish News*. It would be published from my law offices, and would reach the tens of thousands of desperate, hungry, and disfranchised Irish of New York, and mold them into a political force.

"I'm starting a paper for the Irish," I told my father-in-law. "I've been planning to do it for a long time, but never quite had the time, you know. The lectures and law and all."

He was nonplused. "A newspaper? And you're the editor? Can it get a profit?"

"Oh, it will soon, I'm sure," I said a little blithely.

"And how will this be financed?"

"My friends have anted up a little money."

"Will you abandon law?"

"No, but I like the writing better."

"Have you a head for business?"

"I'll hire a clerk to look after things."

"Ah! A clerk. Isn't there a paper for the Irish?"

"Yes, the *Irish American*, but we need another."

"To express your opinions." I saw that familiar glint in his eye.

I nodded. My father-in-law was oozing skepticism. But then he softened. "It could help the party," he said, "and if you do it right, it might give you a return, too, though I cannot for the life of me fathom how a newspaper can make anyone a decent competence. Not like the iron or steel that people need. Aren't editors about one step removed from the bread lines and soup kitchens? I don't know whether people pay for news and opinions, not the way they need rails and boilers. I certainly wouldn't pay to read anyone's opinion. Mine is better informed than any I read."

My father-in-law was thinking about how Tom Meagher would support Libby. But I was thinking of the Irish, jammed into the meanest, dirtiest, most desperate corners of the city, in odorous tenements and firetraps, heaped five or ten to a room, working in the most miserable jobs because no Irishman could find decent employment. They were sick. Most had consumption. The women were even worse off, and many were selling themselves just for a crust of bread. They needed a voice. They needed to assert themselves at the ballot box. They needed jobs and decent wages.

I intended that their plight should be addressed, and that this nation of promise should offer hope to these desperate, sick, dying Irish, who had fled the famine and British oppression only to find another sort of hell awaiting them here.

Thus my own paper was born in my law offices and edited by me. I hired a walleyed clerk from Mayo to take subscriptions and keep accounts, and a feisty little fellow from Dublin to sell ads, and then I began writing. I was receiving very little law trade, so there was time enough to scribble. And I did, employing whatever gift of eloquence I was born to. Twice each week we sent our copy over to the print shop, and soon enough we had our paper on the streets, selling for two cents.

"It is a fine thing you're doing," Richard O'Gorman said to me. "You, looking after the whole flock."

"What else is there?" I responded.

"You want to go home some day?"

"I never stop dreaming of it."

"It shows in everything you write, Tom."

He had spotted my hurt. I lived as with a thorn in my flesh, no matter how blessed my days with Libby. I clapped him on the back, and smiled.

We made our mark, if not any profit. Even at two cents, it was hard to sell a small press run. The news boys got half a cent for each they sold, and hawked them at every corner. Tammany Hall politicians took notice. The state's Democrats saw in the Irish a large voting bloc, and a natural ally. But most of all, we were being heard, and a few jobs were opening up. But we had our enemies too, not least of them *The New York Times*, which mocked my editorials, and poked fun at us.

To one particularly venomous anti-Irish *Times* editorial,

entitled "Poltroonery," which attacked the poorest and humblest among us, I responded sharply in my paper. And that unloosed the accusations that had followed me ever since I arrived on these shores: that I had dishonored my parole. The *Times* rehashed old ground, claiming that even though I had given my word of honor not to escape so I might enjoy a ticket of leave in the penal colony, I had arranged the entire escape while bound by my parole.

Libby read the canard, smiled, and hugged me. I don't know what Peter Townsend thought: we never discussed the matter. He was more tolerant than before, but I never had won his unfettered approval, and was always on probation in his mind. An income of five thousand would have altered his view, I'm sure. I never knew what he said to Mrs. Townsend, but it could not have been so critical, because she always greeted me affectionately.

I had a loyal, fiercely protective wife, and what more could a man want? She was proceeding with her instruction with joy and piety, and would convert to my church as soon as possible. What her father thought of her intentions to become a Catholic I do not know.

I followed with interest the fate of the Young Ireland exiles. Our quiet efforts had succeeded. Some, like me, had escaped and would never be pardoned. Others were enjoying a conditional pardon; that is, they were not free to return to Ireland. But others had received a full pardon: even Smith O'Brien, who could return at last to his beloved estate, Cahirmoyle. John Mitchel stayed briefly in New York and then abandoned my adopted city for the South, where he was becoming a voice of the Irish below the Mason-Dixon line. We stayed in touch. I corresponded with many of my old colleagues and friends in exile.

My law business still did not earn me a competence, and neither did the paper, so I lectured, which did earn me a sporadic living. I was again in demand, sometimes talking to full houses along the East Coast. The oppression of Ireland had not improved, not even after worldwide pressures, and that brought people to the halls.

That year of 1856, the seventh of my exile, had seen a national election, which I had followed intensely, a partisan for the Democrats, of course. Our man, James Buchanan, won handily. He had been nominated in Cincinnati, along with John C. Breckinridge, on a platform affirming the Compromise of 1850. The Know-Nothings had nominated Millard Fillmore and were soundly trounced.

But there was a radical new party out in the hinterlands that worried me. They were calling themselves Republicans, and they were largely abolitionists and those who wanted one way or another to curtail slavery and subdue the South. Their man was Colonel John C. Fremont, the explorer, a man of dubious ability and volatile temperament.

It had been with much satisfaction that I saw this party nipped in the bud. Our man, Old Buck Buchanan, collected over one million eight hundred thousand votes, while Fremont managed only one million three hundred thousand. The new radical Republican party was thoroughly whipped. The country was too intelligent to get swept away by a pitiful novel by Harriet Beecher Stowe. Buchanan had condemned the anti-slavery agitation, had favored nonintervention in the South, and had walked off with the election.

Buchanan had not forgotten his Irish roots. In his inaugural address, he proclaimed that the public lands should be opened to immigrants. "We shall thus not only best promote the prosperity of new states and territories by furnishing them with a hardy and independent race of honest and industrious citizens, but shall secure homes for our children and our children's children, as well as for those exiles from foreign shores who may seek in this country to improve their condition and to enjoy the blessings of civil and religious liberty."

I saw at once the opportunity I needed in all this. I had not established an income suitable for Libby Townsend, or satisfied my skeptical father-in-law that I could support her on paltry lecture fees and an occasional drafting of a will in my Alice Street law offices. What I needed was a situation, and my party could offer me one. I wrote the president-elect:

"I am in rather sad want of a position, with some emolument attached to it," I explained. "For, with all that I can do (and I labour incessantly, Heaven knows!) I find it impossible to make a respectable competence. As long as I am compelled to remain here my time and brain is the property of the public rather than my own. . . . If then, you should not consider it incompatible with the national interests, I would solicit from you a representative position abroad—a consulship, for instance, in South or Central America."

I knew my background might give cause for concern, and sought to allay that: "As for my political sympathies and impulses, you need have no apprehension of their leading me into action which would conflict with the policy and spirit in a few weeks it will be your high duty to initiate. Strict fidelity to my oath of office, to the immediate interests of America, and the letter of your instructions, shall be an obligation paramount to all considerations, sympathies, and impulses. In a word, becoming an American citizen, I cease to be a European revolutionist."

I was hoping for a post in Nicaragua, or Guatemala, maybe Rio de Janeiro, or even Buenos Aires. But I heard nothing. To my old Young Ireland colleague, William Smith O'Brien, I wrote that place-hunting, getting a government position, was acceptable here in America, where I might serve a republican government, even if it was a scandal in Ireland that I had condemned during my revolutionary days.

I still heard nothing, so I wrote Secretary of State Lewis Cass about the matter. I assured him that I would fill any post offered me with great industry and trust. "There will be too many watching my career, for me to waver or be remiss." I had set my heart on Venezuela, but would settle for Quito or Buenos Aires.

I decided that the force of influential friends would carry me to my goal, and solicited them to send letters to Cass or Buchanan. Thus, to my personal knowledge and satisfaction, such fine Democrats as Amasa Parker, candidate for governor, Governor Horatio Seymour, Herman J. Redfield and Richard Schell of the Port of New York Collectors Office; Postmaster Isaac Fowler; plus Charles O'Connor, James Brady, John Van Buren, the historian George Bancroft, John Kelly, Elijah Ward, and others, sterling men all, wrote on my behalf. But for some unfathomable reason, Buchanan did not act.

I wrote Cass again, and then Buchanan several times more, but got no response. I explained to the president that there was in Ireland a great effort being made by powerful men to restore me to the land of my birth, but he could be assured that I would remain a citizen of the United States for as long as I could serve well here.

It occurred to me that Buchanan's silence might have to do with divisions within the party, so I wrote yet again:

"It so happens that my *personal friends* in the Senate are gentlemen who differ in political faith from the government," I acknowledged, but I assured him that these were perfectly prepared to defend my interests. "I am of the same race as your father was," I reminded him, thinking to touch his heart. But it all came to naught, which greatly disappointed and puzzled me. All I could do was wait, as Buchanan's administration settled into office and awarded positions to place-seekers. At least the president had never said no, which was a good sign.

Then at last, some legal business! My law practice took me to Washington to defend the filibuster William Walker who had established a pro-slavery government in Nicaragua and was charged with violating the Neutrality Act. The defense lawyers wanted me for my oratorical skills, and I would deliver the summation to the jury. When the case against Walker was dismissed I was disappointed, because I had done my homework and intended to showcase my legal skills.

Libby, meanwhile, now an ardent Catholic, sailed across the Atlantic, visited my father in Waterford, met my son, and charmed her new Irish family. I knew that henceforth there would be a happy relationship between my bride and the Meaghers, especially my father. They talked of bringing my son, Tom, to America someday, but the boy was doing well there, and my father was happy to care for him, and would eventually school him in Clongowes, as I had been. So the matter was left as it was, and I was content to leave it unchanged. Someday, I would meet my boy. Someday, I would bring him to America.

Libby had not conceived, and I gradually grew aware that our marriage would probably be childless. It did not trouble me, because our lives had become so busy, with so many large events looming, that children would have impeded us. Not that I wouldn't have welcomed them: we were simply caught in a whirl of activity that was to take us thousands of miles from our home, indeed to the slopes of Central America.

12

San José, Costa Rica, set me to dreaming of gold. I met President Juan Mora and his cabinet, along with everyone of note, and judged it to be a country rife with opportunity. The capital itself was set high in the cordillera, and offered a temperate climate and breathtaking prospects.

It wasn't an easy place to get to. One had to sail to Nicaragua, cross that nation by river, steam across Lake Nicaragua, surmount the mountains to reach the Pacific, sail down the west coast, and then proceed by oxcart to the secluded capital. But, ah, what a lecture it would make.

I was traveling with a young friend, Ramón Paez, a fellow Clongowes student and the son of the great Venezuelan rebel Antonio Paez. Our mission was literary and scientific, the advancement of knowledge and the arts, but of course, I was keeping my eye peeled for opportunities, especially a rail route across the isthmus.

What a fine time we had, invited to fiestas unceasing, admiring the handsome people, dining with the most influential and powerful, and of course gathering intelligence, for it had become plain to the world that these narrow nations separating the Atlantic from the Pacific had vast strategic value, especially to the United States. Which was exactly why half the nations of Europe were meddling in the area.

I knew what I wanted there: a fine white casa with a court-yard and a splashing fountain; a host of white-clad servants looking after Libby and me; wine and dinner with people of means, a consulship at the least, a coffee plantation, a sugar plantation, and of course the opening of the nation to those like myself, able to offer it a railroad; indeed, the most important short line in the world. All they wanted was cash; a little cash and they would offer a concession.

Stuffed with impressions, sketches, notes, maps, memories, and excellent food, I bade goodbye to my young traveling companion and returned to New York and the eager arms of my bride.

"Libby, you've got to go there! I'll take you some day. Never have I met such a sweet and innocent people."

"And?"

"Never have I seen such a collection of foreign scoundrels, schemers, agents provocateur, and people who would strangle their own grandmothers for a peso."

"San Jose, here I come," she said.

"We'll get rich. There's a fortune awaiting us there. A bonanza! Coffee! Bananas! Sugar! Pineapples! A railroad across the Isthmus, timber, shipping, good ports on both sides . . ."

"Thomas Meagher, Banana King," she said.

I intended to lecture on Central America, and set about preparing several talks and booking halls and getting advertising out. I also intended to write Buck Buchanan a private letter outlining what I knew of Central America, and where the nation's sympathies might best lie. He would thank me for it.

Alas, I was to learn that Americans are not interested in Latin America, never had been and never will be, and for once my lectures spun out in empty halls. They didn't know the difference between Costa Rica and Nicaragua, and didn't care to learn.

Then scandal struck, and it involved an Irish politician, and I found myself given a rare opportunity. Our excellent New York congressman Dan Sickles, a Tammany man supported by every son of Erin in our city as well as my wife's family, precipitated the greatest scandal ever to wash through Washington, D.C. His wife, Teresa, had formed an attachment to district attorney Philip Barton Key, son of Francis Scott Key, who had written "The Star-Spangled Banner."

Dan, having gotten wind of the liaison, spotted Key signaling to Teresa in front of Sickles's home, tracked Key down and shot him twice. Key died moments later. Sickles surrendered to the attorney general and was jailed.

And there I was, on Sickles's legal team, hoping to get our man off without further damage to himself or the troubled Democratic Party, which was falling apart over the slavery issue. Among my colleagues at law were Edwin Stanton and James Topham Brady.

President Buchanan, tough son of an Irish immigrant, had learned of the murder from a White House page, and swiftly moved the page out of Washington to keep him from testifying. But that was not going to help us much. Much better was the written confession of infidelity Sickles had badgered out of Teresa before he set off to kill Key. We had a delicate problem of our own, because Dan Sickles was a womanizer, and we had to prevent the jury from discovering it.

It took the furious powers of Buchanan's office and staff,

and the exertions of Tammany politicians, to rescue Sickles, the president's close friend, but we managed, mostly by controlling what went into the record.

I was honored to give the summation, pleading against a guilty verdict with all the rhetorical gifts to which I was a most fortunate heir. In very little time, the jury returned, declared Sickles innocent, and it was all over. My skills had carried the day, and for the moment I was much celebrated. Meagher won the case!

I thought perhaps so public a trial, plastered across all the nation's papers, would greatly improve my law practice, but it didn't. I was remembered for my oratory, for reminding the jury of the wounded honor of our man and the justice of his act, but I was given no marks for the strategy, and so my law career languished as before. I was no closer to supporting Libby. Peter Townsend simply stared at me in disapproving silence.

Old Buck Buchanan was in grave trouble. He was opposed to slavery and pro-Union, but felt the states had an absolute right to determine whether they wished to be slave or free, and he abominated abolitionist radicals. His attempts to achieve resolution in bloody Kansas, whose slave and free factions each claimed to be the government, briefly resulted in a slave state there, enraging the north. My party split on the issue, and we lost the House to the Republicans. Buchanan was a veteran lawyer, former secretary of state, a diplomat, congressman, and senator, and held other offices, but all his skills did not avail, and the clouds of war loomed dark and terrible over the Republic.

Opinion had polarized. A man was for the South or for the North, for or against slavery, and few men spoke up for Union itself. James Buchanan was powerless to halt the downward spiral, and even as his administration waned, southern states were arming themselves, and in his last months, several had seceded.

Through all these stormy times I was an uneasy spectator. The Irish of the North didn't mind slavery, and hated abolition and the righteous radicals promoting it. They were poor and uneducated, and knew that freed darkies would snatch their jobs and work for even less, and there would be more misery in the Irish tenements.

There were some Irish in the South, especially my old comrade in arms John Mitchel, who saw the forthcoming secession in just the light that he saw the Irish question: it was time for the Union to back off, just as he believed Great Britain must let go of Ireland and cease to oppress it. And if the Union, or England, did not let go, then armed rebellion was justifiable. I saw the point; all Irish did.

I thought the only solution was the moderation of the Democrats, but I was slowly discovering I didn't know this Republic well, especially its Yankee Protestants, particularly the reformist ones. Out beyond urbane New York was a different sort of American. A rustic from Illinois named Lincoln was debating our little dynamo, Stephen Douglas, and was winning those debates, or so they said.

The Democratic Party was being torn to pieces, along with the other parties, except for the burgeoning new one that was rooting everywhere in the western reaches of the nation, the Republicans. An election was looming, and the Southern Democrats were intending to run Breckinridge, and the Northern Democrats were running Douglas, and any man could foresee ruin for the party.

Libby and I watched all this with helplessness, and even indifference, and for once I felt that my new nation was a mystery to me. As I wrote Smith O'Brien, who was now living quietly at his estate, "I've ceased to be a participator in historic motions. I've become an impassive spectator."

I had other things in mind: my Costa Rica lectures had brought me into contact with a certain Ambrose Thompson, a man interested in building a railroad across the Chiriqui, in southern Costa Rica, thus connecting the two oceans. He already had won an option from the government, had read my magazine pieces about Costa Rica, and wondered if I might be the man to turn the dream into reality.

His proposal, offered across the linen at Delmonico's, enchanted me. I would have a percentage of the railroad, and the result would be wealth unimaginable, as well as public acclaim for making the isthmus passage so easy. I could rely on Sam Barlow's railroad expertise for help, and Thompson's shipbuilding works for material support, and my father-in-law, who liked to think big.

Now there was a prospect to tickle my fancy! And a woman's fancy too. No sooner had I mentioned it to Libby than she was ready to go.

"Just let me get packed, and we'll be off in five minutes," she said, pulling open drawers.

It took five weeks, much of it spent in detailed discussion with Thompson, whilst I made feverish preparations. I even won the approval of Peter Townsend, whose assessing gaze seemed less jaundiced as he weighed me. I might yet please the old gent, especially with a project that would swiftly bring millions to my coffers.

We left on the *Northern Light*, with many champagne toasts to see us off, and wound up in San José by the same tortured route as I had taken before. Libby, ever enthused, didn't even mind the final oxcart ride up the steep grades to the capital.

She fell in love with the hilly town instantly, and made herself at home whilst I began my rounds.

My first task was to persuade President Juan Mora to favor us over a rival. He was a tough-minded fellow, skeptical of Yankee intentions and looking for the best way to get what he could from the competition. I was willing to deal.

Our enterprise, the Chiriqui Improvement Company, was soon chartered by the Colombian parliament (Costa Rica being a self-governing state of New Grenada), and we acquired the right to build our railroad from Bocas del Toro to Punta Mala. I left Libby in San José, a guest of the president, and went off to explore our route, an adventuresome trip among wild companions and wilder country: swamp and dripping jungle, monkeys, gaudy parrots, and cheerful coffee-colored natives, all of which I intended to write about once I returned. From swamps to ridge tops, I probed our route, and came back to San José persuaded that we had a practical plan.

"Libby," I said, "you and I are the bonanza king and queen. We're rich. We're the next Vanderbilt. When the freight starts rolling, we won't be able to spend our pile fast enough."

She eyed me levelly. "I don't know about *that*," she said.

In the summer of 1860, Congress recognized our exclusive proprietorship of the passage, and we could proceed, except for some niggling financial details. We had influential friends who would help us in the Chiriqui. There would be gleaming rails laid soon, across plain and mountain, from sea to shining sea, Atlantic to Pacific, connecting the United States to its distant territories on the west coast, all by ship and rail.

I again left Libby in San José and hastened to New York and Washington, to arrange for one final and crucial piece of legislation. I had promised the Costa Ricans an initial three hundred thousand dollars, to be procured from Congress. With that modest sum, the United States navy would lease Atlantic and Pacific ports from the Costa Ricans, linked by our short railroad, all under American control, all strategic and vital to the republic.

But congress, preoccupied with the deepening crisis, rejected the deal. I was aghast. Thompson and I were out in the cold. I steamed back to San José, determined to win some other concessions, but Mora and his cabinet shut all doors and barred them.

Libby and I headed back to New York, and a nation with a new president-elect, the outlandish Abe Lincoln. Several slave states had already seceded, and Buchanan was trying hard to keep the rest in the Union. The whole world had changed.

13

By the time we sailed into bleak New York harbor, in January of 1861, in the twelfth year of my exile, everything had shattered, and not least, our own hopes.

The nation had shattered. The Democrats had shattered. Tammany had shattered. The Irish had shattered, lining up on both sides, North and South. Even those supporting the North had shattered. Our mayor, Fernando Wood, and the New York cotton merchants were pro-South, and wanted to declare New York City a separate city-state republic, from which Wood would no doubt enrich himself even more than he had already. Other men wanted to hold the Union together at all cost.

Libby and I stepped into a cold new world. My country—I had been a naturalized citizen of the Republic for only three years—had fallen into near-anarchy, and now thunderous storms loomed over the fruitful land. Blood would flow in rivers. A nation bound by geography and tradition had sundered itself.

Peter Townsend met us with his black barouche as we stepped down the slippery gangway into an overcast and bitter world.

"Ah, Libby, Tom, you're safe. We'll have you warm enough in a bit," he said, doing his hearty best.

But he looked drawn. We soon learned that southern customers of the Sterling Iron Works were declining to pay their debts, saying they would do so with the new southern currency whenever it was issued. The works had poured its rails and steel into the South.

"Are we in trouble?" Libby asked.

Townsend smiled. "Do you know what the South owes the North? Two hundred millions, and much of it to New York banks, some of it to me. War, if it comes to that, might help us recover. Maybe even a quick campaign."

We were soon ensconced in our warm Fifth Avenue quarters, and I was more eager for news about the Republic than I was to tell the Townsends, downstairs, about our disaster in Costa Rica.

"What about this man Lincoln?" I asked, after we had settled for liquid refreshment in their parlor.

"Uncle Ape? That's what we call him. The homeliest specimen ever fitted into black frock coat. A true son of the frontier."

"But what does he believe?"

Townsend shrugged. "He's been saying the job is bigger than he is. I certainly agree with him on that score."

"What about the Union? He can avoid war, let the South go."

Townsend shook his head. "He says he's against the secession, but he's trying to avoid war. There are still several slave states that haven't seceded. Seven have. The rebels are getting together to form a government down in Alabama. Jefferson Davis is their man."

I sat in that elegant cream-enameled and wine-wallpapered parlor of the Townsends, there at 129 Fifth Avenue, hearing the distant crash of cannon and the rattle of musket fire and the clank of chains and the clatter of sabres, and the hoarse cries of men dying. Would this shambling string bean Abraham Lincoln unloose all that?

"Lincoln's coming here in a few days, you know," my father-in-law said. "He'll talk at City Hall. And also Moses Grinnell's place, a big levee, raising support for the union. Four blocks away. You can take your own look at the man. I think I will."

I resolved to do it. He aroused my curiosity. What sort of golden-tongued oratory issued from this man, that he could whip the great Stephen Douglas, the Little Giant, in debate? I considered myself an expert at that; I made words pierce and glow, touch hearts. I knew every ornamental embellishment, how to quote the ancients to good effect, how to couch each idea in lofty garb, how to insinuate, how to mock so subtly that my opponent scarcely was aware of it until too late.

I had all the best gifts of my countrymen. Had I not been on the public stage all my life, treading the boards, standing on the hustings, comfortable with podiums and lecterns? Ah, yes, I would go see this shambling frontiersman, and take his measure, but I already knew my verdict: a cunning rube.

Sam and Alice Barlow soon joined us, eager for news, so we sluiced an inch off Townsend's cask of fine Monongehela, added a little pond ice, and made a merry reunion of it. By the time I had soaked the pain out of my travel-weary body, we had concluded that Costa Rica and the Chiriqui venture was an amusing detour.

There was other news, not of war and rumors of war, but of decline and death. Terrence MacManus, my comrade in exile, my brother in Young Ireland, had died in California, and even now his remains were being transported here, and then bound for Ireland. He had not fared well in the Golden State, living there as much in exile as in Van Diemen's Land, and finally his great spirit surrendered. Some there are who can't be uprooted from their native soil, and he was one. Was I another?

A quiet new society, the Irish Republican Brotherhood, planned to make the most of the ceremonies, and I agreed to participate with speeches in upstate New York and Boston. MacManus and I were the symbols of all Irish striving, and I would not disappoint my countrymen. For an hour, anyway, the perilous state of the Republic was not foremost in my thoughts. This new group, which John O'Mahony had started to call Fenians, after Finn MacCool's legendary cadre, made me uneasy, for reasons that were still gelling in my soul. But I had not been called Meagher of the Sword for nothing, and so I went along with them and their dreams of cold steel.

These were portentous times, and I followed them closely in Greeley's *Tribune* and James Gordon Bennett's penny-sheet, the *Herald*, which I deemed more reliable than most of the city's rags. Uncle Ape had left Springfield, on the western frontier, and was wending his way to Washington City, where the electoral college would decide the election on February 13th.

Who was this man? He had a good and historic English name. England was full of Lincolns. Now, upon his inaugural journey, he had surrounded himself with lieutenants and body-guards, but the trip was political every foot of the way. Not a town along the route did he pass but to stop and glad-hand the mobs, review the local militia, the Zouaves, the Yagers, brass bands, fife-and-drum corps, the winsome girls bearing flags, the whiskered speechifying dignitaries in black cutaways, all half hysterical with the nation crumbling into ruin with every passing hour.

He was calling himself "a mere instrument," an "accidental instrument" of the cause that had thrown him into office, as if he had nothing to do with it.

In Cincinnati, just across the river from Kentucky, he sent his message southward toward Confederate ears: "We mean to treat you, as near as we possibly can, as Washington, Jefferson, and Madison treated you."

But in Columbus, he took another tack: "It is not my nature, when I see a people borne down by the weight of their shackles—the oppression of tyranny—to make their life more bitter by heaping upon them greater burdens; but rather would I do all in my power to raise the yoke...."

Abolitionist stuff. I grew impatient with the man, even though what he was saying resonated in me. I knew what he was talking about. But I didn't like the tone. Life was too complex for simple choices. Slaves were property; how could you justly take property away from an owner? A quarter million freed blacks lived in the South, and many of *them* had their own black slaves; some even had large numbers of them. How was Uncle Ape going to sort all that out?

Then, in a tumultuous and intensely southern Washington, still a rude malarial capital with miserable public buildings, Lincoln found himself the winner of the election, as the electoral college votes were tallied. Vice President John Breckinridge, a deep-dyed Southerner, proclaimed Lincoln the winner.

Then Lincoln was off again, his train carrying him in some helter-skelter fashion out upon the bleeding nation. In Columbus, Ohio, he again took a modest stance, declaring himself a man without a name: "There has fallen upon me a task such as did not rest even upon the Father of the Country," he said. "I turn, then, and look to the American people and to that God who has never forsaken them...."

Lincoln's train and retinue worked through upstate New York, coming closer and closer to New York. In Rochester he congratulated the local citizens for the sturdy platform they had made for him, but wryly added it was more of a platform than his speech deserved. I marveled. What manner of man was this?

In Albany, addressing the legislature, he humbled himself once again: "It is true that while I hold myself without mock modesty, the humblest of all individuals that have ever been elevated to the presidency, I have a more difficult task to perform than any one of them."

Then, of a sudden, he was in my city, riding in a procession of thirty carriages sided by five hundred mounted police. Here the crowds were different. They stood silently, hostile faces, many of them Irish. Here no one was shouting himself hoarse. Here were his political foes, entrenched in City Hall, the courts, the whole government of the city.

I went to the City Hall affair to have a look at the gangly man in the silk top hat, a man with a voice not altogether pleasant and smooth. We were jammed in there, and scarcely a man of us favored Uncle Ape. This was Mayor Wood's turf, and he had filled it with his bought-and-paid-for lieutenants.

Lincoln acknowledged at once that he was among his opponents. He graciously thanked Wood for the reception and Wood's remarks about the parlous state of the Union, which he said he agreed with. And then he came to the point: "This Union should never be abandoned," he said, "unless it fails and the probability of its preservation shall cease to exist without throwing the passengers and cargo overboard."

He was virtually laughed out of New York. Mrs. August Belmont made a point of saying she had *not* attended Mrs. Lincoln's reception at Astor house. The barbarian even wore black kid gloves when he attended the opera at the Academy of Music, which amused the whole house.

I didn't know what to make of Americans, but any nation

that could elect an ape like Lincoln deserved what it got. I shrugged off the national calamity and turned to Irish matters. I shared my Anne Street offices with the Fenians, and daily we prepared for our own war—against England.

Meanwhile, I had a living to make, and thought maybe I could get a position, even within the new Republican administration. I had my old friend and mentor Judge Emmet write the new secretary of state, Seward, about a consulship in Venezuela for me. But I never heard.

PART II

War

14

I watched in astonishment as the president-elect zigzagged his self-deprecating way toward Washington, making homely jokes even as the republic sundered itself. When he finally reached Washington, guarded by Pinkerton operatives, traveling incognito, and dodging Maryland assassins in the process, he settled into Willard's Hotel and began to sort out his cabinet choices and entertain importuning office-seekers.

A Peace Commission, chaired by tottering John Tyler, met in February and failed. Old Buck Buchanan could do nothing but stew at extremists and mark time until his term was over. The seceding states had elected Jefferson Davis as their president, and had formed the Confederacy amid wild whoops of defiance and joy.

Down in Charleston harbor, federal forces, one hundred strong, under Major Robert Anderson had retreated to Fort Sumter and had dug in for a siege, while the state of South Carolina rattled its sword, its governor threatened to assault the fort, and Anderson's food supply dwindled. Buchanan had not withdrawn federal forces there, but obviously intended to leave it to Lincoln whether or not the fort would be surrendered.

I watched this from a vast distance, as if through a reversed telescope that made large events small. I sat idly in Townsend's house, sipping cognac, staring out the windows, shuffling through the sensational penny press, scanning black headlines.

The looming American war evoked no passions in my bosom. I could not summon any sympathy for Lincoln, whose flat, dull speeches were so artless as to set me yawning. The Republican Party would get what it deserved: one term in office and eternal disrepute, the blame for slicing a nation in two.

Lincoln was inaugurated in the midst of an armed camp. Old General Winfield Scott, chief of the skeletal army, and his fusty colonels had posted riflemen atop buildings to prevent assassination, which was rumored to occur at any time. Lincoln took his oath from doddering Chief Justice Taney before the scaffolding of the unfinished Capitol building, and the jittery Republicans even managed an inaugural ball at which Mrs. Lincoln wore blue. But of that I cared little.

In the press the next day I studied the man's inaugural address, and found it to be a sordid mixture of threats and olive branches. He must have had the devil to pay with the abolitionist wing of his own party, because he said it was not his intention to outlaw slavery or disturb the arrangements of southern states, but only to let the people of new territories decide whether to enter the Union slave or free. I imagine those hotheads, like Sumner, Wade, Stevens, and Salmon Chase, stewed at that, but it merely amused me.

All I could do was to fill the columns of the *Irish News* with my skepticism.

Events have their own momentum, and even as Lincoln gathered his quarreling cabinet around him and settled into an armed city, the new Confederacy decided the garrison at Fort Sumter had to go. The new nation preempted South Carolina, and sent General P. G. T. Beauregard with five thousand recruits and batteries to ring Fort Sumter round, even as the

Confederates sent two delegates to Washington to dicker for peace, by which they meant secession and nothing else.

It was plain, from press reports, that Lincoln's advisers were arguing furiously about what to do, some wanting to surrender Sumter, which had little strategic value, and focus elsewhere. But others around Lincoln argued that the beleaguered post had symbolic importance, and the Union could not simply let go and bring Anderson's garrison north.

I followed it all, relying on Bennett's skeptical *Herald* to keep me abreast, along with the equally critical *Times*, because Greeley had gone soft in the head and was toadying to Lincoln. The *Herald*, edited by that gaudy Catholic Scotsman James Gordon Bennett, did not mince words: "Our only hope now against civil war of an indefinite duration seems to lie in an overthrow of the demoralizing, disorganizing, and destructive sectional party of which 'Honest Abe Lincoln' is the pliant instrument."

We in New York were powerless in any event: we were out of office, and out of power. My brother-in-law worried about his north-south railroads, and my father-in-law fretted about unpaid bills, and what he would do with worthless Confederate dollars if that was how he was to be paid by southern clients. And when I wasn't worrying about my poverty, I worried about Ireland, where little had changed, and brave lads were secretly forming new cadres to achieve what Young Ireland had failed to do.

There were negotiations between South and North, with Lincoln and assorted southern officers exchanging notes, but it came to nothing. On April twelfth, after Beauregard demanded that his old artillery pupil Anderson surrender on honorable terms, and was declined by his student, the first cannonade of the war sent shell into Fort Sumter. Shot and mortar rained down in awesome barrages, and the dust and shock of all that soon rolled through New York, and the North. They had fired on us!

Federal relief ships sent at last by Lincoln arrived too late, and hovered out of range. Over three thousand shots landed on the fort, while its garrison hugged the earth and breathed through wet handkerchiefs, warding off fumes and heat. And then, on the fourteenth, Anderson surrendered. The last of the provisions was gone, save for a little pork. The enemy was starvation, not Rebel shot and shell.

He marched out, drums beating, regimentals flying, and fifes shrilling, and took a relief ship to New York. The Stars and Bars flew over Fort Sumter. He had lost one man, from an explosion of his own cannon, and with him in his trunk was the Stars and Stripes he had flown defiantly all that while, burned and holed, which, he proclaimed, someday would wrap him in his grave.

That day the cabinet framed a proclamation: the rebel states were now combined in insurrection that fell beyond normal remedies available to governments. "Now, therefore, I, Abraham Lincoln, President of the United States, in virtue of the power invested in me by the Constitution and the laws, have thought fit to call forth, and do call forth, the militia of the several states of the Union, to the aggregate number of seventy-five thousand, in order to suppress said combinations . . ."

One other thing: Lincoln and Stephen Douglas, Democratic contender for the presidency, were closeted for two long hours that day, and when Douglas emerged, it was to give his utter support to the war effort, to the defense of the capital, and to the call upon the militias. The man I had supported so strongly was standing side by side with the president.

We were at war. And bonny Major Anderson was the moment's hero, his hundred men holding out a day and a half against five thousand, his honor enhanced, his devotion to duty applauded, his courage esteemed. And he was a man with a divided heart, for his wife came from a great southern slave-holding family. But he saw where honor must lead, and there he went.

The bombardment of Fort Sumter, which had blown the American flag off its staff, stirred and rocked a nation, and in every hamlet and city of the country, angered men stood up to be counted among the volunteers. There was brimstone in the air.

My father in law, Peter Townsend, no friend of the South, had started calling them Rebels, but I corrected him: When you have eight million Southerners forming a new government, it's not *rebels* they are, but *revolutionaries*, I said. He glowered at me, and once again a shadow passed between us. All was not harmony in his residence. It put him in a fix. He favored his ancestors' revolution against England but opposed this one.

I discovered, as did many of the Irish in New York, that I was now, willy-nilly, a Union Democrat, and the shift had occurred in the space of a week. It was one thing to sympathize with moderation and the South; another to endure a massive rebel assault upon the Republic which had harbored us so generously.

It wasn't our war, but we had some obligations, and we could defend the Republic or not. Many of the Irish chose to defend it. I told Michael Cavanaugh, the young clerk in our Anne Street offices, that I felt obliged to defend the Republic that had offered me asylum—and that if Great Britain intervened, we Irish would be fighting to free our homeland.

"Meagher of the Sword," he replied.

15

Lincoln wanted seventy-five thousand militia for a three-month term, and I decided I probably would not be among them. This war evoked no great passion in my breast. But there were plenty of New York Irish who thought it was their war. Some three thousand of them headed for Prince Street, headquarters of the 69th New York Militia, to enroll.

Its leader, a fire chief named Michael Corcoran, could accept only a thousand men plus officers, and was swiftly up to his full complement. Nonetheless, after some days, I stopped in to talk to the colonel, a hard and steady man. He granted me a few minutes.

"You feel this is our war?" I asked.

"It's our republic. We're needed."

"Irish are the cannon fodder of other nations."

"Meagher, these men volunteered. We turned most away."

"Sure and the Irish have joined the foreign legions of France, India, Mexico, and other nations, Wild Geese they're called, and get themselves shot dead for it. They get shoved into a fight first, ahead of the regulars. That's how it was during the uprising of seventeen ninety-eight when the French landed in Connaught and stirred up our peasants to fight the English. It was the Irish lads, with nothing but their pikes, that ran toward the redcoat muskets and cannon and got mowed down, while the French army waited. The devil's in this, I think."

Corcoran was genial but impatient, with a thousand things begging his attention. He stood restlessly, wanting it to end, but I was someone he needed on his side and I could see him containing his impatience.

"I am thinking, Meagher, that it might be good if these men were to become real soldiers, hardened to battle, *veterans*. Mind you, that's all I'm saying. A good lot of real soldiers, blooded in battle, Irish lads, here in a republican country . . ."

The thought had eluded me. It opened windows. "Irish veterans! An Irish army to free Ireland! You yourself now, are you against the South?"

"If it's slavery you're worrying about, I suppose I am, not liking the buying and selling of mortals, but if it's the Union, and keeping this country in one piece, Meagher, that I am and no doubt about it."

In that moment, I came to a decision. "Colonel, would you accept a company of Zouaves attached to the Sixty-ninth?"

"Zouaves?"

"An elite."

"Led by?"

"Whoever qualifies. Not necessarily me."

"You'd raise it?"

"I would."

He nodded. "Go ahead, man. Keep me informed. Everything."

I left that headquarters with a mission. One hundred Zouaves for Mr. Lincoln. Back in my Anne Street offices, I braced Michael Cavanaugh, our young law clerk.

"Do you know what this war means to the Irish?" I asked. "It means an army."

"Sure and how many of the lads will be coming home?" he asked.

"Even if only one in ten comes home, Michael, we'll have the cadre we need to free Ireland."

"One in ten, Tom? *One in ten?*"

"It's a three-month war. Ninety day service. That's all they're keeping the militia. Most likely nearly all the lads will come home, and well trained soldiers they'll be."

He stared at me with compressed lips, not rejecting it, not accepting it. "Not our war," he muttered.

"Ah, Michael, lad, it is our war. We owe it to the Americans."

"For what? Starving us? Herding us into tenements? Mucking the streets, the girls selling their bodies because they cannot hire?"

Cavanaugh was in a mood, and I left him there. I had business with O'Gorman, Dillon, O'Mahony, Judge Daly, and a raft of others. But first I headed for *New York Daily Tribune*, a paper I reckoned would get the response I wanted, and placed an ad:

One hundred young Irishmen—healthy, intelligent and active— are wanted to form a company of Irish Zouaves—under the command of Thomas Francis Meagher to be attached to the 69th Regiment, NYSM.

I found O'Gorman in his offices and made my case.

"A company of Zouaves, all Irish, drilled to perfection, an elite, capable of training an army in the old country, battle hardened. I'll lead it. The ad's running in the *Tribune*."

"And you want something from me."

"I want Zouave uniforms, green, and some Celtic colors to lead us."

He laughed. "So it's gaiters and balloon trousers and little jackets and fezzes you're wanting, all done up green!"

I was a little put out, and simply nodded.

"Soldier boys!"

"They won't be boys when I'm done. They'll be men, and they'll know arms and war, and they'll be a key to many things afterward, maybe the future of our Isle."

He sighed, smiled, and I saw agreement in him. "Ah, Tom, uniforms you'll be wanting, and green silks, like the jockeys wear in a good horserace, little caps, and a pretty flag." The smile vanished. "I'll see to it," he said. "And what'll I be calling Tom Meagher next? Colonel is it?"

"No, little enough I know about such things. When I was in Ireland stirring up the people, I thought I'd be a good general. No, I'll take a lower rank. A captain is what I'd make."

"Let me talk it around. You'll have your hundred Zouave uniforms in a bit."

I bade him goodbye, and headed at once for Fifth Avenue, to tell Libby what I had done. I found her seated before the sun-lit casement, saying her beads, her fingers working through the decades, the rosary of onyx and gold one I'd given her. I waited. She saw me, bowed slightly, and stopped.

"Good, we need the praying," I said.

"I hate war. My father's in a mood. He thinks he'll be ruined."

"It won't last long," I said. "A quick thrust. A show of force. Why do you think Lincoln's asking for so few, and for such a short time?"

"Because he's dumb."

That was my Libby, brimming with opinions.

"What did you come to tell me?" she asked, knowing that I would not normally disturb her early in an afternoon.

"It's the war, Libby," I said. "I've decided to raise a company of Zouaves. And lead it."

She stared from those warm brown eyes, absorbing that. "Lead it? No, Tom, don't do it. Please don't."

Never had she resisted me. Always, she had said yes, let's go, melding her will to mine.

"It's just for three months, Libby."

"For what? For what?"

"For the Republic."

She smiled crookedly, in a way I had never seen, and the twist of her lips said she didn't really accept my explanation. Somehow, we had come to one of those hinges that turn a marriage in a new direction.

She stood, played with my lapel, and I slid my arms about her.

"This won't last. No one thinks the South will resist for long."

"What of us?"

"Libby, when this is over, you'll be glad and proud that I answered the call and helped hold our country together."

It sounded like a recruiting speech.

"Yes, you'll be fine," she said, but her face had clouded and I knew she wasn't fine. "And I'll be fine too. Don't worry about me."

I felt off balance, and summoned our servants.

"A drink," I said, "for Mrs. Meagher and me. And make it double."

16

Ah, what a sight it was, the New York 69th, almost entirely Irish boys, mustering there on Prince Street, May fourth, to march off to war. A rowdy crowd had collected, and many was the bottle that passed to our brave lads, giving them warmth and cheer and a murderous gleam to their eye. If we could march them off without pain, then we were doing them a small favor.

It was a fine and glorious moment for the Irish of New York, our bonny boys gathering into columns like *soldiers*. And when the last sip had been drained from the last little bottle, they kissed their girls and struggled through the hooting crowds, off to the Battery and the *James Adjer*, which would sail them to hotly secessionist Baltimore. From there they would march to beleaguered Washington, which lay in rebel country, though neither Maryland nor Virginia had seceded.

Lincoln needed men fast; his capital city was scarcely garrisoned, and the South might win the war with a preemptive strike, capturing the government and maybe even the president. And so our fine lads, big and brothy and strong, sailed off to war, along with militias from all over the country, to rescue Mr. Lincoln before the capital was overrun.

I, of course, was still recruiting for the Zouaves and getting the dandy uniforms made up. Dark green trousers, green coats embroidered with gold braid, white gaiters. I intended that my Zouaves would be the best, the finest, the heartiest lads in service. At last, when the recruiting was done and we had selected the healthiest, we met at Phelan's Tavern to elect officers, and there it was that my Irish lads made a captain of me. I had been offered better positions in other regiments, but thought better of it. There would be blood on the hands of any officer who didn't know what he was doing.

For some while, during those first bleak days of war, we heard nothing from the capital; it was virtually shut off from the North, besieged by unruly mobs of Marylanders, threatened by Rebel forces entrenched across the Potomac. But old Winfield Scott had not been idle, and in time we learned that our own 69th was encamped in Arlington, on muddy ground, bulwarking itself against the traitors.

The place was called Camp Corcoran after our colonel. The war was barely a month old, and utter confusion reigned, rations were erratic, and half the men lacked muskets because the rebels had brilliantly raided federal arsenals and commandeered them.

Libby adored my natty green and gold uniform and made sure the tailors got it right. I rather enjoyed it myself; Meagher of the Sword, captain of Zouaves, ready for action.

In June we were summoned at last.

"Three months, love, and I'll be on my way home," I said, to lighten Libby's worries.

She smiled brightly, and kissed me. "You'll be a brigadier before you know it," she said. "Wherever you go, whatever you do, there will I be, and there will my prayers be too."

She rode beside me as I led my bright-clad Irish lads from Beekman Street to the pier, and then came aboard to hug me good-bye. The steamer's whistle shrilled, she and I touched lips and hands, and I escorted her down the gangway. She dabbed at her eyes.

We were off, by sea and rail, to the war. It was an easy ride over coastal waters, but as we progressed into the steamy reaches of the South our trousers bagged and our natty uniforms sagged. At Fort Corcoran, drenched by rain and muggy weather, we set to work erecting ramparts, slogging through muck, and scavenging rations.

Colonel Corcoran welcomed us. "So far, the war's been pick and shovel rather than rifle and bullet," he said. "But we've some West Point cadets here to give the boys some pointers. You'll take instruction with the rest."

And so we learned, sitting in hot grassy fields full of ants, our stomachs growling for the want of anything but hardtack or biscuit, and watched as stiff-legged cadets took us through our drills, loading Springfield muskets, attaching bayonets. We learned to break down the rifles, clean them, and put them back together. We learned the function of every part. We learned how to pull a misfired charge. We learned how to quick-load, how to shoot in volleys. We even got in a little target practice, though powder was scarce and we had only a dozen rifles.

Some regular army sergeants, gravel-voiced veterans, took us through the army names for things, the order of ranks, seniority, discipline, punishments for everything from brawling to desertion, obeying commands, sanitation, hygiene, dress, the contents of our haversacks, traveling light, field rations, binding wounds, foraging for food and supplies, trenching, earthworks, defenses, digging in, following orders, knowing bugle calls, staying alive, keeping an eye out for our officers, aiming and shooting low, watching for snipers, sticking together, helping each other, getting exercise, types of artillery shot and shell and canister, keeping feet dry, keeping boots repaired, letting blankets air, the danger of frostbite, staying warm, what to do and where to report if sick.

I wasted no time setting up comfortable quarters in a wall tent, with a cot, an old rug on the grass, a camp chair, and a cask of good Pennsylvania rye whiskey ready, along with potable water and some tumblers. Ah, that was the life! I soon had a fine parade of guests coming to my lodgings and sharing jokes about the Rebels. Sometimes we could see their pickets. Once or twice we glimpsed their new national colors, a flag with crossed bars, a traitor flag we spat at.

I looked after my Zouaves but there wasn't much I could do. The army's commissary had yet to catch up with the amassed militiamen circling Washington City. Then in July the New York 69th got bad news: their three-month enlistment didn't begin the day they left New York, but when the 69th was mustered in, which was May 9th. They would not be free until August 9th.

Corcoran asked me to talk to the men, raise their spirits, and so I did. It was with quips and jokes I put them at their ease. We'd all been burnt by the southern sun, and so I told my boys the commissary should issue us parasols because our bummer caps weren't enough. I told them that the stuff I had to eat the other day was so peculiar I donated it to Barnum's Museum.

But most of all I stressed that we were doing our duty, and returning to the union the gift of liberty it had given us, and that quieted our men some. But most had hoped to be home in July, and New York had to cancel its welcome celebration for its returning warriors.

At least they were paid. Most of the lads sent their eight dollars back to the city to help their wives and children and parents and not a little of it crossed the sea to Ireland. We finally got our own rifles and cartridges and field rations, and we started feeling like we were soldiers. We were about to march, and knew it.

On July 15, we received our orders, which came down from General McDowell. We loaded our haversacks with three days' rations, and the next dawn we marched toward Fairfax, Virginia, led by the gray-clad engineers, whose task was to clear away the roadblocks. After them, the drummers and then the officers: Colonel Corcoran, Lieutenant Colonel Haggarty, and Captain and now *acting major* Thomas Francis Meagher. Ah, it was a feeling not to forget, these men, over a thousand strong, thumping toward war. It was hot work, and the Virginia sun soon dehydrated us, my men hunted water, and I learned that war is mostly marching and foraging and nursing blistered feet.

It was our misfortune to be placed under a rude martinet of a colonel, a snarling, barking red-haired man named William T. Sherman, a West Point graduate who had returned to active duty after a teaching stint in Louisiana. We had been attached to his 3rd Brigade, along with the 13th New York, 79th New York, 2nd Wisconsin, and 3rd U. S. Artillery, and his fate would be our own. The lads didn't much care for this Sherman.

We reached Vienna and there at last was the enemy, butternut-clad southerners well entrenched in a line along the horizon, men like ourselves but we could not tell one from another.

Beyond the Confederate line was a woods full of Rebel reserves. All these troops were guarding the Confederate flank. I felt that savage stirring of the blood that excites the humors of men at war. We paused a moment to let Ayers's battery get down to work, and soon enough, canister and shell were raining on the Rebels. Then the moment came: Haggarty, Corcoran and I drew swords, rode ahead, and beckoned our men to follow. A throaty cry rent the morning, and my Irish raced forward, howling from their parched throats, and the Rebel line broke. By noon, the Stars and Stripes flew over Vienna. We marched in triumph, our forage caps perched on our bayonet points. The 69th had tasted battle and triumphed.

"Proud of you I am," I cried to them.

Captain Breslin had been injured, but Sherman had allowed us but one ambulance, so we took the captain forward with us instead of back. I protested to Sherman, to no avail. That rude and envenomed martinet cared little about any Irishman, and out of utmost spitefulness had refused us more ambulances. He had shown his malignity toward the 69th, and was roundly hated by the regiment. I intended to let the world know it when I published my account of our engagement.

But the hard month of July was not over for the 69th. We marched through Centreville on the 18th toward a place called Manassas, a key railroad junction where the Rebel General Beauregard had amassed his army and was awaiting reinforcement from General Johnston. A creek called Bull Run ran athwart us, and along that creek the Rebels had dug in, covering every ford up and down the river from the Warrenton turnpike.

Israel Richardson's Fourth Brigade made a probe in force across Blackburn's Ford that day, and fell back under heavy fire. Late in the day we were sent to relieve Richardson's men, and took some bombardment from the Confederates and also from Sherman's mean tongue, but soon we were retreating to Centreville to await rations being brought up behind, and to let General McDowell put his army in order.

On the twentieth, we knew that the next day would be our first taste of real battle and blood and death; not simply another Vienna. Father Cass, a brother of one of our officers, heard confessions from our lads all that eve, within a green bower, and I knelt also, to cleanse my soul and prepare myself, and thus we were shriven and ready for whatever would come.

"Men, we're the Union's Irishmen, and we're enrolled in a sacred cause, protecting this free and generous Republic from its traitors, and we're going to march with great hearts and the courage of the Gaels," I said, for it had fallen to me to rally our troops. "Ahead lies Manassas Junction, where the Shenandoah Valley and the Richmond railroads meet. Defeat the rebels here, and their capital lies open to us, little defended, and we'll have a railroad to take us there. Win here and now, and the war is as good as won. And our battle-hardened and victorious Sixty-ninth will parade its colors down the streets of New York and receive the honor to which we all aspire."

They cheered and I knew they would follow our green silks to the end of the earth.

By dawn the next and fateful day, we were deployed near the stone bridge that spans the creek. There at the middle we were to pin down the Rebels while the main Union thrust would flank from the left.

There in a green field we waited, sweated, munched hard-tack and sweltered, as the hot Virginia sun rose upon a frightful tableau.

17

The sleepy Virginia countryside harbored armies in its bosom. Soft zephyrs slipped through our encampment in the green fields of the valley. Beyond the run lay thick forests, and beyond that a steep rise to various verdant hills, some topped by farmhouses. Here farmers plowed and sowed and harvested, cattle grazed, and butterflies and bees flitted from bloom to bloom.

But we heard no birds this morning, for they had taken flight at the soft creak and rumble of soldiers marching, caissons rolling, iron-rimmed wheels cutting into clay. And the scent of daisies and magnolias had surrendered to the rank pungence of sweat and fear, the sour breath of dread.

The first hours of that fatal July 21st were absorbed in feint and maneuver; at times we saw the graybacks marching on the double, even as our forces switched leftward to flank Beauregard's army and cut off reinforcements.

My men watched uneasily, wondering whether cannon shot would soon shatter in their midst, great eruptions of earth and iron that would topple men and rip open their bodies.

I knew they were all asking why, why this was befalling them just a few days from their August 9 discharge. They were ninety-day men, and nearly their entire term had passed. They had defended the capital in its danger and now wanted to go home.

I tried to think of Libby, back in the enameled rooms of the Townsend house on Fifth Avenue, and could not even summon her image. There is that about war: all else vanishes.

We heard soft rumbles, then deep thunder, as batteries fired, and sometimes the rattle of distant musketry, but the real struggle had not yet begun. Percussion shocked the breezes; the earth under our feet trembled. Colonel Sherman stalked through our ranks, glaring at us, snarling orders, making himself even more obnoxious than was his natural humor. The lads were tired. They had been up since three-thirty, marched from Centreville before dawn to await their fate here.

Then Sherman shouted, and we were off, our bayonets glinting in the sun, wading Bull Run and hiking warily toward the hill beyond, its summit our objective. Only minutes before, along that ridge, we had seen columns of graybacks marching off to our left. We had a tough climb up the bluff of the creek, and then we marched toward that smudged ridge, past sulking woods, across open pasture, naked and exposed.

Ahead of us the Johnny Rebs fell back, using copses of trees as their cover, back toward the hilltop, gray and butternut-clad infantry rolling left as we pushed ahead. They were stragglers trying to reach their main army which was heading leftward; we were an organized brigade heading for the high ground.

They didn't shoot at us; not then, when they were forming up in the woods against the thrust to come on their right. Nor did we shoot at them. We were heading for the crest; it was as simple as that. Our tired blue lines marched upslope unmolested, Corcoran, Haggarty, and I directing the lads with our swords.

We marched toward the white farmhouse above, and that was when Haggarty spotted a Reb straggler, raised his sword, spurred his steed and attacked ahead of our lines, intending to cut the man down. I still see it in my mind. The Reb simply lifted his rifle, and put a ball through the lieutenant colonel's head. He fell, slowly to earth, dead before he landed, and his horse bucked and plunged and headed for the Confederacy.

All this the lads absorbed. For a long moment there was only silence, but then an animal rage boiled through our lines, and the howl that erupted would chatter the teeth of a devil. They shot that straggler. The Rebs, in the copses beyond, returned fire, and men began to fall.

Sherman materialized out of nowhere, yelling at us to cease our fire, wait until the Union's flanking maneuver to the right was complete. Sullenly the lads complied, but they lifted Haggarty's bloody remains and passed him to the rear, out of the war, out of the world.

Then Rebel batteries near that white farm house opened on our lines, blowing great red holes in our ranks. I saw men lifted and crumpled, saw explosions fell a dozen men like tenpins, murderous iron flying in all directions. I felt concussions knock me, push my horse, pound my head.

"Get them," Sherman snarled, but ordered the 2nd Wisconsin to lead the attack. These were gray-clad men themselves; the blue of the union army had not yet clothed the backs of all the militia. Twice they charged, twice the Reb infantry defending the batteries repulsed them, and then in the confusion they began to draw fire from our own lads, and no shouting or explaining could stop the slaughter.

We were next. With a cold gesture, Sherman sent us in.

"We're going to take that battery," I yelled to my lads. "Form up!"

Colonel Corcoran rode his line, getting his men in order, and then swept his sword forward.

My Irishmen rose up with a howl, lowered their muskets,

and trotted forward, even as balls stung and murdered. I rode everywhere, waving them forward with my sword, calling them into the cauldron of fire.

The stronghold ahead was, I learned, Henry's farmhouse, and around it the graybacks had dug in. Riflemen swarmed among the trees, there to protect their murderous artillery battery which was butchering my lads.

Off we went, Corcoran and I in the midst of the boys, pushing them forward. But they needed no pushing. Their Irish howl shook the grasses. At the fore was the lad carrying our green flag, the one Judge Daly's wife had presented to us, and it was a fatal emblem. The Rebs shot the boy, and shot the one who plucked up our colors, and again, until Corcoran shouted and cursed the lads away from that fatal trophy. The flag itself was shot to ribbons.

The Reb battery lowered its barrels and fired canister, blowing iron through us, and I saw New York boys topple, redden, catapult, fall. Corcoran called us back; we retreated to safety, regrouped, and stormed that hill again, and again the Reb battery chopped holes in our line, even as their sharpshooters picked us off. We fell back.

"All right lads, for our country, for the honor of Ireland, for the Sixty-ninth, once again up that hill! We'll silence that battery," I cried. "For the honor!"

But they were fewer now, their uniforms filthy and caked with sweat and blood. Some wore no shirt, some were barefooted. The living wounded, left on that slope, groaned and wept. We had not carried the fight to the Reb battery, which remained unscathed. More of Johnston's men had arrived to reinforce their position, and nearby, Thomas Jackson's formidable force had repulsed all Union attacks.

My weary, staring, blank-faced men collected again, and

once more we walked into battle, slower this time, the energy out of us, but muskets at the ready and bayonets tipping them, this time against a reinforced foe.

We weren't alone. Sherman had thrown in his Wisconsin men and his 13th and 79th New York. Into the maw of death they walked, brave and gallant men, but the Reb battery once more shot holes through our ranks, and this time the lads turned and fled; stumbling pell-mell back toward Sherman's command.

No rallying on my part slowed them. I wheeled my chestnut horse everywhere, until suddenly some terrific force blew the good animal apart, heaving me from my saddle, spraying me with blood. I felt myself catapult up, down, land on my head, and then I went black.

I do not know how long I lay there, amidst a disorganized rout, but I learned later that a New York neighbor of mine, with the 2nd U.S. Dragoons, Porter's Division, plucked me up, lifted me into his saddle, and carried me down the slope and across Bull Run. By the time I came to, the battle was over.

I had a violent headache; I had been concussed by my fall. I stared up into the tender faces of my lads as they inquired after me. My ears rang; my vision was blurred, I had no balance, and my limbs refused to work at first, but I managed to stand, dizzily, and hobble.

I walked toward Washington with the remnants of the red-clad New York Fire Zouaves, and finally got a ride in an artillery wagon. It seemed an orderly retreat at first, men walking quietly from battle, but Reb black horse cavalry was harassing us, and what had been orderly turned into another rout. Our own dragoons covered our rear, but it wasn't enough.

Arnold's battery unlimbered and began firing shot and shell, stemming the Reb assault. But many was the lad who pitched musket and haversack aside in his flight, and many was the wagon ruined at Stone Bridge by the panic, and the whole road back was littered with canteens, broken harness, ragged clothing, tattered shoes, the debris of defeat.

God help us, Colonel Corcoran was not among us. He and several of his officers and men had been captured by the Rebs. The New York 69th had few officers left. All our dreams of glory, our bright uniforms, our martial airs, our illusions, vanished that 21st day of July. The men were stumbling toward Washington like a flooding river, and no officer could stop them. They trudged the twenty midnight miles back to safety, defeated, weary, but determined to reach the small comforts of their bivouacs, their letters from home, a good mess, and real sleep.

I ran into fragments of the 69th at Centreville, but we did not pause, and not until three in the morning of the 27th did the 69th reach Fort Corcoran. I comforted the men, told them they had fought valiantly, restored their honor to them as best I could, but they stared at me, remembering blood and iron and defeat.

Many of the men wanted to leave since our enlistment was nearly up, and Colonel Sherman was forced to guard our camp with his regulars to prevent escape. Any attempt to leave before our enlistments expired would be met with bullets, he said. It brought shame to me, this state of affairs.

There were reports afoot that I had been killed in the battle, and these reached New York; other reports that I was less than gallant on the field of battle. But I would soon give the true bill to Libby and my friends, and there were those among us who would stick up for me.

The toll at Bull Run, we learned, was 16 officers and 444 men killed; 78 officers and 1,046 men wounded; 50 officers and 1,262 men missing. I thought of the dead and the suffering;

the widows and orphans, the men blinded and limbless and helpless.

A few days later, Mr, Lincoln himself visited our camp, flanked by staff and officers, including Colonel Sherman. I mustered my men, every last one of whom was Democrat, and waited to see how all this would avail. We awaited the president as one would a stranger: he was not one of ours and never would be, and when he arrived in his stovepipe hat, men nudged each other.

But Lincoln knew these men had been in the forefront, and commended them for their particular gallantry. He spoke eloquently of the need to persevere and endure for the sake of the Union, and my lads responded warmly to the praise, the personal attention, and the homely tenderness of this big, skinny and awkward man. He commended Michael Corcoran, now a prisoner of the Rebs, for valor in battle. And when Mr. Lincoln was done, he offered to listen to the grievance of any man.

One lieutenant took him up on it.

"Mr. President, this morning I went to speak to Colonel Sherman, and he threatened to shoot me."

"Threatened to shoot you?"

"Yes, sir, he threatened to shoot me."

Lincoln stared at the man, and at Sherman, and then leaned over to the lieutenant, and whispered sotto voce, "Well, if I were you, and he threatened to shoot, I would not trust him for I believe he would do it!"

The officer reddened and retreated. The lads laughed. They gave old Abe a good Irish howl, which irritated Sherman, but no one cared.

In a few days Colonel Sherman would be forced to release them; their enlistment would expire. And I, among them, would be heading back to New York, but not out of the war.

18

Oh, how they greeted us in New York! From Baltimore we sailed by steamer to the Battery, and from there we marched up Broadway, with the 7th New York as our honor guard. The largest crowd ever seen in the city thronged the boulevards.

We were veterans now, some of us coatless, others wearing plasters, our bullet-riddled silken colors borne on a stick whittled from a Virginia branch. We were proud lads, walking high, listening to the heady cheers of our kin, warriors who'd served the Union, who had rescued the capital during its peril. And the bands, the bass drums, snare drums, cornets, were howling our quickstep air, *Garryowen*:

> *Let Bacchus' sons be not dismayed*
> *But join with me, each jovial blade*
> *Come drink, and sing, and lend your aid*
> *To help me with the chorus:*
> *Instead of spa, we'll drink brown ale*
> *And pay the reckoning on the nail;*
> *No man for debt shall go to jail*
> *From Garryowen in glory.*
> *We'll beat the bailiffs out of fun*
> *We'll make the mayor and sheriffs run*

We are the boys no man dares dun
If he regards his whole skin
Our hearts so stout have got no fame
For soon 'tis known from whence we came
Where'er we go they'll fear the name
Of Garryowen in glory.

And waiting for me, when we disbanded for the day amid that cheering throng, was a glowing Libby, and the summer-dressed Townsends, and Sam and Alice Barlow. I hastened to my bride, swept her into my arms, and she pulled me into her own.

"My captain!" she said, pulling back to look at me. "A soldier!"

"Back safe, my love, and you are utterly beautiful," I said.

And so they looked me over. They already intuited what I would soon be doing: there would be a renewed 69th, and I would be going to war with it.

We hiked through crowds to our home, and swiftly broke out the Monongahela, for good war stories require the lubrication of some spirits. It was *Lincoln* they wanted to know about, every detail, every wart: Bull Run they understood. Wire reports had flooded to all the papers. But Lincoln left them uneasy, a mystery, some great inept oddity out of the rural west, a chimpanzee running the republic.

"Saw the president a few days ago," I said. "He came to the camps, with his retinue."

"Is he the bumbler they say?" asked Sam.

I hesitated. "He's a humble and homely man. And he took special pains to tell us of our valor. Every report he received commended us, so he commended us. He knew that Corcoran had been captured, too, and mentioned it. He called us brave men, fighting for a worthy and true cause."

"Well, that's the politicking that presidents do," my father-in-law said, impatiently.

"They do that, but Lincoln was feeling that war, and that defeat, right down to his bones. There was no mistaking his earnestness."

"Is he an ape? They're calling him a baboon," Libby asked.

"No, love, he's a man caught in a bloody mess, just as he says, and trying to make the best of it."

The man who came to commend and encourage us showed a face already etched in sorrow. He had not neglected the wounded, suffering so grievously in various Washington camps and hospitals, and he had seen the awful face of war. Each of those men had received a handshake, a soft word, so it was said, and many a man who lay abed without legs or eyes or hands had wept.

I sucked deeply, letting the rye spirits, chilled with pond ice, comfort my aching body.

"What of the Rebels? Can they fight?" Peter asked.

"They can fight better than we can. The best of the officer corps headed south and it shows. They'll make the most of what they have. It won't be a short war after all."

"The British are thinking of recognizing the new government in Richmond," Barlow said.

"And if they do, every Irishman, north and south, will be fighting for the North."

"Except Mitchel."

I laughed. "Except Mitchel." My old colleague from across the seas and fellow Vandemonian exile was trumpeting the southern cause in his newspaper, and sending his sons into service with the Confederate army. How odd it was: not even in exile could the Irish agree on anything.

The eve was young, and I was still vibrating from that brass band, tuba, trumpet, and trombone parade, all the hosannas, all the gawking children scampering beside us as we marched, all the pretty girls waving handkerchiefs. I was itching to collect my officer friends of the 69th at Phelan's Tavern to plan a future, but Libby was tugging at me, her gesture pointing to our chambers on the upper floors.

I downed another inch or two of spirits, resisting as long as I could. But finally she rose.

"Tom, you're worn out," she said.

The Townsends stood. I soon found myself above, alone with Libby. Our spotless enameled chambers seemed strange after four months of bivouac and mud and sweat. The open widows admitted soft August breezes and billowed the curtains. The great city rested quietly below.

I lit a gaslight and led Libby to the red plush divan and seated her there, and kissed her warmly, and her white hands found my face, my neck, and my own hands.

"I have missed you," she said, throatily.

"Ah, my Libby," I said. "You were upon my thoughts, guarding me in war."

"You are not done with the war."

"No, not done."

"I knew it the moment I saw you; the moment you lined up those men, the look of you in your uniform, the ease. You're a soldier now."

"I have a knack."

"Yes, I could see it. You have a silver tongue, and what is more important than an inspiring word in war?"

That wasn't really it, I thought. It was much simpler.

"I can do it. I can give something to the Republic."

She nodded. The war had bled away any ambivalence I once nurtured, and now I was cleanly, fiercely a Union man, without the slightest doubt. They had killed Haggarty, captured Corcoran, nearly killed me.

I stood abruptly, poured some whiskey from the cut glass decanter, and downed it neat. She watched, her gaze raking me. The spirits didn't take the edge off me, but I took no more.

She smiled, said nothing, and began pulling tortoiseshell pins out of her red-brown hair, until it tumbled thickly about her shoulders and framed her face. I always loved that rich chestnut mane of hers.

"One minute," she murmured, and retreated behind an oriental silk screen.

I paced restlessly, not wanting to take off my hard-worn Zouave uniform. I found a mirror, examined myself, noting the tan of the Virginia sun, the lean look, the ensigns of rank at my shoulders.

Almost before I knew, she slipped back, this time wearing a new wrapper of green velveteen with white piping. A white night dress peeped from her neckline. Her brown hair fell lustrously, newly combed, about her shoulders.

"Come along, soldier," she said, a wry smile lighting her face.

"I'm going to recruit a whole brigade, Libby," I said.

She kissed me warmly, tenderly.

"An Irish Brigade. Not just the New York Sixty-ninth. Lads from Boston, boys from Philadelphia. It'll be the finest force in the Union army."

Her hands found my jaw, which had not seen a razor, and rasped under her fingers.

"I'll meet tomorrow with O'Gorman and the others. Get them all to Phelan's Tavern. We'll form a committee. We'll get some funds together. A thousand dollars. Buy ads. I'll go on a recruiting tour, make speeches, get a thousand men, two thousand."

"Tom . . ."

"Wild Geese we are, the Irish who fight other countries' battles. We'll be the proudest regiment in the army."

Her hands found my hair and roughed it. She found the brass buttons of my coat and undid them, one by one. Her hands found my shirt and tugged at it.

"The boys who went to Virginia, they'll all reenlist. They'll form the core, teach others. We know how it is! We'll need new colors. Sew us a green flag, Libby; a golden harp on a green silk ground."

She didn't reply.

"Ah, Libby, it's a grand life, and you'll come with me. We'll go to Washington. Stay at Willard's, meet the generals. Attend one of the levees. Meet Lincoln. You want to meet the president?"

She sighed, let go, and headed for bed.

19

It would be the most important recruiting speech, and I was ready. We'd been slow to organize, but at last that August day, we held a picnic at Jones Woods, on the upper east side of the city. Twenty-five cents per person was our price, the money going to the widows and orphans of the 69th. But it would also begin our effort to fill the ranks of the Irish Brigade.

The weather was fine, and the largest crowd ever to gather in New York greeted us. The papers reported a hundred thousand. I saw only a sea of faces, mostly Irish, earnest young men, pretty girls in summer linens and muslin, wearing straw hats bedecked with ribbons and bows: all had come to the dappled shade of the green-leafed trees to hear me.

There were ghosts present, and things I knew little about until recently. Plenty there were in the country who did not relish an Irish Brigade; indeed, loathed the very idea. They were mostly Republicans, and some Know-Nothings too, those who dreaded the immigration of our people, who despised "papists," who wished to shut the gates of the Republic to anyone not native, or who spoke a strange tongue. But worse still, there were army men who didn't want an Irish Brigade, and I was tardy in learning the reason.

To a man, our organizing committee had wanted General

James Shields to command. He was Irish-born, a veteran army man who had fought in the Mexican War. He had left the army but now was returning to fight for the Union. We entreated him to take command, yet he seemed reluctant, though he gave our committee his warmest endorsement. In time, I learned why.

"They're remembering the San Patricio Battalion, and so is Shields," Cavanaugh told me. I understood none of that until he enlightened me. The Mexicans had actively recruited Irish soldiers during the Mexican war, appealing to religion and the plight of the foreign-born in the United States army, who were treated brutally, often from Know-Nothing sentiment among its officers. Many Irish recruits had deserted and joined the Mexican army at higher pay and higher rank. Scores were eventually hanged in Mexico by the victorious Americans. Others were flogged. The United States Army officer corps remembered, and still cultivated its prejudices against the Irish. Maybe that explained Colonel Sherman.

We were without a commander, with Colonel Corcoran still in Libby Prison in Richmond.

But now, while I was being introduced from our red and blue bunting-draped platform, I knew I had an even more difficult resistance to overcome, and not even the generous enlistment bounties collected from patriotic businessmen would win us a regiment, much less a brigade.

There was scarcely a Republican in that crowd. And hardly a person in that sea of upturned faces supported Mr. Lincoln's effort to liberate black bondsmen in the South. They were, tepidly, for the Union, but they despised the abolitionists, hated Republican radicals, believed we should be conciliating the South, and were not about to sign up for three-year enlistments, even for a bounty they could send to the old country.

These were my people, the great bulk of them Irish-born,

most of them poor. They were hack drivers, waiters, seam-stresses, street sweepers, ditch-diggers, bartenders, grooms, maids, gandy dancers, ordinary laborers. Little else was open to them. Yet their lot here was a bit better than the one they left behind, and that would be my lever.

"My friends, hear me out this fine day," I began. "For I know your sentiments and understand the way you feel about this Republic, and I share these beliefs with you, along with a common heritage, born to a race of men whose glory shall never dim . . ."

Oh, I gave them an oration. I told them that Mr. Lincoln wasn't my president, but he was the country's president. I told them that the man in office, whoever he might be, was charged with upholding the constitution, and keeping the Union together, and that we, his opponents, needed to support the Union which had nurtured us, regardless of who was in office.

But I could not fathom the feelings of that huge crowd. They were too many, too quiet, too solemn for a bright August day. I had learned to throw my voice outward, so that even those in the most distant ranks could hear me. Now I focused on the most distant, and threw my words to their very ears.

"Never, never, I repeat it, was there a cause more sacred, nor one more great, nor one more urgent."

They applauded politely when I sat down, and I thought perhaps I had lost them. A cornet band played Irish airs, and marching songs, and that seemed to lift their spirits.

It was a good address, but I feared it had all been for naught, and so I retired from that stage, sensing defeat. Soon, though, our Beekman Street recruiting station near the Metro-politan Hotel had lines forming outside of it. Men were pledg-ing themselves to the war and to the Irish Brigade. And we were getting more than raw recruits, too. Veterans of the

British army signed up. Lieutenant John Gosson, from County Dublin, who had fought for the Austrians as a Hussar, joined us. The ranks swelled daily as my countrymen committed themselves. We would defend our new land from those who would despoil it.

I was pleased. My oratory, salted with fat bounties, was creating an Irish Brigade, the child of my dreams. I campaigned in Boston and then in Philadelphia. It was harder there, but men signed up in Massachusetts and Pennsylvania regiments that would soon join the Irish Brigade. Then I was back in New York, orating, talking up the brigade, answering hard questions. I especially wanted the veterans of Bull Run, the old 69th, to reenlist, but that wasn't an easy task, and their colonel was imprisoned in the South.

We had not settled on a commander, and now my colleagues were pressing me to present myself. And so was Libby. I didn't want high command, and told them so at Phalen's Tavern.

"That's for men who have studied war and fought it, who know how to avoid mistakes, how to keep troops alive, who know enough to deploy their men well. What foot soldier would want to be led by any other?" I asked those gentlemen, assembled around a table. I had said much the same thing to Libby.

"But Tom, you can be the acting commander. The one who gets it together," said Cavanaugh. "You can resign the command in favor of an experienced officer when the time comes."

I sighed, and accepted. They made me the acting commander, and gave me a provisional colonel's rank. I was actually little more than a recruiting officer, but they wanted me to have that honor.

Libby was promoting me for even higher stations.

"You must put in for brigadier," she said. "You're just the

right person to become the brigadier. They'll follow you any-where."

I demurred. "That's what I'm afraid of. Libby, an officer has the lives of his men in hand."

"I know," she said sweetly.

We were assigned to Fort Schuyler out in the Bronx. I found myself officially made brigade commander, and other officers were confirmed: Kelly, Condon, Keeffe, Gleeson, Haverty, Stacom. We set up a camp there and started training our menagerie of rowdies, if that's what one can call a nonstop party, with every lad's sweetheart hanging on and bringing in flasks and bottles. The men got their blue uniforms, and next thing I knew they were pinning green cockades to their caps.

"There, you see now, colonel, it's the green of Ireland," announced one sergeant.

The elected officers of the brigade were unanimous in their belief that I should lead it, not as a recruiting colonel but in battle, and again I felt that malaise that always swept me when I heard such things.

Whatever the pressures put on Washington by so many, my name went to the Senate for confirmation, along with the names of such veterans of real military service as George Meade and Winfield Scott Hancock.

But before that, we were ordered out. In mid-November, we gathered before the residence of Bishop Hughes, on Madison Avenue, there to receive our flags. My darling Libby had embroidered the green banner of the 69th, featuring harps and the words "No Retreat" upon it. The gallant lads in the New York 63rd and New York 88th received theirs as well from my wife, and the 88th awarded Libby with an honor. They would henceforth be called Mrs. Meagher's Own. Ah, and did my bride's eyes shine.

We boarded steamers for the capital, and soon found ourselves in General Bull Sumner's Camp California, outside of Alexandria, and a part of his corps. I was proud to be connected to his command. Once again we were hock deep in mud. Very much as before, we fortified and trained, turning our raw recruits into a coherent fighting force.

I telegraphed Washington: "The Sixty-ninth—the First Regiment of the Irish Brigade—were reviewed yesterday by General Casey along with four regiments from Pennsylvania and Maine. The appearance of the new Sixty-ninth was extraordinarily perfect and brilliant. The Irish Brigade leads the way in the National Army, in the hopes and hearts of the Government and people of the American Republic. War with England is imminent: *the Irish Brigade will be the first to meet the music.* . . . Ireland's day has come!—Thomas Francis Meagher."

I got to meet more of my men. Captain Hogan, a carpenter; Private Ginnelly, bartender; Tom Joyce, Pat Phelan, Bill Riley, Jim Ryan, all privates now; Martin Purcell, groom; John Byrne, burly sergeant; Will Coughlin, Jim and Billy Connolly, all from my parish and all coughing through life; Sinclair Breslin, Hugh Brophy, Joseph Burke; Richard O'Sullivan, clerk; Maxwell Hennessy, black-browed blacksmith. Soldiers now, wearing the blue.

They came across the sea in steerage, every one of them; not born here, but fighting here for their new country. O'Sullivan had six children and a sick wife. Brophy a bride of three months, already pregnant. Connolly's uncle was a bishop. Byrne wrote poems when he wasn't shouting at the troop or blaspheming. Purcell took a nip whenever he could, and always made it three nips if he could. Breslin was a pugilist and loved a brawl, and sung ballads in a sweet tenor. Skinny Captain Mulloy looked after them, herding these wild geese through their exercises.

Half were sick with dysentery, and the other half were suffering bruises, cuts, bunions, felons, hangnails, scrapes, sprains, blisters, and trenchfoot. But out of this mass of men came a disciplined corps.

Some had never touched a rifle before. Now they sighted down the barrels of the Model 1842 .69 caliber muskets, ran a thumb along the edge of their bayonets, studied the waxed cartridges. They fitted their haversacks to their backs, tasted and spat out hardtack and dehydrated vegetables and sour sausage. Their sergeants taught them the Manual of Arms, how to clean, load and shoot their rifles. How to aim. *Low! Don't shoot the sky!*

They set up their white tents, learned to ditch the rainwater away, learned to get along with their tent-mates or get tossed into the sleet, learned that their sergeants could usually whip them bare-knuckled and were willing to try, learned to keep their blankets and stockings and boots dry if they could, and if they couldn't, to dry them the next moment the sun shone or the wind rose.

They collected their greenbacks, gambled, drank, confessed to Father Corby, and little was the cash that remained in the regiment the day after each payday. They were tough rollicking Irish out of the tenements of New York, grinning at me as I walked through. They knew me, and the lazy salute was their reminder that we were all immigrants together, all outcasts, all men somehow trampled by the crown, or landlords, or the queen's bailiffs and sheriffs.

I was exhilarated. Here we were, the Irish Brigade, settling into white tents lined up in orderly rows, receiving our issues of arms, duffel, uniforms, boots, bummer caps, forage caps, gloves, cartridges, and muskets. I relished every moment of it, and set about making my headquarters comfortable. I got myself a plank floor, a good bunk, a small trunk, upon which rested my keg of seven-year-old Pennsylvania rye whiskey, a pail for water, and plenty of tin cups. I was soon open for business, welcoming officers up and down the line, getting to know all my comrades in arms. They repaired readily to my tent and sampled my whiskey, and I was alert to keep a cask in reserve. Many was the friendship I made there in my warm tent, as we drilled our men through that wet winter.

Then word arrived: the senate confirmed me as a brigadier and I received my orders:

> Brigadier-General Thomas F. Meagher, Volunteer Service, will report to Brig.-General Edwin V. Sumner, U.S.A., for assignment by him to the command of a Brigade of his Division. By command of Major-General McClellan. J. Williams, Assistant Adjutant-General.

I reported in person to General Sumner, and was assigned the command of the Irish Brigade:

> Headquarters, Sumner's Division, Camp California, Feb. 11th, 1862. Special Orders, No. 14. Brigadier-Gen. Thomas F. Meagher, Volunteer Service, having reported to these Head Qrs. for assignment in accordance Special Order N. 38, Hd. Qrs. Army of the Potomac, Feb. 8th, 1862, is hereby assigned to the command of the 2nd (Irish) Brigade of this Division. By order of Gen. Heintzelman, I. W. Taylor, Capt. U.S.A., A. A. A. C.

We toasted that, my Irish Brigade officers and I, and I hastened into the crowded city to engage some tailors to make me a pair of uniforms and field attire. It was no easy matter; the city was jammed, and the tailors were harried. But I blarneyed one to stitch up one uniform with the promise of another in a few weeks. He measured me up, and soon produced a fine blue wool brigadier's outfit, complete with the gold-threaded star of rank sewn on my gold-braided epaulets, military belt, a blue forage cap, and trousers.

We had a grand review and dress parade, and General Shields addressed the men of the Irish Brigade, followed by a banquet for me, given by my fellow officers. When they toasted my health, I replied with a humble oration:

"It is the hope, the prayer, the inspiration that this Irish Brigade here on the southern bank of the Potomac, together with every other Irish soldier in arms for the American Republic, will be the advance guard one day—and that day not far distant—the green flags and ringing trumpets of which will awaken the soul of Ireland to the dawn of the Easter Sunday which has been so long promised, so faithfully awaited, and so fervently prayed for."

Libby insisted she had to see her general, so I wrestled a room out of Willard's Hotel, thanks to some Townsend influence, and she soon arrived in the jammed city, after an exhausting steamer trip to Baltimore and stand-up rail passage to the capital.

She stepped out of the steam carriage carrying a hatbox, and looked me over, a wild smile building. "My general!" she cried, seeing the gold-thread star on each shoulder, the double row of brass buttons of my tunic.

"Your general indeed. I'm about the least experienced brigadier in the United States Army," I replied.

We got a hack and headed for Willard's. Wherever I went, officers and men saluted me, much to my amazement. I was robed for war.

20

What a fair day it was, and how we enjoyed the steeplechase. Never let it be said that the Irish Brigade lacks amusements. We invited a few officers to be judges, built a reviewing stand, got our jockeys up in bright silks, bet furiously on the nags, and ran the courses.

It was a warm, humid day, brimming with birdsong, the last of May, and we were camped on the Chickahominy River a few miles east of Richmond. There we were, just a three-hour march into the Confederate capital, enjoying the sporting life. The war would be over soon.

Of course the Irish Brigade's hospitality had become a legend in the army. I kept a plenteous supply of good sipping whiskey on hand for general officers and visiting dignitaries, whilst the men organized games, jousts, tournaments, marches, feats of arms, and sometimes some good Irish fiddling or band music, which of course serenaded us all with Irish airs.

Virginia springs are wet; that was our only curse. But the warm sun swiftly dried us out, and the lads all had the new pup tents, each man carrying half, and we survived the drenching.

After a cold, wet spring marching hither and yon and freezing our feet in slush, we finally boarded transports which steamed down Chesapeake Bay to the York River, and then upstream to a point not far from Richmond, which lay to the southwest. From here we would make quick work of the Confederates, under General Johnston, and go home.

Our commander, George McClellan, general of the Army of the Potomac, was in no hurry, and we saw little action all spring. But he had been accumulating matériel and men the whole while, and now we were a part of a grand army. The Irish Brigade was one of three composing General Israel Richardson's division, within Edwin Vose Sumner's II Corps, and we were gradually being positioned for the assault on Jeff Davis and his Rebels.

I had met Bull Sumner only once. "So you're Meagher," he said. "The orator. If words were bullets, General, the whole Reb army would lie lifeless at your feet."

I had taken it for a compliment, but uneasily.

We were in a sprightly mood that day, with the jaunty "Dick" Richardson and General William Henry French in the judging stand. I offered as a prize the pelt of a jaguar I had shot in Costa Rica and there were large purses for the winner of each race. After the races there would be some theatricals, music, and a few games.

Richardson grinned upon seeing our racetrack. "Meagher, I have to hand it to the Irish," he said. "There's supposed to be a war around here somewhere."

"Sure and when it comes, we'll fight," I said. "All right, you're the judge, and the jockeys are ready."

Off they went, followed by more races over the hurdles, and so the day progressed nicely, until, far south, there rose the low thunder of artillery, shocking the quiet. We paused. Israel Richardson frowned and excused himself, along with General French. It was only moments before dispatch riders raced in with orders from General Sumner.

The Rebs had found us out, and were attacking the middle

of our line, which stretched roughly north and south, just east of Richmond, from the Richmond and York River Railroad on the south to the Chickahominy River on the north. They intended to sever the Union army, and the Reb's General Johnston was massing his divisions to break us apart.

Richardson, French and I read Sumner's orders. We could hardly believe them. Move south fast, behind our front lines, and hold the railroad right of way. We were to follow obscure lanes, dodging some marshes, keeping out of sight of the Rebs. We were heading for a place called Fair Oaks. Southeast of there was a place called Seven Pines.

"All right, Gents, let's *move*," Richardson said. "The steeplechase is over."

Move fast, move light! We issued sixty cartridges and field rations to each man, told our lads to leave their knapsacks there and form up.

My groom brought me my sleek mare, Dolly, saddled up and ready, with the blue saddle blanket that bore a gold stripe around its borders, the emblem of a brigadier.

Now the roar of distant battle rolled over the misty land; the low thunder of artillery, and sputter and rattle of musketry. A big fight had erupted southwest of us, and we would soon be in it. Yellow gray smoke billowed upward above the trees.

We formed up and followed the Chickahominy, the boys wet-footed as we slogged through a marsh toward a bridge. Dispatch riders caught us en route, always with news, always urging us to hurry.

The IV Corps, under General Erasmus Darwin Keyes, had dug in at Seven Pines, south of the Chickahominy, set up a battery in an abatis, and was now under siege, along with the III Corps under General Samuel P. Heintzelman. The Rebs attacked about one o'clock, throwing in all of General A. P.

Hill's forces. Little Mac, General McClellan, got wind of it early in the afternoon and sent Sumner's Corps to support Heintzelman and Keyes, and so we were marching to the rescue. I saw a wild light in the eyes of my men: they were itching for a fight.

Even as we marched, word kept filtering to us: the reinforced Rebs were driving General Sedgwick's Union forces back from Seven Pines. At four, the Confederates attacked across the whole front: Longstreet, Anderson, Wilcox, Kemper, Colston, Pryor all supporting Hill's forces. But some of Sumner's lads arrived in time to help retake the ground.

All this reached us through smoke and roar, the dull distant thunder of war; but we did not partake of battle. By that evening, we had reached the forlorn fields, and found ourselves amidst the dead and dying, the gutted corpses of horses, the ruins of caissons and wagons, the screaming of the wounded, the darting of surgeons as they went from one man to another through trampled corn.

It was a haunting night, and the lads hunkered low and gnawed their biscuits in the blackness, watched by the ghosts of the dead, and wondered what the dawn would bring. At two in the morning, officers met in Sumner's headquarters tent, and decided to attack as soon as our commands could get into place. Richardson's division dug in along the railroad: French's Brigade in the first line, Howard's in the second, and mine in the third.

About five the next morning, just when I was talking to a wounded Irish Reb who was waiting for medical help, some Confederate skirmishers showed up before us, and were driven back. Then the Rebs opened up in force, with French's men taking the brunt of it. Howard's Brigade attacked, and was shot up, with General Howard receiving a ball in the arm. They retreated, and the gray wraiths flowed out of the woods, head-ing our way.

The Rebs were shifting left to flank us, and it looked like we might flee. That's when Bull Sumner himself rode in, and urged us forward. "You're my fighting Irish, and I know you'll not retreat!" he cried, his hoarse voice cracking in the dawn light.

We were ordered to attack with bayonets, and so we did, a fine Irish howl rising from our numbers.

I waved my sword, let them know I would be in their midst, and then we marched, pace by pace, through haze and smoke toward that dark and forbidding wood. We pushed forward in a resolute line, straight into musket fire pouring out of the dark-ness across the way. We marched, volleyed, marched, into the jaws of war for the first time, reached the railroad, plunged across the tracks and into those Reb woods and fields beyond, howling in Gaelic. I saw men drop, saw blood bloom, saw men stumble and lie still. But I also saw the green colors advance, and felt the murderous howl of my brigade as it hounded its enemies.

Our old friend Dan Sickles, commanding the 71st and 73rd New York, chocked with more Irishmen from Manhattan, pushed his lads forward next to us, routing the Rebs before him. We watched the Rebs abandon rifles and coats and haversacks as they headed for Richmond, and a fine morning it was for us all. Or so we thought for the briefest of moments.

Captain Lyon climbed a tree, and reported that sometimes, when the smoke lifted, he could see the glint of sun off the capitol dome in Richmond; we were that close. The whole city lay just ahead, with a defeated Reb army scuttling toward its perimeter. Surely the war would end soon.

We had fought a good fight, and I told my lads that we

could be proud. Straight into fire had we walked, never breaking, never wavering. There were thirty-nine who would never
go back to their homes, our first dead in the campaign.

But I learned later there had been no victory; it had been
counted a federal loss, and the war was not over. Most of us had
believed we would be marching through the streets of Richmond at that hour.

We dug in north of the Chickahominy, throwing up a log
fortress, and then we did nothing. There we were, knocking on
the gates of Richmond, the capital in sight from any tall tree,
and we were building defenses instead of ending the war. We
had sent them reeling back into Richmond. But now the Rebs
were reinforcing, regrouping, this time under Robert E. Lee,
because their commander, Johnston, had been wounded.

We didn't lack provisions. I'll say that for Little Mac. He
had his supply boats ready. But his inaction puzzled us. We
could have been marching through Richmond and heading
home. That's what the lads thought, anyway.

But the word I got was that McClellan thought the enemy
was a lot stronger than we were; more men in larger armies,
better supplied, and so the commander of the Army of the
Potomac was bent on forting up his formidable army there on
the peninsula, instead of taking the war to the Rebs.

I heard also that Lincoln was pointedly asking him what
his plans were, when he would move, what more was required.
But Little Mac was content to build up his mountains of
matériel and dig in.

My lads didn't like it. The full blast of Virginia summer was
upon us; heat, humidity, sweaty clothing, malaria. On the
advice of our doctors, I ordered a whiskey ration for our men to
ward off the malaria. But some had taken the temperance oath,

and sure enough, those were the ones who got the ague, and lay shivering and fevering until they died.

And when Little Mac finally moved, this time in another retreat, to the distant York River, it fell upon us to save his departing army from destruction. We did, but with terrible losses to the Irish Brigade. I was learning how little of war I knew, and how much of it I would learn.

21

We marched at night, fought by day, killed men in gray, plugged gaps in lines, held off the Rebs, and felt the murder of their fire upon us. The names clog my mind: Mechanicsville, Gaines Mills, Malvern Hill. McClellan was retreating, digging in, maneuvering us as if we were chess pieces instead of a footsore army. Robert E. Lee, the new Reb commander, knew it, and was determined to destroy the Army of the Potomac and win the war fast.

I was ill-tempered, raging at my men, and for little reason. The lads fought resolutely. General Sumner told me my brigade had rescued the Union army, not once but twice, the rear guard fighting off vicious thrusts by superior numbers while McClellan's marching columns retreated to new redoubts. How often he came to me, with a simple and desperate question: "Are the green flags ready?"

At one point someone above me put me under twenty-four-hour arrest, and I never discovered why. I had my suspicions. On our surgeon's advice we had issued medical whiskey to our men to fight off malaria. Somebody didn't like it. And it was being said I would take a nip before battle, which I hotly denied. It was the curse of the Irish that whatever we did, and whether we succeeded or failed, the world would accuse us of taking the nip.

Then, just as suddenly, I was restored to my command, no explanations, and Bull Sumner was heartily thanking us for yet another valiant rescue of the corps.

The Seven Days cut my brigade to ribbons. My 69th New York began with 750 men at Fair Oaks; by the time George McClellan was through with his wandering across the peninsula, it had 295. My other regiments, the 88th and the 63rd, lost another five hundred. We were given the dubious honor of covering the retreat, guarding the flanks and rear while Little Mac marched. The Rebs met my brigade, and fell.

Then, suddenly, the peninsula campaign was over. My men got issues of new clothing, some hot food, and even some back pay, though the new greenbacks were swiftly losing their value. They licked their wounds, mended their gear, fended off the summer showers, endured mosquitos and flies and wasps, and mustered uneasily, aware that we were a third or half of what we had been a few days earlier.

The Irish Brigade was no longer a fighting force.

In July, I got permission to return to New York and recruit. I took with me Lieutenant Emmet, grand-nephew of the Irish martyr, who had been wounded but was well enough to travel. Things were tense there: the radical press was calling Democrats copperheads, after the deadly snake, and blaming the Union losses on Democrat generals, in particular McClellan, but one could add Hancock, Sickles, Shields, and myself to that list.

It was a hot trip, and New York was at its most stultifying. Libby met the grimy steamer as it docked at a Battery wharf jammed with military gear in crates and casks, and in the midst of our joy, I saw the gloss of perspiration on her face.

"Oh, Tom! Tom!" she said. "You're so thin."

"I guess I am," I said. My blue uniform sagged loosely over me.

I introduced her to Emmet, whose pale face revealed his weakness. It was all Emmet could do to travel, and yet his name, which stirred so much feeling in any Irish heart, would guarantee us new men. He knew it, and had insisted on coming.

We gathered in the Townsends' parlor once again. The family wanted war news. I had nothing good to tell them.

"What are your plans?" Sam Barlow asked.

"I'm here to recruit. We were shot up."

"Shot up," Barlow snapped. "Guarding the rear, far as I can make out."

I didn't feel like responding. The war was changing me, tearing away the civilities. The rear was the front in this army.

"You're recruiting, but Corcoran was here before you," my father-in-law said.

Colonel Corcoran had indeed been here. He had been exchanged for Reb officers, and made his way here to raise a new Irish unit now that I commanded the Irish Brigade. He called it the Irish Legion, and soon had five regiments of a thousand men each willing to follow him into battle. Five thousand!

I would have my difficulties. I wondered if there were still a thousand of my countrymen in this sprawling city who would respond to my pleading.

"He's a good man," I said. "And a Fenian. He makes no bones about it. The armies he's raising can strike against the Queen. The boys he recruits will be tomorrow's liberators of Ireland. He never said it publicly, but that was the word he passed along."

It was odd, discussing this Fenian undercurrent with these protestant Yankees. The Irish Republican Brotherhood was a furtive presence, its name barely whispered by the Irish and unknown to the rest of the world.

They, in turn, told me that New York seethed with unrest, hatred of the war, oblique motives, disgust at Republican radicals, loathing of that ape Lincoln, and now, vicious attacks upon "copperheads."

War, I had learned, spawns war of other sorts: officer against officer, vanity against vanity, faction against faction, rumormongers against those they despise, clan against clan, party against party, newspaper against newspaper. And much of the nation against the Irish who filled the army's ranks. Behind every battle at the front was a fury of maneuvering, ambition, bitterness, gossip, and accusation.

In our chambers, later, Libby nestled her head upon my shoulder and clutched me while I ran a hand through her undone hair. She was eager for the sweet embrace, but I resisted, though I yearned for her even as she yearned for me. But war did that to me. I had been deadened to her touch. After a little, she simply pressed herself close, and clung to me, even as I held her tight.

"I am here beside you, wherever you go, whatever you do," she whispered, and I felt oddly ashamed, for no reason at all.

"I'll be fine. I'm thinking about the speech I'll make," I said.

She didn't reply, and I knew I'd hurt her. Other things preoccupied Thomas Francis Meagher: war, recruitment, Lincoln's blundering generals, the Fenians, the Irish troubles.

"You are my everlasting light, my love, the brightest star in all the heavens," I whispered, hoping my affirmations would be a recompense.

She sighed, released me, and soon I felt her body release its hold on wakefulness.

I drew a fine crowd at the Seventh Regiment Armory, but it was not the sort I was used to. These were hard-eyed men and women who wanted to find out about the war, were skeptical of it, doubtful of me, Meagher of the Sword. I could feel it from the moment I addressed this sweaty and odorous throng, jammed into the cavernous dark hall.

I described our glories. The Irish Brigade had fought hard, stung the Rebs, and every man in that crowd could be proud of the green silk banners that had pierced into the heart of enemy lines.

"Sure, and it's us doing the fighting!" The shout rose from a man in the sweltering crowd. "Us and not the ones that started this!"

"The Irish Brigade's seen no more war than General French's men," I replied. "We've all fought, and hard. There's been no distinction."

But the man wouldn't accept that. "It's not so; the Sixty-ninth has been shot to bits."

"Boys, boys, if you knew the glory, the honor, attached to our green flags . . ."

"It's the Republicans' war, not ours," yelled another.

"Talk to Dan Sickles, as Irish as ourselves. He's recruiting for his brigade, and see if it's a Republican war! Talk to the Democrat General Hancock! Talk to Little Mac, and see if it's a Republican war! It's a war to save the Union, and every man here owes it to the Union to defend it."

But it was of little avail. All my talk, all that Lieutenant Emmet added in support, brought fewer than three hundred recruits. All my efforts had failed to restore the brigade to fighting strength.

Emmet continued on to Long Island to recover from war wounds—and there he died. One hour with us, and then the war claimed him. I rejoined my veterans at Camp Corcoran, awaiting what might come and filled with foreboding.

22

Colonel Gleeson of the New York 63rd reported to me that his regiment was back to full strength. His Fenian officers had little trouble recruiting the Cadres who dreamed of liberating our homeland.

"We've run over fifty percent casualties in my Sixty-ninth," I said. "More war is coming. What Irish soldiers will be left to free Ireland?"

"None if Pope continues to command," he said.

Brigadier General John Pope. A cavalry man elevated by Lincoln to replace Little Mac, had stumbled into disaster at the second Bull Run. Little Mac failed to press the war, but he didn't invite catastrophe.

"Colonel, I've learned something in this Yankee army. It's the sergeants who make an army out of a rabble; the tough sergeants, with big fists and big mouths, and the will to use them, who teach the lads how to bayonet and shoot and lie low and stay dry, and keep their canteens full of clean water, and follow orders. It's the sergeants you'll want to train the Fenian army, not officers."

"We'll have sergeants when the time comes," Gleeson said. "Stephens, in the old country, is making sergeants out of peasants."

"That's my point. The peasants won't make good sergeants. Have a nip," I said, nodding toward my cask.

"I've taken the temperance oath, sir. And I've duties to perform. The recruits know too little of war."

He did not bother to hide his disdain of me. He saluted casually and left my tent, letting in blinding sun as he pulled the flap aside. I poured a nip into a tin cup, and a splash of water, and sipped, angry with the man.

I had a war to prosecute. One war at a time. I had requested that all the Irish units in the army be put under my command, but the adjutant general turned me down flat. I knew why. The war department wanted a Union army, not a patchwork of allegiances.

We idled in Camp Corcoran, mended our bodies, received issues of warm clothing, fed well, and marched. Then one day word came down: Little Mac was back, Pope was out. The lads cheered and so did I.

Then, that early fall of 1862, the war was taken out of Union hands, so to speak, because Robert E. Lee was on the move, pushing north and west into Maryland. I knew that the respite was over, and there would soon be more Irish blood sinking into the soil of America. General Sumner soon received his marching orders, and we headed north, trailing Lee's army, Richardson's division in the van, followed by French and Sedgwick. As usual, my Irish were out front, closest to the enemy and in the greatest danger. We trailed Lee's vast army toward Harper's Ferry, then across the Potomac and into Maryland, through rich fields ripe with crops, a lush harvest in a warm and dry fall, the sort of countryside armies relish for the foraging.

Little Mac had been listening to Lincoln, and was now pursuing Lee, not trying to take Richmond. Lee was traveling farther from his base in Virginia, but had a lush farm country to draw from, and the hope that many a secessionist Marylander would join his army as it approached. He had sent out flyers in advance, announcing his presence, inviting recruits.

On the 14th of September there was some hard fighting, but we were not a part of it. The Rebs were plugging several gaps in the hills, and buying time for Lee to consolidate his stretched out army, which was gathering near Sharpsburg. My men advanced easily with Sumner's corps, until we found ourselves camping along the east bank of the Antietam River, outside of Sharpsburg.

There would be a fight the next day; across from us was General D. H. Hill's corps, the center of the Reb line. Off to the south, on our left, was Longstreet and A. P. Hill; to the north were Hood, Early, and Stonewall Jackson. We thought they were our match in men; little did we realize our forces were about twice theirs. The Rebs as usual had the good ground, Sharpsburg Ridge, rising formidably west of the river.

The morning bloomed sweetly, a fine haze filtering the sun, the scents of field and harvest perfuming the air, along with the dust raised by silent armies marching in great columns. We ate sidepork and biscuits, looked to our equipment, and studied the shrouded fields beyond the river, where the graybacks were well dug in and waiting. Behind us, McClellan set up his headquarters, along with reserve artillery, and quietly positioned his formidable forces, Mansfield and Hooker to the north, Burnside to the south, and Sumner in the center.

A great but restless silence followed until the skies blued and the sun glowed just below the eastern horizon. And then the boom of artillery heralded the day's bloody events. Their brilliant boy artillerist, "Gallant Pelham," opened from a hill to the north of us, and then the angry rumble of our own batteries matched theirs.

There was a battle raging, but it thundered over distant fields while we sat and sunned. My veteran lads were alert, taut, ready. Then word came down from Sumner: head across the Antietam and up the slope ahead. Sedgwick and French's divisions first, and ours, led by Israel Richardson, following.

As Sedgwick's men marched, they were hit with a terrible fusillade from a dark woods nearby, volley upon volley, and could scarcely return the fire. In moments, hundreds of the blue-clads were lying on the ground, leaking blood into the Maryland soil, and General Sedgwick saw his force demolished. French's division, meanwhile, ran against a thick Reb line hunkered down in a sunken road making a natural fortress that protected them from our sting. Reb riflemen scythed French's boys, and repeated charges brought his division no closer to that awful trench that curved into a natural rampart.

We marched toward this cauldron, the Irish Brigade once again facing a murderous fire. And before us was that sunken road, the Rebs barely visible behind the safety of its slope, and it became our awful task to take that natural bastion.

I rode hard, encouraging the boys. They let loose an Irish howl and charged, quicktime, muzzles lowered, bayonets ready, refusing to stop, ever onward, only to be thrown back by awful volleys that spread a sheen of red blood across the grasses, and left my Irish sprawled on the ground, fighting for life, or lost to the living.

We took that sunken road, lost it, took it again, and finally drove those graybacks away. Canister shot killed General Richardson, my friend and my superior, and we found ourselves under the command of General Hancock who told us to hold.

We held, digging in whilst a thousand of the Rebel dead lay at our feet. We slipped and slid on blood.

The losses to the four regiments of the Irish Brigade in those few minutes came to 540.

Somehow I was thrown from my horse in the heat of it. My gelding was shot out from under me, and I pitched free as it stumbled and collapsed. That turned out to be more of a blow than I had bargained for. Later I learned there were those who thought I was drunk; that General Meagher had to fortify himself with a bottle before going into battle, and fell off his mount. Not even the dead animal lying there in the grim red fields stopped the talk. I did not even know such things were being said about me until I overheard it just before a staff meeting in Hancock's headquarters.

23

Never had the burial details faced such a task. The Union and Reb dead filled the sunken road knee deep, heaped atop one another. My men were there, sprawled insensately, often with Rebs half covering them. I could not bear the sight of them, the innocence in their faces, what was left of their faces, the ten thousand dreams and hopes that had vanished in a day's battle.

I watched the burial men disentangle the bodies, looking for the medallion that would identify the departed, often finding no sign. Many a boy in blue was unknown; even fewer of the Rebs could be identified. Many was the body still alive, and these were lifted into ambulances and taken to the hospital, an area near a haystack set aside for the busy surgeons, where they would die by degrees.

I did not want to see the details at their work. Sometimes they paused, weary, stared at me, the author of this carnage, and returned to their grisly task. Sometimes they turned over the body of an officer, and I stared into the pale face of a lieutenant or captain, Burke, O'Hara, Monaghan, Rourke, Byrne—Byrne, pale law clerk in New York, half his face shot away, his widow soon keening. And it would be up to me to write her the news.

Sometimes the crew picked up pieces of a man, their gloves brown with caked blood. All were thrown into carts and wagons after ammunition and personal effects had been salvaged.

How do you bury several thousand men? That's what Antietam came to: over ten thousand Reb casualties, and over twelve thousand Union. There was a place called the Cornfield, north of us, that started as thirty acres of tall corn and ended up as thirty acres of bodies.

Where are the shovels, the boxes for such a task? Where, in that exhausted army, are enough able men to form the hundreds of burial details compelled to dig pits and drag corpses into them? Where are the lieutenants to write down names, gather medallions, collect valuables, identify enemy units, keep records? Where are the officers who will notify the widows, children, parents, and sweethearts?

A sergeant came to me: "These burial details, sir. They've stomached all they can."

"There are living men in there, sergeant."

"Aye, and these man have just fought a battle, sir. That one there, he's puked himself empty, but he carries on because there's no relief."

I sought out Captain Conyngham. "We need to rotate the burial details, captain."

"No men left to rotate."

"Find some."

The captain stared at me, nodded, and headed into the blackness.

The hospital area was worse. The wounded lay in bloody rows, most insensate, some staring mutely, some without eyes, some gasping, some screaming, some weeping, some breathing quietly, one or two laughing wildly, a dozen mad and raving. Their pain smacked anyone who entered those confines. There were tables soaked in blood, red saws, white and crimson bandages. The lucky got morphine. The unlucky howled and groaned and sobbed. In a week, most of those thousands lying there would be dead of mortification.

There was another sort of thunder now, this from Washington, and it crashed over Little Mac and washed him away. He had won; Lee's army had lost ten thousand of its forty; ours was double the size of theirs, and yet General McClellan had not finished the job, ended the war, chased and caught Lee as he was hemmed by the Potomac. George McClellan had not thrown in his reserves, not hunted Lee down and trapped him. And the politicians and the Republican press were railing against Democrat generals soft on the South. Lincoln's orders were to destroy Lee's army, and our commander had hesitated when the bright chance was there.

I understood McClellan's hesitation. His army was not fit to press the fight. He was heartsick and wanted to give his men a rest. He believed Lee had a large force even though his own intelligence efforts suggested otherwise. I knew that Lee didn't have the hundred thousand that Little Mac imagined. So did all our officers.

I wrote Libby that we had been woefully cut up, and urged her to take heart. The brigade had won great honor, holding the center, capturing the sunken road, attacking over and over, never faltering, stinging the Rebs. We could be proud; the green silk flags never had such luster. We were the fighting Irish, and we actually *fought*, unlike half those abolitionist outfits. But what price honor? And where would I get recruits now? Signing on with the Irish Brigade amounted to a death warrant. We were being used harder than any other force in the army, used and wasted.

I brooded the next days, while the army licked its wounds and let the Rebs filter away, cross the Potomac and lick their wounds in the safety of Virginia. Maybe Little Mac was right: bury the dead and fight some other day. I did not know how I could lead my grieving and afflicted brigade into battle once again. But we had no choice in the matter.

In Washington they called Antietam a victory, and Lincoln used it as the platform for his Emancipation Proclamation, a selective freeing of slaves in the rebel states but not in the border states still attached to the Union.

We absorbed that bleakly at first, but then, somehow, it lifted the spirits in my ranks; the war took on purpose and meaning we had scarcely fathomed at first. We would free all oppressed mortals, and by God, they would be Americans like the rest of us, with all the rights the republic had given us. For those of us in the ranks, it became a new banner; for those in New York, it was another act of radical Republican madness.

Finally, after pulling ourselves together, we marched to Harper's Ferry to recuperate and stand guard. We were now a part of Hancock's division, he a regular army man, a Democrat, and a friend of the Irish. And there Lincoln came to us, and again I was struck by the tall and sad man who walked among us, tears rising in his eyes, his heart in every handshake.

There in the mountains outside of the bombed-out town we made a comfortable camp and gathered strength. The good news was that I received a new regiment, the 116th Pennsylvania, led by Colonel Dennis Heenan, and I now had 1,700 in the brigade. Out of it I got a new orderly, an Irish-born private named McCarter who was literate and could swiftly write my messages. As terrible as the toll had been upon my officers, I still had good men: Lyons and Conyngham and Kelly, and so many more. They were restoring the Irish Brigade to its proper strength and health and spirit.

Those were good days, and I entertained Libby at long last. There would be horse races, Irish airs, dinners with officers, and the great healing of the Mass. I met her as she stepped out of the railroad carriage, all aglow with her energies bursting within. She smiled, and yet her gaze searched me, even before we embraced.

"Ah, God, Libby . . ."

"General!"

"You're the only thing here not afflicted by war."

"That's why I'm here, Tom. We have each other for a few hours. Let's steal whatever happiness we can."

I had commandeered a room for her in Harper's Ferry, but I was on duty and our precious moments together spun out in our camp those early autumnal days, pleasant and warm for the most part, yet with the sadness of fall in the air, and the coming of winter on our minds. Each evening I sent her back to her room, while I stayed in command.

We sipped whiskey in my tent, and she enjoyed the acrid smell of canvas and the muted amber light that filtered through the cloth, and my spartan belongings, for I had long since jettisoned most of what I first hauled about, and now was down to a trunk and a cot, an India rubber ground cover, some books and maps, and a few brown woolen blankets. And my cask, for I always offered comfort to my staff and visiting general officers, and to myself.

"Tell me of the war," she said, sitting on my cot. "The things I need to take back to my family. The things not in the papers."

I told her a little of the war, mostly shielding her from the brutality of it. But I told her of my pride to be flying the Stars and Stripes, and in my adopted land, and also how my lads felt now, especially after the Emancipation Proclamation.

"Really? We all think it's awful," she said. "I don't know of anyone who likes it."

I shook my head. "It's changed the war. It is what God would want for us; his design for us."

She smiled wryly. "Then, Tom Meagher, I shall be for it!"

No sooner did I see her off to New York than we were embroiled in a smart little battle. There were some Rebs in

Charlestown, a few miles away, and the Irish had the honor of inviting them to leave. They were perched at our flank and could cause trouble.

We marched toward Charlestown, singing the abolitionist song "John Brown's Body," and were surprised at ourselves for singing it. The lads had responded to Mister Lincoln's proclamation, which gave the war a new tone. It was as if we all had been waiting for that freeing of the slaves, and now that this had come to pass, we would fight and win.

Charlestown was defended by Rebs fighting from every upstairs window and every darkened door, and as my skirmishers approached, they met a hot hail of lead and retreated. I got my staff together and made some plans and parceled out the things we needed to do. We decided to leave the 116th behind to guard the artillery, which would fire canister ahead of us, and then charge, double quick.

And so we proceeded, a great Irish huzzah, and ere long the Rebs fled, a running mass of them retreating, and we took the town with scarcely a shot fired. But the Reb town humped its back against us, and from every window rocks and curses rained down upon my men. We were the invaders. Women spat, boys snarled, dogs snapped. My ears burned with the vile words. It reminded me of the royal constables in Ireland, or the redcoats marching through Tipperary.

And yet, quietly gathered in knots on the street corners were the silent blacks, gaunt and solemn, their children clinging close. My men saw them too, and smiled. The slaves did not know what to make of us, but some day they would.

I rode in at the head of my command, the 69th New York. And from then on, we would lead Hancock's division south, ever south, into the bowels of the Confederacy.

24

Burnside. The word came down that General McClellan was being cashiered, and Ambrose Burnside would replace him. My staff mourned. Several young officers tendered their resignations; they would fight under Little Mac, but not under this big, rough gent from Indiana who, unlike anyone else, wore his brushy whiskers down either side of his face, cropped about at the level of the earlobe. The new style was called burnsides, and some were calling them sideburns.

Our new commander was an experienced major general, elevated after some successes along the Atlantic coast of the Confederacy. My lieutenants and captains all saw disaster looming in Lincoln's appointment, but I would not accept their resignations: "We've a war to win, for a just and good cause, and we'll show the Yanks that the Irish are here for the good of the republic," I said.

Reluctantly, my staff stayed on. But all my men had reservations about this new commander, and didn't hesitate to voice them.

We mustered our regiments one overcast day, and told them of the change in command, spoke warmly of Little Mac, said he was going on to other crucial commands, and asked our men to give a last hurrah to McClellan, and they did. It warmed my heart.

We were camped now, late in the fall, near of the Reb-held town of Fredericksburg just across the Rappahannock, and all of us thought the season's campaigns were over. We would build our winter huts, shiver through a rainy and cold Virginia winter, envy those Rebs in comfortable homes across the river, and campaign in the spring. My brigade was up to strength, with Irish regiments from Massachusetts and Pennsylvania swelling our ranks. We were well supplied, warm-clad, at ease, and ready to win the war come spring.

I sent our battle-ruined emerald colors up to New York to be retired. There would be banquets and toasts to the brigade. Let them see our green silks, with the harps, with the holes where minié balls pierced our colors. Let them see that in New York and reverence the colors of the Irish Brigade, and send us new colors for the spring.

Rank has its privileges. I enjoyed a good watertight tent with a plank floor, some field chairs, thick blankets, and a warm cot. There I entertained staff and general officers from the Army of the Potomac, bonding myself to other officers and colleagues. The Monongahela casks emptied quickly, and I was swift to replace them and keep plenty of tin cups and some branch water on hand. Spirits erased the torment of war, and I indulged myself amid the bonhomie. I especially enjoyed the officers in Sumner's corps, and many was the eve when we gathered in my tent.

On one of those occasions I was the cause of a minor scandal. It happened in this wise: I stepped into the dark to relieve myself, and my aide, Private McCarter, seeing that I was about to tumble into the campfire before my tent, threw his rifle across my path, caught my fall with the flat side of his bayonet, thereby deflecting me from the flame. But his rifle fell into the fire, discharged, and caused a commotion.

I picked myself up, dusted myself off, and quieted everyone down. Later, I commended my orderly, and got him a new musket out of stores. Word has it that I was in my cups, which is of course an exaggeration.

I sip, and so do all of the officers save for the temperance men. I imagine most of the general staff does, and some, such as General Grant out west, are well known for it. In fact, I trust a man who takes a little whiskey more than I do one who never touches it. But the malicious gossip did no good for my standing as an officer, and I worried about it. These Yankees do not understand the Irish.

It was to Hancock that I turned more and more. A fine man, deep-dyed Democrat, my immediate superior, veteran regular army officer, distinguished family, and a friend of all sons of Erin.

He was not above sipping with me, by the light of a bull's-eye lantern in the quiet of an evening, whilst the rain pattered on his command tent.

"What will Burnside do?" I asked.

"I don't know. There's something unfathomable about the man. But I hold him in highest esteem."

"He did well recently."

Hancock nodded. "In a coastal campaign. He's commanding the largest army in North America right now, and he's up against the best general in the world just now, Robert E. Lee, a great commander who has half our men and matériel but matches us."

"Will he do as well as Little Mac?"

Winfield Scott Hancock sighed, shook his head, and remained discreet.

That troubled me. The volunteers were skeptical, but so were the regular army men.

Hancock stared. "I have the best division in the army," he said. "Veteran troops, well trained, fierce, wise under fire, courageous. Many are Irish. What is it you Irish have within you that makes a fighting man?"

"Bitterness," I said, and then repealed it. "I should say, general, hardship and desperation and a clannishness. We hold together when we're not fighting each other. The rowdies in the villages have regular brawls."

He smiled. "All that rowdiness I see in other races. There's something else about the Irish, and I don't know what."

"Poetry, sir. When the Irish make a song or a ballad, it lives in our hearts and takes on force."

"Poetry?" General Hancock was startled.

"Yes, sir, we turn all life into poetry. We follow the green, and it's the poetry of the green we see, not the color. Green is our poem, sir."

"General Meagher, I am lost."

"Ballads, general. We make a ballad for every brave and valorous man. We sing a poem to every hero. There's not a lad born to Ireland but doesn't want a song sung about him. We sing of war and fate, of courage and the blood of Christ."

He shook his head. "Quite beyond me, general. But I know a few things: my men, gathered mostly from New York, Massachusetts and Pennsylvania, are the fiercest and stoutest in the army, and I am proud of you."

"It is our glory to fight and die," I said.

He stared. "There is no glory in dying. Brave you may be, running into the muzzles of ten thousand rifles, but there is no beauty in it. I don't want legends, I want victories. I tell you, general, my object is not to watch my men die in glory, but to win. Let the Rebs die for their treason, not you or your great Irish Brigade."

I felt a great humility flood me. My commanding general was paying homage to the Irish.

"That, general, is the song we crave, the ballad that fills us up."

I don't think Winfield Hancock fathomed any of that. "What will Burnside do?" I asked again.

"One thing he won't do is overestimate the enemy. That was always McClellan's weakness. He doubled Lee's army in his mind, and nothing could shake that from him. Lincoln's been looking for a commander who sees the other side clearly, and Burnside answers."

"Lee's not far away."

"Burnside knows it, and knows what the president wants." Hancock sipped, coughed, and sipped again. "The president wants Lee. Now."

"Now?"

"Burnside's asking questions. And the questions all add up to a campaign."

"What's Lee doing?"

"Fortifying. If we're going to do this, it should be *now*; a day or two at the most. After that, we're up against an entirely fortified ridge."

"The flanks, what about them?"

"Burnside's working on that. It looks like we can turn a flank from the south. But Lee is not a man to leave himself open, and neither are Stuart or Jackson."

"Is Lee divided?"

"We believe he's recalled every unit he has, mostly back from Richmond. All the more reason to fight now, not later."

"Why here, on the worst possible ground? Why in December?"

"You'd have to get into Burnside's skull to answer that. I think he simply wants to please his president, and he's got the army to do it."

I absorbed all that bleakly. Of course, this was not official, not anything but the private speculations of general officers. But I knew, suddenly, that slow, methodical Burnside would begin a slow, methodical attack against lightning-quick Lee, and the Irish Brigade would be in the thick of it.

"General, the men are cutting Christmas boughs to decorate their huts, and sending Christmas letters back to their sweethearts."

"So are the Rebs, General."

"The Brigade's ready; it's always ready, General. It's ready now, as winter lowers; it's ready to fight on Christmas Day if it must. We've bled for the republic, and we'll bleed again. But oh, we are speaking of hard things."

Hancock sipped. "Maybe if we smash Lee's army this December, there'll be peace ushered in upon the turn of eighteen sixty-three. I would wager that General Burnside is thinking along those lines. What better Christmas gift to a war-weary nation?"

25

Hancock summoned his general officers to his command at eleven the night of December 12. I limped through thick and icy fog, aware that events of great portent were unfolding. I had an ulcerated knee, an abscess that was causing me great pain, and our regimental surgeon, Lawrence Reynolds, had ordered me to take a twenty-one-day leave to let it heal. I would not hear of it.

I hurried, wanting the heat of Hancock's tent to warm me. I entered to a blast of foetid air and amber lamplight, and discovered all of his generals and commanders in attendance, crowded around a map lying on a crate. There I learned that the entire Army of the Potomac would throw itself at Lee's Army of Northern Virginia in the morning. General Franklin's Grand Division would tackle Stonewall Jackson's Second Corps to the South; Sumner's Grand Division, including ourselves, would attack Longstreet's corps entrenched directly ahead on the heights just behind Fredericksburg.

This was no surprise. For two days the Rebs had harassed our engineers as they built pontoon bridges across the Rappahannock, sometimes employing their infantry, sometimes with artillery. But the job had been done, and then the Union army had filed into Fredericksburg, occupying the abandoned city and looting it, no matter that officers forbade the looting.

There was something brittle in Hancock's voice, the sound of a soldier who disagreed violently with his superiors but was doing his duty and the best he could.

"I sent Colonel Nugent of the New York Sixty-ninth out to reconnoiter last night," Hancock said. "He was able to get close under cover of darkness. He reports that those heights are well fortified. At their base is a sunken road, and in front of it a stone wall, with infantry behind it. There are rifle pits above, several layers of them, and artillery on top. They command open fields, without cover save for one low embankment. Their artillery will reach Fredericksburg and any woods along the river. They can put canister down any east-west street in the city."

"Surely Burnside knows this!" I exclaimed.

"He knows it. He believes Lee's army is divided; the major part in Richmond. He believes their lightly manned works can be stormed."

I had, for days, been studying that slope beyond Fredericksburg with my glass. For two weeks the Rebs had been digging in, throwing up earthworks, fortifying their batteries on top, turning the ridge called Marye's Heights into an impenetrable wall.

"What does he believe will happen?" asked General French.

"Franklin will turn their left flank. We will storm the heights and drive them toward Franklin."

"After two weeks of fortifying the whole ridge?" French's skepticism laced his voice.

Colonel Zook asked the prickly question: "Why are we fighting on Lee's ground? Why not pick our own?"

Hancock was impatient. "Those are our orders, and you will all carry them out to the utmost of your abilities. At dawn, we will deploy for battle as soon as the fog lifts. If there is any."

"Who goes when?" I asked.

"I was coming to that." Hancock's voice was rough. "The honor will fall to General French; General Kimball, General Andrews, and General Palmer; followed by Colonel Zook, General Meagher and General Caldwell. Howard will be behind us, and Hooker behind him."

There it was.

"Who do we face? Is it known?" asked French.

"Longstreet commanding. Kershaw on the ridge. Cooke below him. General Cobb, we believe. McLaws on his right. Jackson's farther south. Anderson on the north."

"What infantry behind the stone wall?"

"We believe the Eighteenth Georgia, the Twenty-fourth Georgia, probably the Phillips Legion, and the Twenty-fourth North Carolina. All veteran men."

"Some Irish," I said. "The Reb Irish."

"On the heights, Porter Alexander's artillery," Hancock said. "None better."

"We will have artillery?" Zook asked.

"All we can get. There will be another engagement to the south, you know. Against General Jackson."

"And their artillery commands our approach?"

Hancock nodded.

I felt a dread steal through me. I remembered how my staff officers had tried to resign en masse when they heard Burnside would command the Army of the Potomac.

We went over the plans for another hour, and then General Hancock grasped the hand of each of us, shook it heartily, and wished us every success. He was saying good-bye. Some of us would not live through the next day.

"General Meagher," he said. "I'm counting on the green."

I stepped into a cold black fog, well after midnight. Icy mist hung in the air. I could not see ten paces. I had things to do. The men would be awakened quietly at three. Most were awake even now; there was no concealing the muffled rumble of wagons, the creak of harness, the thud and splash that were all that my veterans needed to know to piece together what would come.

Let them sleep.

I stopped at the tent of our chaplain, Father Corby, and awakened him.

"Who is it?" he asked, throwing open the flap.

"Meagher. Tomorrow is it," I said. "The lads will want a mass and confession."

The father nodded. "I will ask a blessing upon our lads."

I had my aide, Conyngham, awaken my staff. Not that they needed awakening. Soon they collected in my tent, where a candle-lantern lit their unshaven faces. I saw a great weariness among them: Heenan, Kelly, Nugent, a dozen more.

"We're attacking in the morning, and Sumner's corps will attack those heights," I said.

"Those heights? Which they've been fortifying for two or three weeks?" Kelly asked.

"We will do the best that is in us, and for the best of causes. I want the regiments formed up by six, because I will address each one. This will be our day to be proud."

"But the colors . . ." Heenan said.

Our colors had been retired; they had been holed to ribbons.

"Yes, the colors! You know what it means to the men of Ireland, following the green, seeing the harps, the silks?" said Congdon.

"It's a bad omen for sure," Kelly said.

It troubled me. If my men didn't see the green shining in

the light, didn't see it ride the tide toward the Rebs, there would be no glory.

They were looking at me, as if I could conjure up green battalion and regimental colors on the spot. Well, maybe I could. I nodded to them and bade them wait, and stepped into the blackness. A few paces away was a boxwood hedge, its evergreen leaves intact, even in December. I broke off a few twigs, and found my way through the inky night to my staff. Within the tent, I lifted my kepi from my head, and tucked the sprig of boxwood under the band, which shone green and shiny in the lantern light.

No man said a word. Every one of them would return to their regiments, and before the brigade marched into battle, there would be green decorating every forage cap: the green battalion would stay green.

"Those of you who are mounted: General Hancock does not recommend that you ride horse tomorrow," I said.

They nodded.

I shook hands with each. Within hours, their ranks would be thinned, or maybe my own life would end. I would be out in the midst, limping across that field of fire, no matter the painful boil on my knee.

They retreated into the fog, which lay so thick a lantern scarcely cast light twenty feet. The grim gray dawn rose imperceptibly, and with it the muffled sounds of war. The Rebs knew something was afoot; it was not possible to conceal what was happening along the river, and now Reb skirmishers were firing randomly into the town, toward the slight, sharp rattle of movement.

Thunderous cannonades erupted to the south, where General Franklin had the task of putting Burnside's orders into effect against no less a man than Thomas Jackson, the best field commander in the Reb army. But for us, the time had not yet arrived.

The regiments stirred early, quietly awakened by noncoms.

The men flocked to Father Corby's outdoor chapel and listened solemnly as the priest sang the Latin and absolved them all of their sins. I stood at the rear, attending even as I awaited orders from Hancock. But then our priest's hasty mass concluded and I ordered the regiments to form up in the soft fog.

To each of them I offered encouragement. "This may be the final blow against the traitors," I said. "The blow that smashes Lee's army, the blow that restores this good republic, the blow that frees black men so they may live a life of liberty and equality. We're the Irish, and we know what oppression is. And now, as we go into battle, we will carry in our hearts the pride and glory of our race, the bonds we have to one another, the love we share, the fierce courage we possess, the courage that will win through, until the Rebs break and run toward Richmond."

And so I addressed them, regiment by regiment, even as the sounds of war heightened about us. Every last man wore a sprig of boxwood in his cap.

Some ate hardtack and bacon or drank coffee. Others prayed. A few wrote letters, entrusting them to friends. Some stared mutely, lost in reverie. Some fingered their beads. Some buried their heads in their arms. One hummed an Irish air but no one joined him. Most didn't want to eat. Not a man of them was unaware of the long odds they faced that foggy morning. And then the fog began to burn away.

26

The column has reeled
  but it is not defeated.
In front of the guns,
  they reform and attack.
Six times they have done it,
  and six times retreated,
Twelve hundred they came,
  and two hundred go back.
Two hundred go back now
  with chivalrous story.
The wild day is closed
  in the night's solemn shroud.
A thousand lie dead, but
  their death was a glory.
That calls not for tears
  —the green badges are proud!
—NINETEENTH-CENTURY POEM ATTRIBUTED TO JOHN BOYLE O'REILLY

       The band blared *Garryowen* and then Reb canister chased them into Fredericksburg. We huddled on the north and south streets; case shot raked all the east and west ones.

French's men had charged boldly, wave after wave of blue, only to topple like tenpins. None even got close to that deadly stone wall. Kimball's brigade fell a hundred seventy-five yards short; Palmer's charged and toppled. Andrews's brigade fell, butchered by Reb cannon and those muskets at the wall.

All across that killing field, downed men writhed or cried piteously in the blinding noon light. There was only one slight refuge, a low ditch where a man might lie safe behind the embankment from the hail of lead a foot or two above. And there the injured stumbled and fell. We could not help them.

French's men, whipped around by their officers, rallied and tried again, and met with the same devastating fire, scything the ranks, minutes after the late-morning assault had begun. One by one French's regiments marched and died, and now the wounded crawled and walked past us, in the city, streaking the cobbles with their blood.

It was Hancock's turn. Colonel Samuel Kosciusczko Zook's column attacked and got no farther than the others, and soon was reduced to a shadow of itself. Canister from Marye's Heights sometimes dropped a dozen men at a crack, hurling their bodies in all directions. General Caldwell's brigade attacked, got farther, then retreated, leaving the dead and dying all over that sere ploughed farmland. Brave men, lion hearts, stopped by canister and muskets.

A colonel of my acquaintance, Nelson Miles, of General Caldwell's staff, had been watching through a field glass.

"The Rebs are firing in volleys," he said. "Perfectly coordinated. One line loading, one line firing. That stone wall's got a sunken ditch behind it, and nothing's killing those bastards."

"More artillery, lower?"

"It's not just the wall. They're entrenched."

"A running bayonet assault?"

He nodded. "Only chance."

"We will run, then," I said. "How close has anyone gotten?"

"Not a hundred yards."

Miles shook his head. Zook's men were stumbling past, some sobbing, others mute, a few dying, most of them bloodied and defeated and terrified. I slipped aside and wetted my parched throat from a flask. The spirits clarified my head.

Then Hancock's order arrived: The Irish Brigade will attack at once, attempt to rescue those in the field, hearten them, and sweep them forward against that stone wall.

I nodded at Hancock's lieutenant and turned to my staff.

"Now, and God be with you," I said. "For the brigade, for Ireland, for the republic, for oppressed men, for all that is sacred. Quick time, bayonets, running will save us, wait upon the bugle. Roll the other boys with us, French's and Caldwell's boys out there. Be ready in five minutes. For the green, show them what we're made of, my good men, my comrades in arms."

I saw fear in their white faces.

"This may be my last speech to you, but I will be with you when the battle is fiercest, and if I fall, I can say that I did my duty and fell for the most glorious of causes."

I would be with them, but on foot. An officer on horse wouldn't last thirty seconds. I watched them prepare for war, nearly in tears. My knee was worse and I could barely walk, but I could be there with them, somehow, running as they ran. The pain was lacerating me so much I couldn't ignore it, and I fortified myself as best I could, in my last private moments, at my temporary command in an enclosed porch. I slipped the flask in my warbag, and limped into the racketing world.

There was no time. Zook's and French's and Caldwell's survivors were trapped and being picked off by sharpshooters on Marye's Heights.

The canister never stopped raking Fredericksburg, making it difficult even to form into a column. We were dying even before we formed up. Canister exploded in the midst of the New York 88th, killing several. Another shot wounded Colonel Heenan, of the Pennsylvania 118th, and killed his orderlies. Major St. Clair Mulholland took over. The man had been a police officer in Ireland. And even as our sergeants lined up our lads, screams pierced the air. And then, at my nod, the bugler sounded.

"Quicktime, quicktime, never slow," I cried, as the great wall of blue, topped with sprigs of boxwood, sprang forward into that murderous bleak ground.

The New York 88th and New York 63rd attacked, their howls reaching the ears of Johnny Reb.

I was with my own New York 69th Volunteers, my regiment, commanded by Colonel Nugent. Now the band struck up *Garryowen* and the rowdy lyrics set us howling:

> *Our hearts so stout have got no fame*
> *For soon 'tis known from whence we came*
> *Where'er we go they fear the name*
> *Of Garryowen in glory.*

Clouds of noxious fumes choked us as we ran; the rattle and thunder of war hammered our ears. We gasped as foul air seared our throats. We half-heard the screams, saw our brothers and kin topple. We crossed that ditch and embankment, crossed a ploughed field, and away we went. We felt our rage explode in us.

We felt lead whisper past our ears, pierce our clothes. We

saw the hot vapor of our breath in the December chill. We sobbed and ran and saw the green of our numbers stumble. We fell back, regrouped, attacked again until we were closer than any others had come to that black bleak wall of stone, with a thousand muskets belching death at us.

I had Nugent send two companies to the right flank to skirmish, and he put them in charge of Captain Donovan, a veteran who wore a black eyepatch. We ran into the jaws of death; riflemen up on Marye's Heights picked us off, men died beside me, in front, behind. We caught up with Zook's and Kimball's trapped men, huddled behind the slight rise that offered cover, rallied them, and attacked, only to fall.

We formed again, and attacked again, nothing daunted, while my heart burst with pride and awe at their gallantry, rising again and again to assault the breastworks of the traitors. Never had I seen such courage, such ferocity, such glory. They trotted ahead, both laughing and murderous, even as the Reb artillery found its mark and shot great holes in our line. I heard the strange chill murmur of war about me, as my lads clambered over the dead and dying.

I limped along behind the 69th with my command staff, my knee agonizing me, my duty being to rally the lads, see to the opportunities, direct the thrust. And then I felt hot wet blood at my knee and thought I had been wounded, and I stared at my bloodsoaked trousers, and knew suddenly I hadn't been wounded; my ulcerated knee had burst open.

"Wounded, sir! I'll help!"

A corporal shielded me with his body as I lay on that slippery grass.

"No, it's the abscess . . ."

"Wounded. Gin'ral's down, get him back!" he yelled, as a half dozen others, including my staff, crowded over me.

Someone slit my trousers, and I saw gore and pus, but my leg was intact.

"There, you see?" I cried. "It's the boil."

"We'll help you back, gin'ral."

And they did; two blue-coated boys shouldered me and I limped away.

My men raced to a point forty yards from that stone wall before a deadly volley felled them. Even so, they leveled their bayonets, crouched, howled *Erin go bragh!* and attacked. The toll was desolating: O'Neill, Nugent, Kelly, wounded and being helped back. Horgan took command. We were too close to the wall for the Reb artillery to touch us, so they began battering Zook's retreating troops.

At that point I could walk no further; I could barely stand, was a burden to my own staff. My regimental commanders were down, my men adrift. Captain Condon took command of the 63rd, but he found only nine men left. My lads of the 69th under the command of Captain McGee, younger brother of D'Arcy McGee, my comrade in Young Ireland, had dug in and were exchanging shots with those behind that wall. Lieutenant Patrick Callaghan was the other remaining officer, and all three of them were wounded.

Still, the 116th and the 88th struggled forward, firing at that stone wall, the men now under Major Liam Horgan, who took over when Kelly was taken back. Then Mulholland rallied his Pennsylvanians under their blue banner and rushed that wall, howling *Faugh-au-ballagh*, clear the way, and Horgan's 88th responded and joined the assault. I could see little of it because of the smoke, and because pain clouded my vision.

But back behind, Hancock had glimpsed our dying progress through the smoke and our entrapment behind what small islands of cover we could find. He ordered Caldwell's column to our rescue, and the Rebs were astonished to see yet another wave of blue ran toward the muzzles of their guns.

And so my Irish Brigade, stumbling over bodies, came within a dozen or so paces of that stone wall before we died. No Union troops got closer; no troops paid a higher price.

My captains and lieutenants at the front passed word along: get back to safety if possible. We were too few to fight, and they wanted to save the remnant. But they were pinned down until General Howard's 2nd Division came to their rescue by feinting to the left, drawing fire in that direction so my lads could straggle back. I had returned to my horse, got off my bleeding leg, and was able to rally my lads from my mount.

But of my thirteen hundred, less then three hundred reported from the field that terrible December day, and as I watched them muster, I wept. Some of our companies were down to handfuls.

Later, they honored my brigade, calling our assault the most gallant of the war. But they did not honor me. One hot-headed war correspondent, Henry Villard, called me an *arrant coward*. There were other reports that I had recklessly imbibed, or that I had plundered Fredericksburg for whiskey and passed it to my men. But Francis Lawley, of the *London Times*, summed it up: "Never at Fontenoy, Albuera, or Waterloo, was more undaunted courage displayed by the sons of Erin."

It had all taken twenty minutes.

27

Libby's loving gaze found mine. We were abed, safe in the bosom of the Townsend residence, a vast leap from blood and death.

"The war has wounded you," she said.

She was not talking about the abscess on my knee.

Ever since returning to New York on sick leave, I had been taut as a wound-up clock spring. Our poet and surgeon, Lawrence Reynolds, had put me on a three-week furlough, certifying to my commanders that I had a ferunculous abscess of the left knee that was impairing my ability to discharge my duty.

I was home, but not at home; the battles still raged around me; the shot and shell, the racket of rifles, the whisper of minié balls, the screams of the wounded, the sobs of the dying. All these I had brought with me to this peaceful bedroom.

"You have seen too much," she said.

"I have seen stupidity," I replied. "Little Mac would never have slaughtered thirteen thousand men by throwing them against that wall."

I was saying things to her I would never say elsewhere, not even to Peter Townsend. For three days I had been camped in the headquarters offices of the New York 69th, writing letters of condolence to the widows of our dead officers. The widows of enlisted men deserved such letters too, but that was beyond my ability or strength. And with every letter penned to a grieving widow, describing her husband's courage and honor and gallantry in battle, I sank deeper into my own harsh judgment of this army, this war, this folly, and especially the incompetents who formed the officer corps.

Dear Mrs. Horgan,

It is with deepest sorrow that I write to you of the death of your husband, Major Liam Horgan, on the 13th instant, at Fredericksburg. Your husband fought gallantly, bringing great honor to himself and the 88th New York, and he advanced to within twenty-five feet of the Rebel line, as far as any Union man got. He was, at that moment, in command, and led that final effort to storm the enemy's works. I personally grieve his loss and we of the corps honor his courage.

Sincerely,
Thomas F. Meagher, Brigadier, USAV.

Dear Mrs. Young,

I grieve to report to you the loss of Adjutant John Young at Fredericksburg, December 13, 1862. Adjutant Young gallantly led his fellow soldiers of the New York 88th to within fifteen paces of the enemy works, and there his remains were found. He fought valiantly for his country, was fearless and courageous in all that he did. I grieve his loss and we of the corps shall always honor his memory.

Sincerely,
Thomas F. Meagher, Brigadier, USAV

"You mustn't torture yourself, Tom," she said. "You've done everything in your power."

I choked down a sharp word. She was trying to comfort me, but I didn't want comforting. She was trying to love me, and I didn't want loving. I wanted to rattle bars, rebuke the high command, restore the fallen to life, get through one night without ghosts and terrors.

"There is no Irish Brigade left," I said. "I need a new one. I need to recruit. Then I need to spare them from bad generals."

Her hand soothed me, finding the stubble on my face, and smoothing my hair. Libby was a marvel. Somehow, my causes became hers, my beliefs consumed her. She was a better Catholic than I could ever be; a better Union Democrat, a better voice of the Irish. Wherever I turned, there she was, because we had become one, and not because she lacked a mind of her own. I had married a woman of such astonishing soulfulness that our minds and passions had melded together.

I wanted to be grateful; instead, I drew into myself and stared into the soft, lamplit gloom. We had not made love; we did not make love any more.

That afternoon, at the recruiting offices of the New York 69th, I received a visitor, a young and worn woman with two children, one at hand, and one upon her breast. Mary Flannery was her name, widow of private Martin Flannery of the 69th.

"And what am I to do now?" she said. "I a widow, two children and another coming, and I with the consumption?"

I had no consolation for her, and words failed me.

"Sure and you recruited him, you did, with all your fine sweet talk of gallantry and courage and fighting Irish, and now he's dead and me a widow and if you'd just left us alone to live our lives . . ."

"I know it's hard, madam—"

"*Hard,* you call it, losing the man I loved, my sweetheart, the only good thing to come to me in a bitter life, hard you call it."

"I think the regiment will help you, madam. My heart goes out to you."

"Goes out to me, does it? Then why are you here filling the newspapers with talk of glory and honor and all that, when all you're doing is sending poor Irish boys to their doom, and making tears for widows and orphans?"

"I can only assure you that your husband's sacrifice was to a great cause."

"Great cause, was it? What has it to do with us? We've troubles enough without you adding to them. And now you're luring another batch of good Irish boys to their doom, like the serpent, with all your silver-tongued talk of glory! What glory?"

She would not depart, and stayed on, pouring her invective over me and not until her infant began to wail was I freed. When at last I watched the pale woman in widow's weeds stalk into the winter, I buried my face in my arms.

I didn't know what I believed any more. I rolled out of our four-poster, stalked the room in my nightshirt, scratched a lucifer, lit a lamp, and headed for our parlor, where a cut glass decanter always awaited. I poured half a tumbler of rye and added a dash of water, and sipped. No peace stole through me, so I kept on sipping until I had downed the tumbler, and then I returned to our bed. Libby was awake, well aware that I had taken spirits into me.

A squeeze of her hand over mine made communion. I could not sleep, and what was tormenting me was the dark presence of something else. There were hints of dishonor cropping up regularly in the press, even the more responsible journals. Villard's caustic comments were just one. But Villard, a German by birth, was an ambitious and obnoxious man, willing to write sensations to advance his own career. He lacked scruple, would go far, and others would suffer for it.

There were darker innuendos cropping up. When Fredericksburg lay abandoned and naked, its residents in flight, Union troops ransacked and looted the city, plunging crazily into private homes, commandeering everything from jewelry to whiskey. My brigade was not innocent, but we were not alone. The most severe response by our officers failed to stop the pillage, and not even confiscation of the booty slowed the troops down. It was a madness wrought by the certitude of death: when men knew they were going to die facing that gray rock wall the next day, all the ties of civilization loosened.

But the Irish got the blame, and the untrammeled Yankee press even laid it upon me: I had permitted the pillaging, this shameful hunt for spirits and loot. The charge was contemptible, but found circulation across the Republic. And it was more because we were Irish and Catholic and alien to these protestants than to any basis in fact. For, in truth, the pillaging of Fredericksburg was the work of several commands. But we suffered for it, and my honor suffered for it.

How long would it be until the Irish would be accepted and honored in our new home? How much would the Irish suffer, how much blood must we spill, how much courage and gallantry must we show, how much allegiance to the nation must we proclaim, before we might find esteem among other Americans?

What was this dark thing, this whispering about the Irish Brigade? Why did some generals consider us cannon fodder? Thank God Hancock was not among them. He treasured us as his finest and fiercest unit. I felt myself an alien in this Yankee army, shunned or misunderstood.

On the 15th of December, in the ruins of a theater in Fredericksburg scarcely three hundred yards from the killing field, while the last of the battle still thumped around us, the surviving commissioned officers in the Irish Brigade held a banquet to which twenty-two generals came, and there we poured copious spirits, and there, too late, we celebrated the arrival of our new colors, our emerald harps and shamrocks, and there with raised glasses we mourned our dead. As my staff officer, Halpine, put it:

> And the room seemed filled with whispers
> As we looked at the vacant seats,
> And, with choking throats, we pushed aside
> The rich but untasted meats;
> Then in silence we brimmed our glasses,
> As we rose up—just ELEVEN,
> And bowed as we drank to the loved and the dead
> Who had made us THIRTY-SEVEN.

I presided. On the stage, at two tables, were seated my officers and their guests, and these were served by military waiters. At first my colleagues could not fathom such a banquet at such a time and place, but soon they discovered purpose in our celebration.

I offered a toast. "Generals, brothers, officers, and comrades of the Army of the Potomac: fill your glasses to the brim. I have the honor, the pride, and pleasure, to ask you to drink to the health of my esteemed friend on my left, General Alfred Sully. And I want you to understand, gentlemen, that he is not one of your 'political generals,' but a brave and accomplished soldier—who attracted his star from the firmament of glory—by the electricity of his sword!"

They sat silently, and then cheered me, at first for my kindness to General Sully, and then, after a few heartbeats, for the
deeper meaning of my remarks, for they had slowly fastened
upon my phrase, "political generals," and knew at once the purpose of our brigade's Death Feast. And they got a further lesson
in our purpose when the waiters brought the dessert: on a salver
rested a hot Rebel cannonball which had landed nearby only
moments before.

Thusly did our guests fathom that we Irish hold wakes, and
in our drinking and our song, and in our terrible laughter, we
grieve the dead and keep the darkness at bay and say good-bye.

For the general staff of the Army of the Potomac, our banquet two days after the slaughter, while thousands still lay suffering, while surgeons were still sawing off limbs and patching
torn bodies, was yet another mark against me, and the tongues
wagged.

Now, in our chamber, I sipped and remembered. I am not
given to brooding. There were things to do while my knee
healed. I sought out reporters to write up some true accounts of
the gallant Irish Brigade. I started a recruiting effort, but met
with little success. Who would join a brigade known for its
casualties more than for its honor? It was like buying a lot in a
graveyard. My efforts pained my superiors, who, I learned, were
thinking of dissolving the remnants of my brigade and assign-
ing them to other depleted units. There it was again: they
didn't want the Irish fighting together as an Irish command,
bonding to one another as Irish. They didn't much care for our
silken green flags, our harps and shamrocks, which they saw as
an alien presence.

I busied myself, planned a New York banquet to honor our
brigade and our fallen, and arranged as well for a Requiem Mass
at St. Patrick's Cathedral. We would honor the dead.

That proved to be an event to touch the meanest heart. Rossini's *Cujus Animam* wrought tears in my eyes and most others that solemn moment. We prayed for the souls of a thousand dead, and many of their widows and children prayed beside us that sorrowful hour.

We adjourned, my staff and I, those who were in New York, to Delmonico's for a reunion and refreshments, and there we toasted the brigade, the dead, the dream.

They asked me to speak, and so I did. But strange thoughts flew unbidden from my mouth: I acknowledged the gallantry of *both* armies, commended the Irish for all they had given to their new country, and for a cause to which they had not been wedded at first.

And so we drank to that, and to our lost brethren, and to our nation.

Halleck telegraphed me, demanding to know why I was not on duty. I responded with a medical report saying my infected limb was not yet healed and I was not yet fit for duty. I wondered if I would ever be fit. And so the winter passed while both armies healed themselves far to the south. And then, in February, of 1863, I again kissed Libby adieu and reported for duty, knowing I was not the man I had been on December 12th, and knowing that Fredericksburg had been a watershed for the exile, Thomas Francis Meagher.

28

Mr. Lincoln crossed the crowded room to greet me, and that was as much as I could hope for that bleak February of 1863. I was attending one of his usual public receptions at the White House, at some risk to myself because I was late reporting for duty at our winter camp at Falmouth, near Fredericksburg. But my obligation to my brigade was more compelling than the reprimand I faced.

He took my hand. "General Meagher, I'm glad to see you hale and well," he said. "You are reporting back to the brigade?"

"I am pleased to report, sir, that I am hale. Yes, I'm reporting, but I paused here to raise a matter with you."

I knew Lincoln heard a hundred petitions a week, and never more so than at these levees, but I knew also that I must try, here in the public chambers of the White House, among silked and jeweled women, well-coiffed gentlemen, officers resplendent in blue and gold, and waiters politely serving punch.

"Sir, the brigade I am honored to lead has suffered grievously, having fought gallantly in a dozen engagements. We are greatly diminished and in need of a furlough, or light duty whilst we recover. We're a proud and loyal brigade, sir, and every last one of the veterans would recruit others while on furlough. They've earned it ten times over, and winter's the time to do it, Mr. President."

He clasped my shoulder, smiled gamely. "Ah, General, I heartily agree with everything you say about the brigade. But I've learned to defer to the wisdom of my commanding officers. Here's what I can do: I'll pass the request along to General Hooker. Will that help?"

It would help. I thanked the president, who was already working through a dozen other seekers of favors, a man unable to satisfy a hundredth of the petitions that reached his ears. He seemed stooped by war now, and I watched his bent, black-clad back as he handshook his way through the clamorous and designing crowd. He was as humble a man as ever.

General Joseph Hooker had succeeded Burnside as the commander of the Army of the Potomac, which was the only good thing to come out of Fredericksburg. Maybe Hooker would have sense enough not to assault impenetrable Rebel works after a three-week wait while the enemy dug in. I hastened to rejoin the brigade, and was immediately brought before a commission for being late to report. But my explanation sufficed, and my fellow officers suffered me no rebuke.

There were huzzahs when the lads saw me. But the entire brigade mustered only a shadow of its strength, and could not even be called a brigade, nor even a regiment. Sadly, I addressed its thinned ranks, studied men who still wore dressings or reported for duty not yet whole.

"You have given your all," I said, after reviewing them. "I will devote my attention to getting the furlough you richly deserve for your valiant service to this country."

And so I did. I addressed my petition to Secretary of War Stanton, noting we were down to 340 effectives, 59 sick or wounded, and 132 on extra duty. But Hooker returned my petition to me without comment. I petitioned once again, this time for a few days leave to make my case in Washington, and was again turned down. I could give my men nothing. I turned then to recruitment, seeking time in New York to rebuild the regiments, and failed to obtain permission.

Thus rebuked on so many fronts, I sought other means of heartening my bloodied men. St. Patrick's Day was coming, and for this quintessentially Irish saint's feast I arranged for grand and gay festivities. Libby arrived, bringing with her my white beaver and blue swallowtail, and then we made ready for the feast.

First was the Mass, as always, and then lunch, and then the races, with a few tons of generals in the stands, including Hooker, Sickles, Sedgwick, and Butterfield. The brigade's own show it was, but ten thousand men in blue watched as we ran the heats, and the betting was thick for the last one, the Grand Irish Brigade Steeplechase.

With Libby watching fervently, the breezes tossing her hat, and I as clerk of the course, the old Brigade showed its mettle once again, celebrating our day and our fate and our race.

The long-faced generals cheered, bet, and eyed me with strange reserve, as if the worst-bloodied brigade of the army ought not to be celebrating anything, but should be staring into its ashes. But my brave Libby, the darling of the Brigade, won a thousand cheers.

Hooker tarried through the winter, planning a campaign to sweep Lee's army away once the mud of spring hardened. But my brigade gained few men and the remnant grimly waited. In April I finally obtained permission to recruit again in New York, and hastened north.

Ireland was on my mind. The famine had visited again, at least in western counties, blighting potatoes, and something else was rotting grains. Rains had flooded the bogs, making it impossible to cut and dry peat, so peasants froze in their cottages. Landlords were evicting again, confiscating crops for rent, and the troubles so recently passed beset my native soil once again. I would speak, not only for relief efforts, but against the whole vicious system of landlords. For the pain in Ireland was my own pain, and while one Irish peasant suffered, so did I. That is what everyone who wishes to understand Meagher must grasp.

For that moment, Ireland consumed me, and then I was called back to Falmouth, in the shadow of Fredericksburg, and once again I was enmeshed in war. I knew what was afoot: Hooker would soon attempt a great sweep around Lee's army while feinting a new campaign at Fredericksburg; and Hancock's corps, including the remnants of the Irish Brigade, would be a part of that flanking movement.

At the end of April, we slipped out of our winter quarters before dawn and silently headed northwest toward a place called the Wilderness, and a little crossroads town called Chancellorsville, marching thirty miles through mud, fording the Rappahannock en route. At Scott's Mills we fortified and made ready, even as Hooker's remaining forces back at Fredericksburg made a great show of renewing the assault on Marye's Heights.

I watched my veterans returning to war, brimming with cocky humor, ready for anything. Maybe Hooker was the man Lincoln needed; the lads were putting some stock in him. They liked this type of war, marching to the flank, catching the enemy in a vise, rolling up a Reb line. There were Irish airs in the breeze as they cut loopholes in the mill and threw up earthworks. The silken green colors, the harp and shamrock, were fluttering.

There was battle noise round about that third day of May.

We heard the fighting, but for the moment our fortified mill lay peacefully in the sun. What puzzled me most was that a sharp fight was underway west of us, where I least expected it, as well as south and east. I learned at last by courier that Stonewall Jackson had swept around *our* flank, and was driving straight toward our fortified mill, pushing our routed troops before him. Lee had outmaneuvered the North once again.

I turned to Kelly. "The Rebs have caught Hancock on three sides, and have us cut off. That's Stonewall Jackson west of us."

"I'll set up a recruiting office," he said, eyeing the defeated bluecoats drifting by.

Swiftly I ordered my men to form a picket line to stop the rout and return these fleeing men to their own columns, but we were being assaulted by vastly superior forces, and orders arrived from Hooker to march to Chancellorsville to defend the only field pieces Hooker had available to him, the 5th Maine Battery.

We quicktimed to an open-field crossroads where the Chancellor house stood, passing the debris of war, ruined wagons, caissons, and stumbling men, and threw up our perimeter through an orchard. We instantly found ourselves in the heart of the battle when Confederate artillery on three sides opened against our sole battery, which was firing canister at grayback infantry only two or three hundred yards distant. I caught a glimpse of Hooker himself standing at the house only to flee moments later for safer ground as the enemy artillery rained hell on us. The place was too hot for the command, but not too hot for the Irish.

We had stumbled, once again, into the hottest place of the war, but dug in quickly, using whatever shelter was at hand in the orchard, while shot and shell rained down on that battery and its brave boys, whose five field pieces continued to fire at Reb lines, even as thirty Confederate pieces rained shot upon it, and us. For over two hours we were raked by this Reb cannonade, which took a heavy toll among us, while one by one the 5th Maine's guns fell silent as gunners fell or caissons exploded.

I could not comprehend this twisted and unfathomable battle, with fighting in almost all directions and a vast confusion of men and arms. The graybacks saw our confusion, saw those field pieces, knew how few of us stood between those prizes and themselves, and resolved to take them. But they had not counted on the Irish Brigade, or Captain Mulholland of the Pennsylvania 116th, or a score of others who knew they had to rescue those pieces before they fell into enemy hands.

Hancock was sending reinforcements double-quick straight into the middle of that hell flanking the Chancellor house, and I fathomed at last that we were at the crux, the center of the fight. Hancock was fighting on two fronts, east and west, and separated from the rest of Hooker's army to the south, and my depleted brigade was holding off powerful Southern infantry, but couldn't last long.

Choking smoke filled the area; exploding canister raked us, blew out our ears, toppled any man standing. The enemy artillery seemed to track me, their shells exploding wherever I had just been, yet nothing touched me.

We cheered the last two boys of the 5th Maine as they continued to fire their last piece until enemy shot blew their caisson to pieces, and then the rush for those field pieces began, with our lads struggling against Virginia mud to free them before our lines were overwhelmed. The gallant Irish once again were in the thick of it, and I ached as I saw them fall, by pairs and dozens as they wrestled with the pieces, at last freeing one and dragging it toward safety, and then two more, and finally a fourth, but paying a fearsome price for it.

We dragged those pieces down the soggy road just ahead of the Reb advance guard to the safety of Dan Sickles's III Corps, and there they cheered my boys for saving the field pieces.

We formed a new line east of the road, well fortified with timber and brush, and threw up works, even as Confederate infantry peppered us, the balls striking here and there with frightful slaps and ricochets. But the main fight was elsewhere, and we dug in for the night. I set up a command back away, and had my men fortify my pup tent with sod and logs because minié balls still whipped through the darkness. They were making a great racket to let us know they were there.

I dared not light a lamp within, but sat in the close warm darkness, disgusted once again with the whole war and our command. It was obvious that Hooker's grand design to flank Lee's army had not only failed, but that Lee had *flanked us* and beaten us out of Chancellorsville with terrible loss, and did it all with an army half our size. And in that killing field where we defended the 5th Maine Battery, my boys had been slaughtered.

I dug in my duffel and found the silver flask, and poured fire into me to still the pain. There was not enough whiskey in that flask or a dozen more to quiet my torment, but I swallowed what was left, and sent Private McCarter for more from regimental stores far to the west. I would, I decided, nip what I needed and never a drop more, or dull my wits with drink. It was the pain, and that was the whole of it. All night I lifted the flask with metronomic clocking.

And so the night passed, and the next day we were ordered to guard the rear, defend the ford, as Hooker's mauled army retreated. I rallied the lads, ducked Reb volleys, and did what I could. Lee and Jackson had outmaneuvered Hooker on every field, and now a fifth of my depleted brigade lay dead or wounded, all for nothing.

It had started to rain, and the rain built in slow cold gusts as my soaked and weary Irish formed the rear guard, holding off the Rebs once again while Hooker's hapless army fled. It was an honor, being chosen by Hancock to guard the rear, which was actually the front, but I was sick of honor.

My brigade was lost again in the mud and mire.

29

                                             I drafted my letter of resignation as brigadier of the Irish Brigade:

> That brigade no longer exists. The assault on the enemy's works on 13th December last reduced it to something less than a minimum regiment of infantry. For several weeks it remained in this exhausted condition. Brave fellows from the convalescent camp and from the sick beds at home gradually reinforced this handful of devoted men. . . .

I went on to say that the treatment of the remaining men had depressed me to such a degree that I felt unfit for command. I added that in resigning from command of the brigade, I was not abandoning my service to the Union. When I had at last made my case, I sent it off to the adjutant general's office and awaited the response.

In a few days it came: resignation accepted by the President of the United States, effective at once.

Just like that.

On May 19th I gathered my men, formed them into a hollow square, with my staff and my guest General Caldwell in the center, and spoke to them of their glory and gallantry, and made them a promise:

"The graves of many hundreds of brave and devoted soldiers, who went down to death with all the radiance and enthusiasm of the noblest chivalry, are so many guarantees and pledges that, as long as there remains one officer or soldier of the Irish Brigade, so long shall there be found for him, for his family and little ones, if any there be, a devoted friend in Thomas Francis Meagher."

This farewell brought me nine impassioned cheers from the men, and then each of the commissioned officers shook my hand, some of them with tears in their eyes. The band of the 14th Connecticut played fine airs for the occasion.

I shook hands with them all, each of my four hundred brave men, saying "Good-bye and God bless you" to each, and turned the brigade over to Colonel Patrick Kelly.

I suddenly was a civilian again, without a command. I fought off melancholia and headed north to Libby, torn and alone.

They treated me kindly in New York, where I was much celebrated, even by the new mayor, the Republican George Opdyke. The city council offered me the "hospitalities of the city" as a token of the esteem in which I was held by the people. And then General Birney presented me with the Kearny Cross, given in honor of his friend General Kearny, who had always taken an interest in the brigade. The cross was fashioned of silver, with buckles and clasp of gold, on a heavy scarlet ribbon, and inscribed, "To General Meagher of the Irish Brigade. Kearny's friend and comrade in the Old Division."

So I had been honored, but I remained restless, pacing about the Townsend home, at loose ends, exiled from the world.

"Libby," I said one evening, "I belong in the army. I'm made for the army. I'm a good soldier. And here I am."

"Will they call you?"

"Not unless I pull strings for a new command."

"But not the brigade?"

"That would be the last place they'd put me. Maybe I can rejoin Hancock's division. He's a true friend."

She pulled me to a velvet love seat. "Tom? Only days ago you wanted to get out of it."

A bitterness welled through me. "We have the most miserable general staff ever calling itself a command," I said. "It's not Lincoln's fault, either. He's the commander-in-chief, but he can no more budge the generals than anyone outside the War Office. He told me as much."

Weeks of restlessness slid by; I made speeches, shook hands, toasted the corps, was guest of honor at banquets, boosted the war effort, fended off criticism in various papers, such as *The Irish American,* which was now scolding me for being too close to the awful Mr. Lincoln. I most certainly did share one objective with the president: I wanted a Union victory, *now,* fast, and with the union of the states preserved. And I said so where I could, and to ears that didn't want to hear it.

New York was a luxury and comfort. I slept in soft beds and ate delicacies, and lifted ruby port to my lips, and listened to flattering speeches, and heard the lilt of Ireland in women's voices. But my heart was aching for the bivouac, hard ground, the brigadier's star, the grooms saddling my horses, that band of gold around my saddle blanket, and the proud marches behind the silken green flags.

Gettysburg came, the Brigade fought once again in the middle of things under Hancock, its task to seize the Wheatfield and Stony Hill beyond, and it acquitted itself well, taking two hundred prisoners and killing hundreds of Rebels. But it suffered another two hundred casualties. The Confederates were roundly defeated, and once again the Union failed to take advantage of that and destroy Lee's trapped and disorganized forces which were far from Virginia and safety.

Lee's army had received a terrible blow, and Grant delivered another one to the Rebs far to the west, at Vicksburg. We were all slow to realize it, for the Southerns seemed as puissant as ever for the moment. And yet, the Reb hourglass was spilling the sand now.

I itched to withdraw my resignation. I wished to raise three thousand Irish from the eastern cities, wished to rejoin the war effort. I sent my letter by messenger to Secretary Stanton, another to President Lincoln, buttonholed who I could, got endorsements from friends, and waited.

I did at last hear from the president: "To General Thomas Francis Meagher, Your dispatch received. Shall be very glad for you to raise three thousand (3,000) Irish troops, if done by the consent of and in concert with Governor Seymour. A. Lincoln."

But nothing came of it so I went to Washington in early July, finding room at Willard's Hotel, and set out to win a command. I sent messages to Secretary Stanton, and waited.

But on July 14th, it all came tumbling down.

I watched, aghast, as headlines screamed. New York was in an uproar because of the draft. What had started as a protest against the draft lottery being run by my friend Colonel Robert Nugent, convalescing in New York from his Fredericksburg wounds, turned into the ugliest several days in the city's history. Rioters, ordinary workingmen from the tenements who wanted no part of the war, feared black freedmen as rivals, and hated abolitionists and Lincoln, stormed the draft office on 47th Street and destroyed it.

They torched buildings, tore up street railways, ripped out telegraph lines, and even cheered Jeff Davis and the Confederacy, all the while being goaded and inflamed by Peace Democrats and Copperhead politicians.

The street battles turned brutal. The rioters attacked and

burned an orphanage for colored children, and only because priests rescued and harbored some of the children were any saved. The insurgents lynched black men on sight, burned the houses of Lincoln-supporting Republicans, rallied before the residence of General McClellan, looted Brooks Brothers and Lord and Taylor, and ruled the streets.

When Colonel Henry O'Brien of the New York 11th emptied the streets with a howitzer, killing a woman and child, they revenged themselves by beating him to death.

Not until five regiments invaded the city and rooted out the rioters building by building, meeting violence and death with more violence and death, was it over. But the seething hatreds remained, and in the aftermath there was blame, and the blame fell upon the *Irish*.

Those cheers for Jeff Davis reverberated across the country, giving every Know-Nothing more reasons to drive the Irish out of the Republic. Working men had rioted and murdered orphans and other blacks, and most were undoubtedly Irish. I could scarcely bear the shame.

I didn't even receive an answer to my request to raise three thousand Irish troops, and knew I never would. Except for a handful, like Hancock and Sickles, the army had no use for the Irish and distrusted us. Now, with the riots looking like outright treason in the eyes of most Yankees, the stigma was a thousand times worse, and cast a shadow over my chances.

When I returned, a few days later, the *Irish American* poured its boiling invective over me, labeling me a Lincoln man and blaming *me* for much of the trouble. The riots were my doing! I spoke in whispers to shaken and bitter friends, their hearts divided, their minds seething with loathing of the United States and the Lincoln administration. They would not be conscripted. They would not march off to be killed in a war not their own.

The Fenians were busy making the most of it that fall. They never much cared for the struggle of the Union to preserve itself, and even less did they care about black slavery. My smouldering friend John O'Mahony set to work recruiting the bitter and insurrectionary Irish of the devastated city for his revolutionary brotherhood, and enrolled them in droves.

He approached me, wanting an ornament of Young Ireland in his corner, and I at last swore out the Fenian oath, filled with misgivings. He had not seen war. I had seen nothing but blood, death, and graves. He did not know the grief of widows and orphans. I knew both. But my dream of a free Ireland compelled me to utter those words binding me to Irish revolution. He wanted me to attend a Fenian convention but I put him off, saying I was still a brigadier and on call.

I did visit Washington, and did look for a berth. I visited my old friend and commander, Michael Corcoran, at Fairfax Court House, where his legion was encamped. He accompanied me back to Washington on horseback, said his good-byes, and then tragedy struck. On his way back, he tumbled from his horse, landed on his head, and died a while later even as my train was carrying me north. It was whispered he was drunk, but I had come to realize that this was said about any mishap that befell any Irishman. Corcoran was a great and loyal soldier, wedded to the cause of the Union, and admired by every man in his legion.

I grieved that Christmas of 1863. I officially withdrew my resignation, making myself an active-duty general in the army. The Irish Legion needed a commander and I made myself available. But I heard not a word from the War Department. I remained a general in exile, my pacing echoing through the Fifth Avenue house.

30

Eventually, the War Department discovered it had an unemployed general of volunteers at hand, and shipped me west to Tennessee, where I would assume some unknown command under a man who was no friend of mine, Major General William T. Sherman. I was back on a general's salary and feeling that again I could support Libby as she and her father might expect.

1864, the fifteenth year of my exile, was an election year, and my brother-in-law, Sam Barlow, was General George McClellan's campaign manager. I was often to be found sharing a platform with Little Mac in his campaign against Lincoln's Unity Ticket. That did not endear me to Lincoln's staff, but neither was I forgotten.

On the other hand, the Copperheads and peace Irish in New York were sniping at me more and more for not being a pure enough Democrat, or not putting the interests of the Irish above all else, including the interests of the American Republic, as if no issue or belief or national disaster could possibly be more important than their own.

The *Irish American* even found in my funeral oration for Colonel Corcoran some seeds of perfidious Lincolnism, and thereby denounced my wavering fealty to all causes Irish, proclaiming that I had fallen from my pedestal.

I was weary of their sniping, and tired of the Irish and their lockstep politics. Could the editors find no virtue in independence of mind? I fortified myself with some Pennsylvania rye and fired a salvo at the *Irish American*:

"As for the great bulk of the Irishmen in the country I frankly confess to an utter disregard, if not to a thorough contempt of what they think or say of me. . . . To their own discredit and degradation, they have suffered themselves to be bamboozled into being obstinate herds in the political field. . . ."

The *Irish American* never got over it, and I found myself entertained by their apoplectic sputtering. It was all about betrayal of Ireland, and how I had fallen from my pedestal of fame and honor, and how I had *failed Hibernia*. I read it there at 129 Fifth Avenue, and I didn't give a damn about their rant. But I was never so exiled, so separated from my own.

The War Department finally sent me out to Nashville, Union territory under constant threat from the Rebels. My actual assignment would be decided by General Sherman when I got there.

Libby saw me off. I kissed her, boarded the steam coach, and began an arduous and cold winter journey that would take me by rail and steamboat on the Ohio and Cumberland Rivers, to my new command.

It did not help that Sherman had no use for me or for the Irish or for any union Democrat, and hadn't changed his views since Bull Run. The gallantry of my brigade meant nothing to him. I learned he had a private name for me, *Mozart Hall*, after the peace faction of Tammany. How little he knew me. But I was prepared to do what I could for the cause, and presented myself to my immediate superior, Major General William Blair

Steedman, a Union Democrat and war hero, who welcomed me heartily but had no command for me.

I did not fail to broaden my acquaintances while I waited, and soon Governor Andrew Johnson of Tennessee, a Union Democrat, invited me to address the state's House of Representatives, and I did so, with an oration I entitled, "The National Cause and the Duty of Sustaining the National Government and the War." There I let it be publicly known that I supported President Lincoln's Unity Ticket, even though I admired General McClellan.

I knew that would excite the *Irish American* to mouthfoaming rage, and they would call me a traitor to my own party, but I no longer cared what that narrow-focused paper thought.

My assignment was settled swiftly. I was sent south with a provisional division of battle-shocked troops to guard the Chattanooga and Atlanta Rail Line extending from Chattanooga south to where Sherman's forces were cutting their swath through the South.

"These are troubled men," the general told me. "They aren't deemed suitable for combat, some still weak, barely out of the infirmaries, some anguished by war, some afflicted in their souls by battle, some unruly or rowdy or misfits, one step away from the stockades. Some are outright reprobates and scoundrels. You'll need to inspire, heal, and discipline the whole lot, and keep a sharp eye out for desertions. And even though they're half-ready for war, they must be brought to a peak of readiness."

I nodded. I had a way of inspiring men, and now I would seek to inspire this band of misfits. They had not called me Meagher of the Sword for nothing.

I entrained my troops, settled them at stations along the

way, and began a ruthless patrol of the seventy miles assigned to us. So thorough was our vigilance that we had little trouble from Reb guerrillas infesting the whole area.

I spent time talking to these war-rattled men, some half-deranged, some still weakened from wounds, some cynical and inclined to desert.

"Some day, long after this is over, every one of you will be remembered and honored for your effort to save the Union. Some day, every man who wears the blue will parade in great victory marches, and never be forgotten. I will never forget you," I said, as I visited with one and another of these companies of the afflicted.

A few weeks later I found myself with a much larger command over the whole Chattanooga district, twelve thousand infantry, three cavalry regiments, and two hundred field pieces. Steedman was supporting General Thomas, whose task was to thwart Confederate General Hood's thrust north, the South's desperate effort to force Sherman to turn back and defend his rear.

On Christmas Eve, 1864, Thomas defeated Hood, and we celebrated exuberantly, knowing the war was nearly over. I held a fine banquet for my staff, in which we toasted General Thomas and his brave men. We were in the merriest of moods, and good cheer kept flowing.

Soon we were ordered to move our provisionals and other men to Savannah to help Sherman, and I spent the early weeks of 1865 arranging transport on river packets plying the icy Ohio River, and finding room on the overburdened railroads to move seven thousand troops. Because of weather and crowding, it was a slow task, but eventually my troops were moved to Annapolis and put on ships for North Carolina, their new destination.

Little did I know that my critics, as usual, were claiming

that my command was disorderly, which was their way of saying we were unmilitary. Some fever-swamp journalist in Cincinnati, with a hatred of the Irish in him, was publishing canards about the disorder of my command, all of which reached the attention of General Halleck. There were withering queries from the War Department, and no response from my staff or me sufficed.

Another incident at Annapolis troubled me. I would not let the *Ariel*, the steamer bearing my command, sail south until all my troops were loaded in other vessels, but I was overruled by a certain transport Major Scott, who wished to ship troops as fast as they were loaded, and who had reached Halleck about it. As a result my orders were ignored.

I had had a nip or two in the comfort of my headquarters ship, and to this day am not certain how I was overruled by a major, but whatever passed through the War Department did me grave harm. First they criticized me for stringing out my command along the Ohio in disorderly fashion; now they assailed me for pulling my command together and shipping out as a cohering unit! What sort of malice was this?

At last, in mid-February, I delivered my troops to General Palmer in North Carolina, only to find that for me the war was over: I was summarily relieved of command, and *dismissed* from active duty, but with a commendation from General Schofield. Just like that. One hour a general, the next, relieved from active duty, and the war not yet over.

"General Schofield," I said, determined on gallantry to the last. "This is a fine and gracious good-bye you give me. I've done all in my power for the Union cause, which I regard as sacred to mankind everywhere, to rid the republic of the pernicious black slavery and rebellion that afflicts us. And now, I find myself commended, and return to my home with a heart well satisfied. Sir, I turn over my command to you with a grateful heart."

He nodded and shook my hand, eager to be about the business of crushing the Confederacy in Sherman's pincers. In a flash, he and his staff were back to their planning in an old Carolina mansion, and I stood alone in a sunlit anteroom, where a sentry eyed me lazily, and motes of dust caught the light.

It was an odd thing, being cashiered before the war had ended. I was free to return to New York. Grant, now in command in the east, was still harrying Lee's weakened and faltering army, while Major General Sherman was storming invincibly through the South, severing the Confederacy and administering the death blow. And there I was, a brigadier's star on my shoulder, a civilian, a man without a clear perception of his own future, financially distressed and vaguely dishonored for what cause I did not know. I turned and walked away from the army, away from the war, and took a crowded packet north.

They would be glad to see me in New York. I would take up where I left off, practicing law, maybe getting into politics, making use of what honors had come to me from war, supporting the party of Democracy. But war inevitably changes a man, and I looked ahead to that life with little enthusiasm. I cared not for stuffy law, and could not earn much from lecturing. My best bet was a place in government.

What is there for a cashiered general to do?

Free Ireland? My country still lay under the heel of England, and I still supported independence in every way possible, yet the war had stolen my passion; I was an American now, by war and blood and belief, and I wondered whether I could ever again muster the young passions that had propelled me into a life of rebellion.

William Smith O'Brien had just died, after warning Irish

against involvement in the American Civil War, and I grieved his loss. Some day, I knew, he would be seen as one of the founders of the Irish Republic. I knew little of John Mitchel, my other Young Ireland colleague, who was still penning anti-Union diatribes in Richmond, and rallying the Irish to the dying Confederacy. I admired him, even though we had taken different sides, and stared down gun barrels at each other.

Libby greeted me exuberantly. Her warrior had come home at last, but I could not match her spirit. Peter Townsend welcomed me with his usual reserve. All of New York, it seemed, honored my contributions to the Union cause, and once again I found myself invited to speak, to address banquets, to tell stories of war and suffering, and to honor New York's finest, the men of the 69th.

Then, at Appomattox, it ended. The South lay prostrate. All born to the stars and stripes were freemen. All this I watched in a metropolis still sullen and defiant, a city in which Mr. Lincoln was still the ape—until that eve, at Ford's Theater, John Wilkes Booth put a ball into Lincoln, the last and cruelest casualty of the War of Rebellion.

We grieved our president, I more than my Democrat family, perhaps because I had known him, seen his frustration with an obtuse military organization, seen the disappointment and patience etched deeply in his face.

Even as the war was ending, he was already beginning an effort to reconcile the South, heal the wounds, restore its people to citizenship, though his more radical cabinet wanted to inflict as much humiliation as it could upon the defeated enemy. He foresaw what a vengeful and vindictive North would do to the healing of a nation, and tried to prevent it.

So my friend Andrew Johnson of Tennessee was president. Lincoln had created a unity ticket, making his running mate a

Union Democrat rather than a Republican, to help cement the border states and minimize factionalism during the desperate struggle. Suddenly a Democrat with views similar to my own was in office, and I saw the opportunity in it.

I was summoned to Washington, where all the general officers of the army formed an honor guard for the fallen president, in a most solemn, tearful and bleak ceremony. It was there that I once again felt the great power and courage of this republic, the natural patriotism of its people, the love that was borne in their hearts for this president, and the respect accorded him even by his opponents. Suddenly, the man they had called an ape was discovered to be one of the greatest of Americans, and I saluted proudly as the cortege passed by.

The War Department required the resignation of all generals of volunteers, and I submitted mine, receiving a card of acceptance from the White House. But I wrote my friend, Major O'Bierne, now Johnson's aide, seeking another star. O'Bierne made the effort, requesting a brevet major general commission for me, just as soon as possible. And we continued to correspond that summer of 1865, as Johnson settled into office.

"Let me have the delightful satisfaction of wearing my two stars on the Fourth of July and showing that the Government is true to Irishmen who are true to it," I wrote.

I was restless, waiting word, uncertain what to do with myself. I thought a military governorship in the conquered South might be well worth the effort, and would enable me to conciliate and reconcile the defeated southerners. But nothing materialized.

I hung my blue uniforms and field dress in my armoire, along with the old Zouave uniform I had tailored for me at the start of the war, and other field attire. Each of those blue uni-forms told a story: each had been worn into battle. One had been extensively mended. Balls had passed through its fabric. Blood had been shed upon the wool, and the stain never quite vanished. Saddle grime had worn into the trousers of both. My boots were scarred and no longer took a blacking well. My kepis rested on a top shelf, and each still retained its sprig of box-wood. My gold-thread stars glimmered in the shadow of the armoire. My yellow sash, insignia of my rank, hung separately, somewhat stained, mostly by endless bivouacs, but also by spir-its. The brass buttons on my tunic glowed. I had always made sure I lacked none. I had removed my precious medals, ensigns of honor, and the Kearny Cross, and now they reposed in a glass-front case at our hearth, attestations of my character and courage.

When I tried to close the door of my armoire upon these relics of my life, I could not, and left the door open so that it could not separate myself from those robes of war and honor. Maybe soon I would thicken at the waist and no longer fit into them. Maybe some day I would wear one in some grand parade down Fifth Avenue. Maybe I would even end up with a second star. But now, in that poignant moment of life, my uniforms and I were one, and I felt naked in mufti.

Then, while reading the *Tribune*, I discovered that the gov-ernorship of Idaho Territory, some vague and vast dominion out in the Northwest, was vacant. Gold country, mountains, Indians. I wrote O'Bierne once again: "Entreat the president to let me have it, and all will be forthwith right and glorious with me. Urge this at once," I wrote.

Go west! That was what Greeley had been advocating. The West was the hope of frustrated and disillusioned men everywhere, and the West would repair me, if only I could go with a solid federal salary in my pocket.

And then I spent the summer on Long Island, with our old friends the Dan Devlins, waiting for word from the Democrat, Andrew Johnson, but it didn't come.

PART III

Mystery

31

A great huzzah greeted me in St. Paul, the Queen City of the West, where I would speak to the Irish immigration society at Ingersoll's Hall during the sixteenth year of my exile. Soon after I stepped ashore from the Mississippi riverboat *Keokuk* I was serenaded by the Great Western Band, which played lively Irish airs, and then welcomed by the mayor. These kindnesses and tokens of esteem paid to my person exhilarated and inspired me.

To all these rapt people crowding around me before the hotel, I expressed my hope that immigrants would abandon the squalor of the cities and settle on the verdant and fruitful frontier. I had come to the understanding that the virgin West offered salvation for the starving Irish, and might receive tens of thousands of my countrymen to their great benefit if only they would venture forth.

I was there for another purpose. My acquaintance Captain James Fiske was organizing another expedition to the goldfields of Montana and Idaho, and I was on hand to see to it that the government helped him in this great, public-spirited venture. I believed I had some considerable influence in Washington, with the president as an esteemed friend, so I telegraphed Andrew Johnson requesting troops to escort Fiske and his party westward through dangerous Indian country. But I received no answer.

I was well acquainted with Washington's silence, having received no word of my appointment to be secretary of what was now Montana Territory. I needed to repair my fortunes, having been reduced to the intermittent rewards of lecturing. A place in Johnson's administration would be the answer. Old Peter Townsend was squinting at me again, and even Libby urged me to find a competence swiftly; retired generals need look neither hard nor long for employment. But nothing came my way. I was sick of being the supernumerary in the house on Fifth Avenue, and growing desperate.

My speech in St. Paul enraged the New York Irish press once again. I asserted that "the black heroes of the Union Army have not only entitled themselves to liberty but to citizenship, and the Democrat who would deny them rights for which their wounds and glorified colors so eloquently plead is unworthy to participate in the greatness of the nation."

At this, the *Irish American* was frothing and ravening, and it denounced my supposedly radical and undemocratic doctrines, and my new political creed, all of which was heresy to the white Democrat partisans of New York. I certainly considered myself a Union Democrat, but not the variety of calculating Copperhead that inhabited New York, those tough saloon-headquartered bosses still seeking to oppress black freedmen, still so clannish that their Tammany society could not bear the slightest dissent from orthodoxy, and no interest had validity save their own.

I didn't much care. Let them fulminate. I was gazing westward. There was a vast, fabled land stretching endlessly to the west, beyond the horizon, beyond the *known*, brimming with gold and silver and opportunity, and the Irish could populate it or not, settle on homesteads and farm or not, enter into the spirit of the new land or not. Here was the miracle of America, and I was eager to share the good news with my countrymen.

That selfsame evening, August 2nd, a telegram from the president reached me, delivered breathlessly by a Western Union boy in snappy blue. The secretaryship of Montana was open if I wanted it. I considered the two thousand per year stipend and accepted. I telegraphed my response to Colonel Browning, Johnson's aide:

"Thanks to the Presdt for complimentary and friendly remembrance. I accept secretaryship of Montana, hoping to prove useful in that capacity, shall proceed at once to Bannack city, as cavalry & escort section of artillery are required, shall Genl. Sibley furnish it? No time should be lost."

As usual, I heard nothing, but proceeded to query Captain Fiske about his plans, only to learn that he was much delayed. I concluded that I must proceed west at once, by whatever conveyance I could manage, and without an army escort. I proudly wrote Libby of my new turn, boarded a rail car, and arrived at the railhead at Atchison, Kansas, August 23rd, and then caught the Holladay Overland coach the following day.

Stagecoach passage requires fortitude and a ruthless discipline exerted upon one's own body. It cost a frightful six hundred dollars to Salt Lake plus the price of barbarous meals, at one or two dollars apiece. Worse, the firm allowed me only twenty-five pounds of baggage; anything over would cost $1.50 a pound. Even so, I crammed my lengthy self into those tight hard seats, three of us in the space for two, and soon we were swaying and rolling, bouncing and careening, raising up a fine cloud of dust behind us and ahead of us and over us and beside us, heading into a vast grassland.

Comfort was surely the last item that could be ascribed to

this form of travel. For as we drove relentlessly west, we were engulfed in dirt that could scarcely be scraped off with the foul towels provided us at horse troughs during our brief rest and horse-changing breaks. It was too hot or too cold. The food en route left something to be desired, and one worldly companion, a whiskey drummer, informed me that what passed for chicken was probably roast prairie dog, shot or trapped a day or two earlier.

I had tried to engage my companions, all male, in some sort of talk to pass the time, but found them a taciturn lot. Whilst I genially declaimed upon all that I saw, my first buffalo, a coyote, some pronghorns, grouse, eagles, endless tan grasses, dust devils that struck us sharply, cactus, and the absence of the red Indians I had expected to see, they mostly nodded, grimaced, or stared. I fathomed that most were southern, judging from the outlandish dialects that affronted my ears.

I could scarcely move my cramped legs, or relieve a tormented back or arm or bladder, so crowded was our bone-jarring conveyance. But on August 29th we rolled and rattled into Denver, and I took time to scrub up, walk about the bustling town perched on the South Platte, and sight-see.

I let them know that General Meagher was enjoying their fair city and admiring their lofty mountains, and they paid me many a compliment. I wrote Libby, voicing my delight at this oasis and the continental journey and promised her more letters shortly, all designed of course for publication.

But I had urgent and important federal business to attend, and boarded the Overland stagecoach for Salt Lake City on September 6th, this time traversing dry reaches and sagebrush-covered flats, all of it guarded by grim naked mountains. I missed the green of the east. But I was most curious about this Mormon Zion, and when at last we rolled out of the pine-clad mountains into the holy Mecca of the sect, I discovered that my arrival had been anticipated. The worthy citizens serenaded me, and I made some kind remarks, expressing my gratitude and objecting that I was only a small part of a great effort to defeat the South.

The *Daily Telegraph* of that metropolis noted that "The Major General looked hale and hearty to those who saw him in Salt Lake." I did not correct their impression of my rank, expecting momentarily to hear that the president, my fine old friend and political colleague, had granted me a second star.

But soon it was time to abandon that dry, comfortable "city of Saints," and proceed northward to Bannack, through the wildest and most isolated desert country I had ever seen, fit only for lower species. That cost me an additional hundred dollars. My dusty Overland coach rattled up long valleys between isolated ranges. We passed days without seeing the slightest sign of habitation save for the stage stations, but finally we rolled into a dry hollow where Bannack lay, rude and unpainted, a hamlet crowded with saloons and eateries erected from rough-sawn lumber nailed together in the board-and-batten manner. Was this jerry-built camp the premiere city of Montana?

There I was met at once by the cadaverous and dour Governor Edgerton, a most restless and twitchy fellow, itching to be off for the east on the same stage that had careened its way to this most remote metropolis. Sidney Edgerton proved to be a well-educated and cultivated fellow, but one plainly trapped by this grim outpost and itching to depart.

He scarcely bothered to apprise me of the state of the territory, grunting his general disapproval of the entire population as he thrust a few papers into my hands as soon as I had collected my portmanteau and a spare bag from the coach. These, I learned, were his official notes, seals of office, and edicts, and the whole lot fit into my breast pocket.

"Capital's going to move to Virginia City, seventy miles east," he said. "The legislature did it. You'll set up there. Little office over a store, all I could find, and you'll need to hunt up some living quarters, assuming there are any. Crowded place, miners pouring in, sleeping six-deep in bedbug parlors, drinking red-eye whiskey night and day, half of them former Rebels, maybe still Rebels."

He eyed me, knowing both my war record and my politics. "The southerners outnumber the Yankees two or three to one. You know Sterling Price's Reb army in Missouri never surrendered; it just dissolved without paroling itself, and I assure you, half the men with a southern list to their voices were pointing their rifles at Union men a few months ago. They tried to call that place Varina, after Jeff Davis's wife, but that was politely disallowed by a federal magistrate wandering through here, and it became Virginia City.

"Just thought you'd better know that. And you'll learn soon enough about an organization of vigilance that's kept the lid on, more or less. The whole lot are Masons. I think they're mostly men of probity, but they're operating an extralegal cabal, and need reining."

All this while, we watched hostlers harness some ugly-looking broncs.

"Names, sir," I said. "Who in your estimation may I rely upon for confidential advice and unquestioned loyalty to the Union?"

Edgerton pursed his lips, and for a moment I feared he would say there was no one worthy of trust or counsel. But then he ticked off a few:

"Sanders, Wilbur Fiske Sanders, young lawyer and wise head. He's the main one to talk to, close to the vigilance committee, put an end to road agentry, good man, fought in the war."

"Good. Sanders, then. Who else? Good solid men?"

Edgerton laughed nastily. "Good solid men! You'll come to your own conclusions," he said. "Good solid men, haw!"

"As bad as that?"

But Sidney Edgerton was cackling in a most unseemly manner, and I hardly dared ask more questions. A roustabout was wiping down the coach and readying the fresh team of wild-eyed nags, while a new and lordly jehu chewed and spat and eyed his passengers, most particularly Edgerton.

"I assure you, sir, I am grateful for your confidential information, and I will serve my term as acting governor with all the greater intelligence and wisdom because you have shared your concerns with me," I said.

But he was scarcely listening. I never saw a man so itchy to escape a place, and I wondered why. Everywhere about me, men carried pokes of gold washed from the creeks. I thought that I had never seen an easier way of getting rich, though I soon came to laugh at that proposition when I discovered the labor that went into collecting a single ounce of dust, and the prices of goods at this remote end of the line of supply.

Within an hour, the Overland stagecoach had been made ready, a fresh team harnessed, a new jehu was perched onboard, and then the passengers, including the governor, were boarded and their baggage secured in the boot. I watched uneasily as the coach rolled out of Bannack, leaving me alone, friendless, a pilgrim new to these remote wastes, and the secretary and acting governor of an unruly land where most males wore Navy Colts, Red Indians lurked, and greed governed.

I repaired to a saloon and imbibed the red-eye, coughing some down, sputtering. Thus fortified, I negotiated passage in an Overland Company mud wagon, an open-sided but canvas-roofed carriage operating between Bannack and Virginia City, seventy miles distant, and soon we were rattling east, over great low divides, into twisting drainages formed by the isolated mountain ranges. We passed a peculiar rock the locals called Beaverhead, after the snout of the animal, though I didn't see the connection, and then ascended the valley of the Stinking Water River, where I saw thousands of ragged men feverishly engaged in washing the gravels, animated by a wild energy that I found astonishing.

These were mostly Confederates, war-dodgers and veterans alike. Captain Fiske had told me that the Southern men had made a great effort to ship gold to the Confederacy during the war, and had been largely thwarted by Union men, well aware of the threat. Indeed, the gold of Alder Gulch had done much to finance the Union side.

We rattled through small outlying towns, Junction City, Adobetown, Granite Gulch, and most notably Nevada City, and arrived at last at the Overland stage office on Wallace, the main thoroughfare of Virginia City. Here was a thriving, clamorous and fairly civilized town, nestled again in a barren gulch and surrounded by naked slopes that reached upward into thick pine forest. The towns of Pine Grove, Highland, and Summit lay further up Alder Gulch.

I stepped off the mud wagon into hard clay, liked the sharp clean pine-scented air with a touch of winter about it, heard music emanating from a dozen saloons, waited for the cheerful driver to unload my valise, and knew I had come to a most bracing and delightful locale, even if no brass bands or official delegations or newspaper reporters or military aides were awaiting the acting governor. Indeed, I had arrived unheralded, and that might be all to the good.

I was as thirsty as I get, and set about to remedy the want as soon as I could engage a room.

32

It was all I could do not to pro-
claim the presence of the acting governor to these hale and
hearty citizens of the territory, but I contained my gregarious
instincts, put my duffel in the care of the skinny and cynical
stage office factotum, and asked about the places the best men
gathered.

"Best men?" he said, looking me over. "How long you been
on these shores?"

"Eighteen fifty-two."

"Well, Ireland, the men in Virginia City are pretty much
alike, only some more so than others."

I laughed at his witticism. "Then I will raise a glass to
them."

"Try the Virginia Hotel."

The bustling city was built of log or board-and-batten, as
well as mortared stone. I strolled past a dressmaker's shop, a
general merchandise store called McGovern's, the Elling
Clothing Store, a blacksmith's shop run by a man named
Prasch, and the City Bakery. A one-story Masonic hall
anchored the midtown area, which consisted largely of false-
front stores selling merchandise of all descriptions, while the
lower gulch harbored livery barns, blacksmiths, and coach and

wagon yards, artisans and mechanics. Several saloons dotted that area.

The through streets above and below Wallace, named Cover, Idaho, and Warren, were lined by well-fashioned cottages. I saw at every hand the marks of progress; rude log buildings stood cheek to cheek with finer ones, many of which even had gingerbread on their broad porches, and good four-panel doors brought up from Salt Lake.

I located the future seat of government easily enough from Edgerton's description. It occupied the second floor of a stone building, a merchant's establishment. I obtained a key from the proprietor and ascended a narrow dark stair to the upper rooms, which consisted of a small office overlooking Wallace Street, and a larger room behind it. A pair of potbellied stoves heated the place.

I headed for the grimy windows, enjoying the sunlit view. Below, crowds of bearded men drifted by; scarcely a woman among them. They wore slouch hats, butternut, flannel shirts, square-toed boots, and sported facial foliage in abundance. I saw a few Reb shirts, one with some stripes ripped off, and a few Union sack coats. I was better dressed by far, and would probably have to mend my ways to get along here or they would take me for a dandy. I descended that cold stair again, satisfied that I could run the territory from that humble aerie, returned the key, and strolled Wallace Street. My territory!

The bracing air put me in fine fettle, and after casing twenty or thirty resorts offering refreshment, I repaired to a respectable-looking saloon called the Cork according to its gilded green sign, for a nip and also for information. I thought an incognito governor might worm some valuable insights before flatterers and fawners got his ear. I did not know a single soul in the entire territory.

A foursome of unscrubbed argonauts played poker under a smoky lamp at the rear, and a bleary-eyed loner sulked at his mug at the far end of the plank bar.

"What'll it be, your honor?" asked the keep, a man of Irish mien.

"Ah . . . you know me?"

"No, but soon I will if you choose to imbibe. By the cut of your duds, guv, you're not going to sleep away the night in a shanty."

"Whiskey, double."

"Red-eye, one-bit, or better?"

"Better. Rye if you have it."

"No rye. Four bits for the double."

He poured a generous dollop into a battered tumbler and handed it to me neat.

"Ah, a splash."

He grinned, dipped some water from a bucket, and filled my glass. I sipped and sputtered. "This is your best?"

"Valley Tan, brewed by the Saints."

"The Saints don't drink."

"But they know how to cook a product to sell to the heathen."

"Then what's your worst?"

"Sure and you wouldn't want to know," he said.

"Irish, you are," I said.

"Sure and I'm from Donegal," he said, examining my greenback with distaste. He would have preferred dust.

"County Waterford," I replied. "A stroke of luck, finding you."

He shrugged. "Luck!" he said.

"I'm new, just off the Overland coach. Looking it over. Business, you know. Opportunities."

"Ah, a man who's looking for opportunities. Gravel's not giving much dust to a lone man any more, all cleaned out, but there's plenty to be had for any man with a dredge. Money, friend, money makes money."

"Dredge?"

"Dredging up the riverbed and washing the rock. It takes steam equipment on a barge."

"What about commerce? Freight?"

"Monopolies. Holladay's Overland, some big teamster outfits, big ranches like Kohrs up to Deer Lodge."

"What else?"

"Way to get rich now is a toll charter. Build a bridge or scrape a road and get yourself a toll license from the next legislature, and sit back and get rich cleaning out the travelers a dollar a horse on your ferry, or across your little teetery bridge. That takes politics, greasing some hands."

"What about road agents? I hear there were plenty."

"Still are, but the Republicans caught most."

"Republicans?"

He turned silent a moment. "Like you?"

"Union Democrat."

He smiled. "The vigilantes are Masons, Republicans, but the town's solid Democrat, both Union and unreconstructed Reb itching to start up the war again."

"Who's Wilbur Fiske Sanders?"

The barkeep squinted at me. "Who'd you say you are? I'm Dan Connell."

"Oh, Meagher here, Tom Meagher."

"Mah-er?" The man looked startled. "No, no, not here. Thought you might be a fine somebody that's known to me."

I nodded. "Sanders?" I said.

"Ah, Sanders. Lawyer, Republican, candidate for this and that. Very respectable. May I ask . . ."

"He was recommended to me as a sound man."

Connell grinned. He lacked some incisors. "Some would say so," he said.

"Virginia Hotel a good place to stay?"

"If you can handle the tariff, one-fifty, and I imagine you can."

"Rentals available?"

"If you have a purse." It was a question. He eyed my empty tumbler, and without bidding, refilled it, and took the change lying on the battered pine bar. I sipped. The Valley Tan smoothed out with sipping, but it would require a *lot* of sipping before it tamed itself to my tongue.

I whiled away another hour, and thanked Connell.

"Here," he said, pitching me a brass token. "I give these to pilgrims just in. Little courtesy." I could not imagine what it was for, but I discovered, stamped into the brass, that it purchased Beans, Bath, or Bed from Minnie's Bathhouse on Cover Street.

"That isn't all it gets you," Connell said, leaving me puzzled.

I headed for the Virginia Hotel, discovered that I could have a room if I was willing to share it, and that nothing else was available.

"My fine fellow," I said, addressing a bag-eyed old imbiber, "you have the honor of receiving as your guest the secretary of Montana Territory, and its acting governor."

"Edgerton?"

"No, he left for the east. I'm General Meagher, fresh out, and here are my credentials." I dug into my breast pocket, but he waved me off. "A room for one, sir, would accommodate me."

"Sure enough, governor. Three dollars."

"But the rate—"

"For two."

"Ah, for tonight, then."

I had not received any sort of funds from the Treasury, and had with me only my lecture cash, and that much depleted.

"I shall write up a voucher payable on the Treasury, all right?"

"No, cash. Don't want to wait half a year."

So it was that I engaged a room at great cost, knew at once the necessity of finding suitable quarters, knew that at these outlandish prices my two thousand per annum salary would not stretch far. I signed the register, General Thomas F. Meagher, Secretary, M.T. He turned the ledger around, read the name without recognition.

"A pen and ink and paper, send them to me, sir."

He nodded.

Ensconced in my own room at last, if the cubicle could rightly be called a room, I wrote President Johnson to declare my arrival, and then Libby about my trip and first impressions of Virginia City.

"My dear, contact President Johnson at once. I believe Edgerton is about to resign, and I should like the appointment, if a vacancy should occur. Tell him as well that this turbulent territory requires a regular army garrison.

"Come swiftly, my dear. There is opportunity here to get *rich* very *fast*. This is a place to delight the heart and fill the wallet."

I signed it and posted it, and headed for Minnie's Bathhouse over on Cover Street to soak, and see what other wares the place offered.

33

I called upon Wilbur Sanders the next morning, finding him at his Idaho Street offices, which he shared with another attorney named Baggs.

He greeted me effusively.

"Why, General Meagher, my uncle told me to expect you!" he said, adding a hearty handshake to his welcome.

"Uncle?"

"Sidney. Sidney Edgerton."

"I see," I said. "He recommended you as a sound man and one I should consult."

"Well, General, I'm flattered. Here you are, a hero of the war, veteran of many a hard battle, and here I am, a struggling attorney in a frontier town."

He poured such effusions over me at a steady pace for some while, whilst I took the measure of this muscular, energetic, and remarkably confident young man. If there was any issue he was doubtful about, I did not encounter it on that occasion.

I was utterly alone, and in need of a friend and counselor. So I asked him to give me some sense of the state of affairs in the territory, and he plunged in at once, sometimes pacing his spare offices, at one point flinging off his suit coat though it was chill out and no fire burned within. He radiated a vast energy, enough to make me wilt, but I ascribed it to sheer youth.

"General, this territory's in good hands, thanks to a legal fluke," he said. "The legislature, mostly mischief-makers I must say, failed to enact a regular date to reconvene itself or hold elections, and that means it *cannot* meet, nor can we hold elections, and the territory has, for the time being, no valid government—save for you and my uncle, of course, and some reliable judges. Think of that! Why, that's just the way to keep it for now. Convene a legislature and the scoundrels would soon be at it again."

"At what?"

"Sedition." He eyed me. "You're a staunch Union man, I gather."

"I have been from the beginning of the war, sir."

"Well, this territory brims with traitors, rebels, sneaks, who slipped out of Sterling Price's army in Missouri at the end, and were never paroled or discharged.

"Before anyone knew it, they had put themselves into the legislature, and sent Colonel McLean off to Congress as the territory's delegate."

"What was he colonel of?"

"Ah, he fought for the North, General. A Union Democrat, at least that's what he says."

"You say there is no government?"

"Well, General, the Organic Act, enacted by Congress, provided for a series of steps by which the territory moves toward its own laws and institutions and elections. My uncle set it all in motion, called for elections, seated the first legislature, which was heavily Democrat and seditious. But he vetoed their organization bill, you see, and that leaves us in a legal limbo. I assure you, you have no powers to call a new legislature or election, which means that things just go their merry way."

"I have no power to summon a legislature?"

"Most definitely not, general. I take it you're an attorney? Then consult the Organic Act. I have a printed copy of it right here, just have a look." He waved it at me. "But it's our considered opinion, and those of the appointed judges in the territory, that until Congress offers a remedy, there can be no elections or legislatures. My uncle will deal with the situation as soon as he reaches the east. It may take a special bill."

Sanders smiled, and I had the gratification of seeing a true friend emerge in that smile. "You'll do fine, and I'll introduce you to men you can rely on. You might also consider a few trips, one to Last Chance Gulch—that's a gold camp north of here, Helena it's called—to talk with more good men. The things that beg your attention are crime, road agentry, and Indian troubles."

"I thought crime had been dealt with."

"You're referring to the citizen organization that looks after public safety. It still is maintaining its vigil, General, and will for quite some while with unblinking eye."

"Then crime's not a problem?"

"Worse than ever. Road agents, petty theft, footpads, dissolute behavior at every turn."

"Who are these vigilance men, Mr. Sanders?"

"Their names are secret, General. I scarcely know the names myself. When the territory obtains a strong peace system, the vigilance committee would gladly abandon its heavy burdens and slide into peaceful pursuits."

"Is there no constabulary?"

"None, apart from two or three county sheriffs, and of course some federal marshals and deputies."

I thought again of the army. What was needed here was a garrison of the regular army to patrol roads in and out of the territory and keep an eye on these Missouri Rebs.

"Well, you must know some vigilantes. I wish to meet with them and begin a transfer of power to federal peace officers."

"Can't be done. They're sworn to secrecy."

"Are you one, Mister Sanders?"

He shrugged. "If I were, I would not say so."

"If crime's a grave problem, I presume the magistrates will have court records I can examine."

"I imagine. But you see, little of it surfaces, and what the magistrates deal with is only the smallest fraction."

"Who commits these crimes?"

"Southern men, general. Bitter, disaffected Confederates. Mostly Missourians. One was hanged here a year or so ago. His last words were, 'Hurrah for Jeff Davis!'"

"How do you know they're all Confederates?"

"Friends connected with the vigilance organization, one way or another, keep me apprised."

"Who defends these criminals when they're brought to trial?"

Sanders smiled. "It doesn't work that way, General. They're invited to leave the Territory. If they see the sign, Three, Seven, Seventy-seven, scrawled on their door in chalk, they know what it means. They supposedly have three hours and seven minutes and seventy-seven seconds to vamoose."

"What do the numbers mean?"

He shrugged. "No one knows except the vigilance committee. There's much speculation. It could be the dimensions of a grave."

"What happens when a miscreant sees those number chalked on his door?"

"He takes fear, packs his duffel, and catches the next stage out of the Territory. If he has any brains, I should say."

The more I talked with this energetic young man, who

never ceased his pacing, the more certain I was that he had close connections to this vigilance organization.

I got from him the names of other substantial citizens whom I might rely upon for counsel and wisdom. He named for me the merchant Sam Hauser, the Deer Lodge cattleman Conrad Kohrs, and a sawmill operator named Nathaniel Langford.

"What persuasion are these gentlemen, Mr. Sanders?"

"All solid Union men."

"I will talk to everyone, humble and influential, of all persuasions, until I have a grasp of the troubles."

"A noble sentiment. General, it has been a great pleasure meeting you, and please call on me at any time for whatever information or favor I may impart."

Thus dismissed, I retreated into a cold sun, conflicted about this young fellow and his advice. If the territory was truly beset by Rebels who had not been paroled or oath-bound, then Sanders might just be right. But still, the idea that I was powerless and the territory had fallen into legal limbo seemed extreme, and I intended to parse the law closely.

A chill hung over the gulch this October morning, and I knew I would soon face a mountain winter. Smoke curled lazily from a hundred stone chimneys and black stove pipes poking up from the buildings along Wallace street, perfuming the air with winter's pungence. The wan October sun hung low over the mountains, casting long shadows, and I imagined that in midwinter, Virginia City would see little sunlight. I made my way past Dance and Stuart's Store, Gohn's Meat Market, Hussey, Dahler and Company, and a shaving saloon, feeling cold air eddy through my clothing.

I made one more stop that morning, at the ink-stained offices of the *Montana Post*, a thrice-weekly sheet. I thought the best way to assume my office was to make my arrival public.

I poked into the grimy press room and found a small, fragile young fellow at a battered desk.

The man spoke with a familiar flavor to his voice, which I recognized at once as Oxonian, and it turned out he was an Englishman named Dimsdale who had come west to the mountains to cure his consumption. He had made his way conducting a school for Virginia City children, and was now writing the territory's first paper, an avidly Republican organ it seemed.

"Pleased to meet you, General Meagher," he said in a soft voice, offering an ink-stained hand. I was not impressed by the sincerity of his salutation, and thought at once that he was not inclined to favor Irish revolutionaries or escapees from the English penal colonies of the antipodes.

"I simply wish to announce that I have arrived; that President Johnson appointed me territorial secretary, and in the absence of Governor Edgerton, I am the acting governor," I said. "I shall make myself available at my office on the second floor of Stonewall Hall. I would like to hear from people with concerns about the territory, and to greet people."

"I'll put this intelligence in the next edition," he said. "And after you're settled, I do hope we can chat. You must have things to say about the recent war, and perhaps news from President Johnson to impart. . . . I might be able to steer you away from certain elements, and put you in touch with the good men here, help you in certain confidential ways. A newsman has resources."

"Your counsel is appreciated," I said.

I left, determined to locate housing and set up office. The chill I had encountered here pervaded my spirit, but I have never shied from trouble, not in Ireland, and not in the seventeenth year of my exile.

34

After a few weeks enduring life in a cramped room, I rented a suitable house on Idaho Street, a log affair with actual plank floors. I was lucky to get it; renting in the gulch is all but impossible, but a landlord made way for an acting governor, preferring me to a fly-by-night teamster with a large brood, which would tax the outhouse overmuch.

Libby would have to wait for spring, it being too late for overland travel, and I would need some while to put the cottage in proper order. Such was the gubernatorial mansion that it would require new chinking in the logs and a new privy before being suitable for a woman, especially a woman reared in comfort. So my cabin, not much better than a bivouac hut, became my bachelor quarters that Montana winter of 1865–66.

I wrote her at length, describing my new quarters, urging her to come in the spring as soon as grass was up and the stages were running. I warned her that comforts might be lacking, but opportunity wasn't: "This is a rich territory, and *anyone* who puts his mind to it can make his fortune! There is a want of every sort of good and comfort, but plenty of gold dust to pay for scarce sundries. I have never seen such opportunity to prosper. So fly here as soon as the snows melt, my love, for here I am, the acting *general*, with my future in hand. And be sure to tell your father, and all my friends, that I am the *governor* of a rich land. And think where that might lead!"

The *Montana Post* announced my arrival in picayune type, which I took as an indication of where I stood with that Republican sheet, and I soon had my hands full. Petitioners arrived by the dozen and they all wanted something I could not give them, especially county offices. Edgerton had beaten me to it. I had no staff apart from Edgerton's recording clerk, who was still in Bannack, and alone constituted the executive branch of the territory and all its departments, branches, offices, and functions.

I ordered up a few reams of paper, some pens and ink, some ledgers, some furniture, and set up shop. I did discover an account in Henry Elling's bank, and became the territorial treasurer, too, by virtue of necessity. Federal salaries had not arrived for months, and I made do with promises to pay. I soon learned the various judges out in the counties were clamoring for their long-delayed wage but I could do nothing except wing a letter on its way across the continent.

I brimmed with ideas but needed more understanding, and spared Secretary Seward my sound advice for the nonce until I had fashioned a program. But soon I would be penning letters, and starting to put the territory in good order.

When at last I walked into Dan Connell's saloon one November eve he greeted me warmly.

"Sure and it was you all the while, Meagher of the Sword. I was thinking it could not be, not so far from the States, the man who risked death for the old country."

He handed me a whiskey, poured himself a double, and set his tumbler across from mine. "To Erin," he said, leaning close, a keen gaze in his bright eye. "May it soon be free. And maybe it soon will be, if what I hear is true. Is it that certain men are drifting toward Canada?"

I smiled, seeing the network of red veins in his nose, and decided not to reply. "To Ireland," I said, and lifted my glass.

It was Montana Territory that absorbed me now. If Sanders could supply me with one viewpoint, Connell could supply me with another. So I steered the talk in the direction I wanted.

"Ah! The things to tell, governor. The blithering Republicans! They sent Edgerton out here, fine decent fellow, full of puritan principles and hatred of anything resembling a bit of pleasure, if you gather up my skein of thought. Ah, indeed, from Ohio is this man, college-educated, bringing his proper nephew Sanders, his various long-nosed relatives, and a fine Methodist holiness, and a little Know-Nothing in him too.

"Anyway, this Lincoln man, he follows the letter of the law, the Organic Act making the Territory of Montana, appoints himself a privy council, saws up the territory into districts, counties, brings an election for a legislature and delegate to Congress—and gets himself a mess of Democrat lawmakers he has no use for, half-witted Republican fool that he was.

"He knew full well who's in Montana washing gold out of every creek, it's Johnny Rebs, draft-dodgers but Rebs even so, itching to make trouble and ship the gold south to Jeff Davis by hook or crook. And they elect Sam McLean to represent the territory to Congress, Colonel McLean, they call him, and he tells the Congress in Washington, boys, watch out, treat us right, if you annoy the fellows in Montana, they're likely to join up with Canada, ho ho! And then where will the gold go?"

I grinned, and he refilled my tumbler.

"And, guv, one of them that get elected to the Assembly that was meeting solemn and legal, and in riotous disorder, in a little whiskey parlor in Bannack, was a bona fide Reb named Rogers, and this traitorous fellow flat wouldn't take the oath not to lift his angry hand against the republic, and that made old Edgerton wrathy, and he declared, he says, there's no legislature I'll recognize until they get this Rogers out of it, and he refuses to deal with them. Well, Rogers, he resigned before he'd swear an oath not to take up arms against Lincoln's government, so the legislature's back in business without him.

"And then the Democrats got down to the impawtant monte game of handing out toll road franchises, bold as can be to favorite sons and bold bribers, tolls clear to Salt Lake City, fixing to charge a poor traveler plenty to get in and out of the territory, and maybe make some Democrat rich."

"I've been talking to some of the businessmen. They want things to stay the way they are," I said.

Connell laughed. "Them that has good businesses, banking, merchants, assayers, lawyers, they're doing fine keeping things just as they are, no Democrats passing laws. But it won't last."

"What'll happen?"

"They can't pretend this territory's got a proper republican government if there's no elections. The Republican congress has itself a problem: stick to the Constitution and the law and see Montana go Democrat, or just do nothing."

I downed another couple of Mormon whiskeys, blessed the polygamous Saints for supplying the nasty stuff, and Connell wouldn't let me pay a nickel. He even thrust another three or four tokens for Minnie's Beds, Beans, and Baths at me.

I headed back to my cabin, knowing that at last I had a good grasp of the tangled politics of the territory.

That evening I lit a coal oil lamp in my cabin and fetched

the Organic Law from the mounting stack of papers on my desk. What powers did I have? I hadn't the faintest idea.

In 1864, in the middle of the war, Congress created the Territory of Montana, severing it from Idaho, and set in motion a means to govern a territory whose gold was crucial to the Confederacy. The idea was to curb the flow of gold heading toward Richmond.

I turned first to my own powers, and the language was clear enough:

"And in the case of the death, removal, resignation, or absence of the governor from the Territory, the secretary shall be, and he is hereby, authorized and required to execute and perform all the powers and duties of the governor during each vacancy or absence, or until another governor shall be duly appointed. . . ."

Good. I was thus empowered to be commander-in-chief of the militia, and Indian superintendent. I could grant pardons and respites for offences against the laws of the United States until the decision of the President might be made known. I could commission all officers appointed under the law of the territory, and I was charged with faithfully executing all law.

That was fine, but why could I not call a legislative session? I found the trouble at once, in Section 4:

"And the persons thus elected to the legislative assembly shall meet at such time and place as the governor shall appoint; but *thereafter* the time, place and manner of holding and conducting all elections by the people . . . shall be prescribed by law, as well as the day of the commencement of the regular session of the legislative assembly."

We had no "thereafter." Edgerton had vetoed the organization bill.

That was daunting. Sanders and his cronies were right. I could find nothing empowering me to do a thing except warm a bench. Well, if they were right, then I would play along with them. I wasn't anxious to put myself in harm's way. I set aside the Organic Law, intending to peruse the rest of it at my leisure, but not at night by the light of a coal oil lamp. I thought a soak at Minnie's Bathhouse would suit me well.

35

I did not lack visitors once I opened my offices. They flooded in from all over the territory. Most anxious among them were Virginia City's leading citizens, who embraced me as one of their own, with many a hearty handshake and arm about the shoulder. It was an old game, and I listened closely as they steered talk in the direction they wished.

"Ah! General! The territory is in fine hands, sir. A man of your abilities, why, nothing will go undone!" Nathaniel Langford said one day whilst we lunched. "Keep a lid on those traitors, get funds out of Washington for our purposes, and you'll win the admiration of all the sound men."

"I'm honored by your esteem."

He leaned forward. "You fought them tooth and nail at Antietam and Fredericksburg. We're still fighting them here, sir. They've never admitted it's over, they lost. A villainous lot. A certain society of good and sound citizens is always at your beck and call, general. We've assisted in the past, and will again, in concert with the administrators of the territory."

"I'll welcome your counsel, Nathaniel."

"Good! No man arrives from the States with a finer reputation as a patriot than you, general. Your eloquent speeches attest to a heart given wholeheartedly to the Republic. We shall expect the best."

I had the sensation that General Meagher was being catechized.

I was calling myself "the acting one," since Edgerton remained governor. I did not know whether he would return, or whether he had abandoned Montana for more hospitable climates. In any case, I was swiftly forming my own plans. I wrote General Sherman of the Department of the Missouri, urging a cavalry garrison, which would patrol the roads, deal with Indians, and keep a sharp eye on ex-Rebels who had their own schemes afoot. I wrote Secretary Seward, seeking presidential appointment of various officials, ranging from marshal to surveyor.

I discovered that I was being closely watched, but paid it no heed. These bushy-bearded, staring gents were simply curious about their acting governor. But it seemed odd that I could scarcely stop at a resort for a libation without having some local businessman studying me from a perch a few paces down the bar but close enough to hear my conversations.

"Have a drink," I said to one, a local hardwareman and noisy Republican named William Chumasero whom I had yet to shake hands with.

"No, thanks, General, I'm just having a sarsaparilla. Wet my whistle. My little woman's awaiting me, and she waves the tomahawk when I'm late for supper." He deposited a few bits on the planks, and walked out.

But it was Sanders who undertook my serious instruction. He was a teetotaler and never showed up in a saloon but made a point of stopping by with news or insight into the territory.

"Some Indian trouble at Fort Benton," he would say. "The heathen are still a menace."

"What have you heard?"

"Oh, a man can hardly leave Benton without the redskins trailing him, wanting tolls or money or whatever."

"I've written General Sherman," I said. "I want a thousand light horse cavalry."

"There's hardly a thousand cavalry left in the whole Union army, I hear," he said.

"Mr. Sanders, have you heard from your uncle? I'm pressed on all sides. New camps want a town marshal and a surveyor. Old camps want a post office. Every camp wants roads and bridges. Everyone in the territory wants a court that will adjudicate mining claims. The territory has yet to enact laws governing land, land sales, and all the rest. We need a legislature. We need a system of taxes, and we need to support public officials. Where can I find a territorial attorney?"

"You come have dinner with us, General. People for you to meet, good solid men. Let me check with my wife."

I went, but I didn't feel at home there, amid all that primness. No libations. Kind, hearty people, unacquainted with the Irish, and I felt myself being scrutinized, right down to my table manners.

I had scarcely settled into office before I was out on the road. Gad Upson, the federal Indian agent for the Blackfeet, had called for a big powwow with that hostile tribe at Fort Benton in November, and as the territory's Indian agent, I had to go. There had been trouble earlier; the Blackfeet had slaughtered some woodcutters at Ophir, and several Fort Benton residents had butchered a few Blackfeet in return. Governor Edgerton had attempted to raise a five-hundred-man militia without much success, and I determined to get on with it, put soldiers on the roads for safety, and deal with the Bloods, the most militant and dangerous Blackfoot band.

We set off in pleasant weather, a cheerful contingent of territorial officials, including two deputy United States marshals, X. Beidler and Neil Howie, and a lawyer named Hedges. We paused in Helena, where I got my first look at a city of small log cabins and shops crammed into a mountain gulch. Miners were furiously washing gold no matter what the weather. The rudeness of Helena was even worse than the rawness of Virginia City, if that were possible. But I was greeted cordially by the miners, who knew me for a Democrat and moderate.

The weather turned, and at Sun River a blizzard forced us to find refuge for several days in old St. Peter's Mission, where we visited with Father Francis Kuppens. With better weather we proceeded to Fort Benton, a rustic metropolis on the north bank of the Missouri River, occupying a wide flat and surrounded by cream-gray bluffs. And there, to my amazement, I beheld thousands of savages, their conical lodges dotting the whole flat, the smoke from their fires hanging over the waterfront. I rode amongst them, grateful I was wearing my brigadier's blue for this occasion. They were certainly displaying their war honors. Savage braves were accoutered in their finest ceremonial clothing, eagle feathers, hawk feathers, bone chokers, scalp shirts, quilled and died leather tunics, bright with blue, their favorite color, but rich with garnets and scarlets, blacks, earthen colors, their dyes gotten from local clays and mixed with grease.

The women were comely; indeed, these were a proud and handsome people, even if a murderous lot, and as they crowded around our party, I was aware that these prideful savages were people of passion and ceremony. Their urchins ran beside us, firing mock arrows, and it was all I could do not to flinch.

But the warriors worried me. They stared dispassionately, some wrapped in gaudy blankets, some braving the cold, and their assessing gazes awakened me to peril. Here we were, two hundred white men in a sea of bronze faces that my friends were estimating at four or five thousand.

I left the ceremony to Upson and his peace commissioners, who gathered the chief men around them at the waterfront, called Front Street by optimists who considered it a street, with row after row of warriors behind them, and the dusky women and children banished to the perimeter. Never had I felt so vulnerable. Even though these warriors had left their trade muskets at their lodges, along with quivers and bows, they wore knives and could turn the Missouri blood red in moments.

But Upson made a grand talk, with much waving of arms, promising them generous gifts and food from the Great Father in Washington, far to the east, if these people would agree to move north, away from the Missouri, and live in a reserve that would be theirs forever, between the Grandmother Queen's possessions and a line well north of Fort Benton. All this was slowly translated, and it was clear that the savages were more interested in the heaps of gifts in crates along the river than in the oratory. And yet they listened solemnly to Upson, and to me.

"My Indian brothers, I am here to make peace, and protect my people as well as yours," I said, and waited for the burly translator in buckskins to turn all that into their tongue.

These were mostly Piegans, largely friendly to whites, and Bloods, who weren't. The other Blackfeet, the Kainah, lived in Canada, and were not present in large numbers. As I surveyed this vast tawny horde, I knew what I must have: an army in blue, rifles and bayonets and cavalry horses and sabers and cannon. And I knew that every white man in the territory would agree. I saw opportunity in it, too: Meagher, the man who plucked the territory from peril, would be a good name on a ballot.

The parley dragged on and on, and I learned that savages are masters of their own oratory, and that I, in a camp chair, had to sit through the chill and listen to their slow orations, as each chief and subchief and headman contributed his ideas.

"How's it going?" I whispered to Upson.

"In the bag," he said. "That stack of blankets buys what we want."

Indeed, an enormous stack of cheap and gaudy blankets had been mounded close to the water, a small inducement to behave themselves.

Off toward the old adobe fort still operated by the American Fur Company out of St. Louis, a dozen Diamond R teamsters had collected, with a string of mules and packhorses. They were hauling goods from Cow Island, down river, which was as far as some of the steamboats could get that low-water year. They were a tough lot, afraid of nothing, bearded ruffians who could hold their own in any fight, and even welcomed the chance. The Diamond R packed goods into the mining camps and made a fat profit at it, and dominated transportation in the territory. Never had men so cheerful, profane, and tough collected under one flag, unless in my own brigade.

"The army's arrived," I whispered to Upson.

"There'll be no trouble. This is going as I planned," he said.

"When do the savages get that booty?"

"Soon as they put their mark on this sheet of parchment," he said. "It's a treaty, and treaties have to be ratified by the senate, and that's tough to explain, but I'll manage."

I donned spectacles and studied the document, and found it straightforward. The Blackfeet would hightail north; they would be guaranteed a homeland in perpetuity. They would receive gifts, and annuities, which would be distributed each year.

The early twilight of November was settling by the time

the chiefs and headmen wound up, and I wanted to get back to Virginia City. But I was forced to spend the night in the old adobe post, well aware of the thousands of Blackfeet, some of them angry and vengeful and barely controlled by their chiefs, the hundreds of fires dotting the flat, the drifting sour cotton-wood smoke, the scent of roasting meat, and the vulnerability of every white man in Fort Benton. The next day would wind up the affair. I wanted to wander among them, especially to enjoy the tawny beauty and grace and shining black eyes of their women, but decided against it.

By noon the next day, the hordes of savages were again assembled around Upson and the treaty goods, and now the chiefs made their mark on the parchment, usually scratching an X with a quill. I was pleased to see the proud Little Calf, of the Piegans, make his mark. He was an influential fellow. Then, at last Upson signaled for the distribution to begin.

There was a blanket for all the headmen, mirrors and beads for everyone else, and a generous issue of knives, fire steels, and awls for prominent men, all distributed by Upson and his agency men. One by one, they picked up their gift, stared at it, pulled the blankets open, or ran a thumb along the edge of a skinning knife, and walked toward their lodges.

When that was complete, a deputy marshal named X. Biedler approached us. I had heard he was a vigilante.

"General, the Diamond R boys have a little scheme in mind to put some respect into these red devils," he said. "They've got a little four-pound brass howitzer mounted on a pack mule, barrel pointing rearward. They're thinking maybe these savages might be impressed by a little white men's magic."

"What have you in mind?" Upson said.

"Why, tugging that sleepy old mule down to the riverfront, pointing him toward us, so the barrel aims over the water, and putting a ball into the bluffs across the river. Let the savages see that."

"Ah! Splendid idea!" I said.

Upson stared doubtfully at us. "That mule calm?" he asked.

"That's the sleepiest old mule this side of the Rockies," Beidler said. "He'll be a little surprised, but it'll all be over before he wakes up."

Upson nodded, and the grinning Diamond R teamsters set to work. I thought the whole affair would be a grand finale to the ceremony, and make an impression on these staring savages.

There were plenty of the territory's finest merchants on hand to watch this, and I soon saw them grinning and licking their chops. A little white men's magic. That's what would put the fear of God into the bloodthirsty Bloods and Piegans.

The boys led that sleepy mule to the river and turned him so that the little brass howitzer faced the river and the distant bluffs. They fetched some powder from the fur post, poured a generous charge down the barrel, patched a ball and rammed it home, and prepared a lengthy fuse, which would give them all time to settle the mule and aim the piece.

Upson got into spirit of things, summoning the savage horde back to the river for this finale to the treaty conference. It was a fine fall day, with clear skies, no haze, and the whole camp was in a cheerful mood. Finally, when all was ready, the little Dutchman who was master of ceremonies lit the fuse. It hissed and sparked, and suddenly the sleepy mule was no longer asleep. It craned around to see what menace was threatening its southern end, and turned the cannon this way and that, while the teamsters fought valiantly to keep the barrel aimed over the river.

I saw the crowd edging away, and did so myself. Then the mule, now truly alarmed, began whirling and bucking. The bore of that cannon scythed around in circles as the fuse spit fire, round and round, whilst savages and white men scattered. The beast began bucking as it whirled, front down, rear up, rear down, front up, and that black bore gyrated every direction, leaving no point of the compass unattended.

I hit the ground, safest of all places, whilst teamsters scattered. I saw Fort Benton's finest hit the water. There went Mose Solomon with a splash, followed by Carroll and Steell, and Helena's Colonel Broadwater, Hi Upham, and Joe Healy, while Baker, one of the peace commissioners, fled for his store, making record time.

At the moment when the mule's four feet were all off the turf, the cannon discharged with a mighty crack. I peered up from where I had flattened myself, found myself whole, and looked for blood elsewhere. The old fort's wooden sign, a buffalo, had been shot to pieces. The mule had vanished; there was naught but a trail of bubbles rising from the river. A dozen gentlemen were paddling to shore, or otherwise shaking the cold water out of their britches with vast and tender dignity, and pretending they had not done what they just had done.

I hastened back to civilized Virginia City and Dan Connell poured me three just because he liked the story.

36

Winter lowered over the
northern Rockies and piled up snows around the peaks, and
later, the valleys. I watched ice form in every puddle and knew
it would stay there until deep into spring. The hardiest miners
continued until the creeks and rivers froze up and they could
no longer wash gravel. And even then some of the diehards
would doggedly melt water, or hoist it from a dug well, and
wash gravel in their rockers and long toms even as the mercury
plummeted.

I could scarcely bear to go outside, even as hardened as I
was by army life. On cold gray mornings, wood smoke hung
over Virginia City like a pall, souring the air. I heard talk of
shortages, even famine. The great flour famine was fresh on the
minds of the miners, and with every new snow layering in the
passes, many there were who worried whether the trails to Salt
Lake would stay open, or whether once again the city would
starve and prices would rocket through the ceiling.

I talked to freighters to find out, and learned that so far, at
least, there were no great hazards. I grew to appreciate a tough
Scots freighter named Neil Howie, who captained his own outfit back and forth from Salt Lake. Edgerton had known him,
too, and made Howie the leader of the militia, rank of colonel.

I corralled Howie one day when he arrived in town, half

frostbitten, icicles dangling from his red beard, and asked him to see me when he could. The next day he appeared in my offices.

"Sorry it wasn't sooner, General. My ox teams were so froze up I had to rub them down and grain them. I can't use them for a week."

I offered Howie a drink, but he refused it. "Never touch it, sir."

"Sidney Edgerton said you're the man to command a militia. Now I want to proceed. There's Indian trouble. Soon as spring comes around, we'll be suffering again. Can we recruit five hundred men?"

He didn't smile. "Recruiting five hundred men, training them, keeping them in one meadow for more than two days, is like recruiting five hundred goldfish from a lake without a net."

"We need an armed force, Mr. Howie."

He didn't deny it. "Pay them enough and maybe they'll put aside the long toms for a couple of weeks."

"What else?"

"Make every third man a sergeant and every tenth man a major, add a hundred captains and lieutenants, and maybe they'll all show up. Nothing like having one's little platoon to order around. Every officer can have two privates and a corporal."

"All right, I'll see what can be done about pay. Some men might be willing to serve if they at least get biscuits for breakfast."

He smiled wryly. "You won't get a merchant to advance a pound of flour, not on a public account. The territory owes nearly every merchant in Virginia City. I don't think they'd give the territory a pound of gunpowder even to save their hides."

I felt that old wave of frustration seep through me, and resolved to write Washington once again, more forcefully. But Howie did not disappoint me. Before he walked out, we had a plan to raise a volunteer militia that could respond swiftly to trouble—at least on paper.

By mid-January Virginia City was shrouded and isolated. But the stores were better stocked than they had been in the hectic early life of the camp. Everywhere, men looked to their tins of tomatoes and sacks of flour, and to their cordwood. For the cold soon grew so pervasive that not even a roaring potbellied stove would warm a house. My second-floor territorial offices never did warm up; the stone walls sucked heat out as fast as I fired the stoves. Montana winter was *mean*.

But if Virginia City seemed to be suspended in an isolated pocket far from the rest of the world, one would never have guessed it from walking into any saloon. There, in the cheer of a glowing potbellied stove, and the dim light of a double coal-oil lamp suspended from the ceiling, the mining fraternity gathered, gambled, drank, brawled, but mostly gossiped. Rough men they were, in their flannels and woolens and canvas trousers and square-toed boots. Rough and boisterous men, squandering the dust they had so doggedly won from the river gravels.

They came from all over, not just the south. The fragile ones had fled; the hardier, bolder, braver ones stayed on, huddling over games of poker or monte, trading lies, boasting, joshing, and waiting out the blizzards and blasts of arctic air, and getting into as much trouble of the bruised-knuckle variety as possible.

I found them good company, and made a regular evening tour of the resorts up and down Wallace Street, usually managing to stop at the Cork and visit Connell. They were good fellows, generous to anyone down on his luck, and many was the lucky miner who found himself outfitted with a new coat, or had his boots resoled, or found a pair of good woolen blankets on his bunk.

They weren't Irish, save for a handful, but they were my kind, and most were Democrats, with a sprinkling of old Whigs, Know-Nothings, and eccentrics among them.

"Gov'nor, let me buy youse a drink," they'd say, and I was never a man to turn them down. And like the local merchants, they had their own lists and demands. Top among them was a way to reconcile claim disputes, curbing pilferage from their camps, and honest scales (half of them swore that the scales used by merchants to weigh their dust were crooked).

But largest of all among their many antagonisms was the iron grip the appointed officials had on the territory; ordinary men wanted a legislature that would give them a working government, they wanted it fast, and they raged at the manipulation of the territory by those who wanted sleeping dogs to stay asleep.

I saw in this some opportunity.

"Show me a way to call a legislature," I said to a Hellgate merchant named Cornelius O'Keefe, who had brought a load of potatoes to town. O'Keefe was a man of parts and ideas, and a load of potatoes straight out of his Hellgate fields made him a hero in those precincts. Men poured out gold for potatoes.

"You ever look at the Organic Act, General?" he asked. He was not one to call me governor.

"Yes," I replied.

"Then you saw what it says there: the legislature can meet but once a year, unless the governor calls it into session because of unusual circumstances."

He smiled. I smiled. I would soon repair to my rooms for a

closer look. In truth, I had not examined the act since arriving in the territory.

" 'Nother way around it, general. A statehood convention."

I sipped, downed my glass, refilled from the bottle, and downed another. A *statehood convention.*

"Like California," O'Keefe said. "They bloomed right into a state, hardly pausing to be a territory. 'Bout the time it took to visit a crapper, they made themselves a state. It's the gold, general, the gold that does it."

"How is it done?"

"Petition congress; draft a constitution, and send the whole thing to Washington."

"Would the Republicans in Congress make a Democratic state?"

"A little problem, is that one. The trick is to get a Republican territory to come in at the same time, balance the scales. That's how it was done before the war. One slave, one free, come in together."

"O'Keefe, you're a man of great discernment."

"No, General, just Irish. Potatoes and politics are my life."

That fetched us a fresh round of drinks.

Even as I settled into office, I chose to do what I do best, which was to engage halls and address my constituents. I drafted a speech that I thought would please all sides, engaged a hall in Virginia City, and made plans to address the idle miners and winter-bound settlers in Nevada City, Hellgate, Last Chance Gulch, and Cottonwood, as soon as weather permitted.

But it was in Virginia City that I could polish my talk and at the same time get to meet more of my people. I got a good crowd one January evening, and addressed them warmly, with a simple message: I wished to heal divisions, and as their acting governor I would recognize no Republican, no Democrat, no

Rebel, no Missourian, in the discharge of my duties. "The war is over, and I will not plant thorns where the olive has taken root."

I supposed the Republicans would not be entirely happy with that, but little did I realize what storms my civility would bring down upon me.

37

When that winter of 1866 retreated and the passes opened, I was able to travel more, visit the mining camps in my dominion, and address the citizens. The trips were lonely, cold, and hard, and usually by horseback because few public conveyances operated anywhere.

The territory consisted of a few rude camps snared in desolation. I found the mountains cruel and lonely, the streams icy and painful to cross, the wide valleys desolate, the silence and hollowness of the wilds forbidding. But the camps were entirely an improvement over nature, for there the genial lamp was lit for the traveler, and companions abounded, and at every turn, good humor and good whiskey.

I found welcome audiences wherever I went. In Helena, which had been called Last Chance Gulch, I was warmly applauded by miners when I told them that my administration would treat all evenhandedly.

But even this simple declaration of republican principle and goodwill wrought distemper among the Republicans, and I soon found myself denounced in the press, warned by my erstwhile friends among the territory's elite, and my character blackened. These men wielded potent pens, and I knew there were letters winging their way to Congress and the president and his secretaries.

I wrote the president: "I am well aware that the radicals and extremists of the Republican party of the Territory, who, animated by the same malevolent and bitter spirit that confronts your grand policy, and would inflict eternal proscription upon the South, regard no Federal officer with favour, or with ordinary fairness even, who refuses to be a mean tool or mischievous firebrand in their hands."

And then I warned him of what to expect. Their malice moved these men to "*disable me by slander*, or overthrow me in Washington by *scandalous misrepresentations*." I asked one favor of the president. "*All I ask is that you appoint no one else until you afford me a full opportunity to meet, contradict, and utterly refute the base calumnies which these disturbers of the public peace may have, through their agents at Washington, the dastardly spite or reckless audacity to submit to your consideration.*"

I repeated my hope that, if Governor Edgerton should resign, I might be appointed governor of the territory.

But I heard nothing from the president or his secretaries, and could not fathom what was transpiring in Washington. On the other hand, I found myself welcome among the numerous Democrats in Montana, and we shared a common program, which included moderation toward the defeated South and reconciliation as a national policy.

But more clamorous by far was their wish for a legislature. The territory was virtually without law, and remedies were needed at once to settle mining and land disputes, commercial questions, toll franchises, and a host of other urgent business.

The clamor became so insistent that I took a fateful step. Clearly, the Organic Act permitted the governor to call a legislature into session if there were unusual circumstances, so I did: I proclaimed it and set March 5 as the day it would be convened in Virginia City, and proclaimed as well that there would be a statehood convention in Helena convening on March 26, in which a constitution would be drafted and application made to Congress for admission to the Union.

That set it all off. Now I was depicted as a turncoat, a Rebel sympathizer (I who had fought them tooth and nail on the murderous battlefield, ball for ball, bayonet for bayonet) and a menace to good order in the territory. The vile press labeled me a "Missourian sort of Democrat," an unsubtle reference to Sterling Price's rebel army. It was as if I had never fought for the Union, risked my life for the North, never led a brigade into mortal battle.

The new editor at the *Montana Post*, Henry Blake, penned scurrilous assaults on my good name until I was ready to whip him, just as I had whipped McMaster long ago.

But I knew the real trouble was not what appeared in the territorial press, but what was being written about me and sent privately and furtively back to the Republican congress, that I might be condemned without even knowing what was laid against me. I had weathered calumny before, and would again, and did not shy from my plan to put the territory on its feet. The legislature would meet in the spring at Virginia City; the statehood convention later.

Nathaniel Langford dropped by, this time on a mission: "General, every judge in the territory tells me a legislature is flatly illegal, and you're overstepping," he said. "I can't spare you the consequences if you won't listen to our highest tribunals."

"Nathaniel, I have the authority; nothing shall stay me in the course of my duty, and you may tell them that."

He stared sharply, and whirled away without so much as a good-bye.

My erstwhile counselors, all Republicans, did make one last effort to allay the inevitable. Thus did learned letters heap up on my desk, but I had a simple answer: Section 11 of the Organic Act, which stated that "there should be but one session of the legislative assembly annually, unless on an extraordinary occasion, the governor shall think proper to call the legislative assembly together."

"I think it proper!" I said to every hostile editor who asked.

We were suffering Indian trouble, and that was an extraordinary occasion. I certainly believed it was proper to call the assembly together, and so did every other Democrat, of whom there was a generous majority. I wrote the president at once: "On more maturely considering the powers vested in me by the Organic Act and the laws of the territory, I came to the conclusion that a legislature did legally and constitutionally exist here, and that it . . . was within the scope of my prerogatives to summon it into action."

I didn't doubt that the sophists and hairsplitters and obfuscators would set to work on that, and pummel it half to death. But I took pains to inform Secretary Seward of my plans, my grounds, and my reasons.

And so the legislature met, while girded about by the rage of the territorial judges and their ilk, who were threatening to declare the session invalid and throw out the entire legislation. That meant war, and I readied myself for a new round of furious letters denouncing me.

Up in Helena, Judge Lyman Munson was proclaiming that *he* would decide whether the legislature's acts were valid. I responded furiously, and in public print: "I do not and shall not hold myself in the least accountable to you for my official acts." And I wrote Seward that Munson and his fellow conniver Judge Hosmer should be removed from the territory, or banished to wilderness districts where they could make laws governing sagebrush and savages.

A legislature is an animal unbridled, and it soon was enacting new toll road franchises, intended to favor a few at the expense of many, but I vetoed these, which didn't win me friends in some Democrat quarters. But on the whole, the legislature enacted most satisfactory laws, enabling me to provide necessary services to mining camps, ranging from township and district and county peace officers to clerks, and to levy taxes.

In some quarters they were cheering General Meagher!

Of greater interest to me by far was the statehood convention whose delegates would soon be elected. For in it I saw a pathway around the cabal running the territory, and also a glittering prize: the United States Senate. Where better for Thomas Francis Meagher to seek such office than in a new state that is heavily Democratic? Where better to get a living suitable for Libby? I had come west determined to make my fortune, and in that seat would I find comfort and means.

"Ah, love," I wrote my wife, "imagine ourselves in a coach and four, riding through Central Park. Imagine ourselves on my yacht, green flag flying, bounding over the main. Imagine your dutiful husband, fulfilling to his utmost the calling of high office in Washington! Imagine the opportunities arising from good connections with men of means. Here lies the future, and whilst life is rustic in the extreme, you will not want for comforts soon, and you will enjoy these enthusiastic, rough, fierce miners. Come swiftly!"

I soon heard from Libby: she would be en route by March, coming up the Missouri by river packet just as soon as the river rose with spring runoff.

I set about turning my bachelor quarters into a cozy home suitable for a lady. I had done nothing to the place; it was little more than a bivouac all winter. I found a seamstress to sew curtains for the windows, bought a regular marital-sized bed, got some rockers and a table from a Salt Lake dealer, and added some rugs.

I repaired to the Cork more frequently than ever, still entrusting my confidences to Dan Connell over a few libations.

"Guv," he said, leaning close. "You are a watched man. See that bloke over there?"

Even as I stared, some fellow in a baggy serge suit turned away. He was an angry-looking man, with a mean eye, and some sort of fury burning inside. The war had produced plenty of those.

"What does it matter? You worry too much, Dan."

"Guv, let me offer some humble advice, yours to toss aside, knowin' you live in a finer world. But I keep me ear to the ground, as they say. Legislators come in here, and say things, thinking maybe a barkeep has no ears. You've made enemies, and mean ones too. They're waving the bloody flag, saying you've gone over to the secessionist rabble. Since you're a Union war hero and a brigadier, that doesn't fetch them much, but keeping an eye on you might."

"Dan, old friend, I am most pleased to see a true friend before me," I said, pushing my tumbler at him. He filled it slowly, for once, and reluctantly.

38

I watched the pilot maneuver the *Walter B. Dance* into a slot on the levee, no mean feat considering that half a dozen other steamboats lined Front Street, the Missouri current ran at nine miles an hour in the spring, and there was little room to spare. Passengers lined the deck, among them a woman I knew.

In time, with the help of scores of men with gaffs and ropes, the packet slid to its berth at Fort Benton, a vast distance from St. Louis, its embarkation point. The crowd surged forward to the edge of the water. Around me were heavily armed miners loaded with gold and heading back to the States, and virtually every denizen of Fort Benton, including those from the saloons.

With a final blast of its steam whistles and a huff of bleak smoke, the packet nestled into the levee and a dozen men secured the hawsers to posts, while the deck crew slid a gangway to the shore.

It was June 8th, 1866, a blessed, sunny, warm spring day in the northern territory, and one that lifted the spirits. I caught Libby as she stepped ashore, swung her into my arms, and hugged her.

"Oh, Tom, I can't believe I'm here. Day after day of prairies, elk, buffalo . . ."

"Well, you're here, my love, and soon we'll be in Virginia City."

"Is it long?"

"A couple hundred miles. There's a regular coach now."

She peered for the first time at the roughly dressed miners thronging the boat.

"Is it safe?"

"Libby, those are rich men returning to the States! Just you wait! We'll do fine here, Libby. I have connections. With a little cash, I'll buy into some of the claims, or maybe a freight outfit or a toll road outfit. Then you'll see what the West can do for a man."

She laughed. She was so glad to see me she couldn't stop touching me, sliding a hand over my cheek, clamping my hand in hers and squeezing it.

"Where are the Indians?" she asked.

"They've been pretty much chased out of Fort Benton," I said. "But they're a vexation that needs to be dealt with. You'll see them."

"There, that's my trunk!" she said, pointing at a stevedore. "That's it?"

"No, five more."

"Five?"

"Well, you said I needed something for all seasons."

"Five trunks! I'll have them all sent by wagon. Do you have a satchel?"

"Three."

I sighed. At two bits a pound, they were going to cost a pretty penny loaded on top of the coach. I was as penniless as the whole territory. My federal salary didn't stretch far in this country, where things cost five times what they did in the States.

"Why do all those men have guns?"

"Because they're carrying gold dust."

"But where's the policemen?"

"Libby, on the frontier, it's each man for himself."

"They look fierce."

"If you approached their wagons, they'd look a lot fiercer. Every one of these boats heading back to the States carries a fortune in gold."

She stared at me, wondering if I was teasing her. I trusted that my serious mien told her I was not.

We arrived in Helena two days later, and Virginia City a few days after that. When at last we pulled up, stiff and hot, before the Overland Express office on Wallace Street, she seemed melancholic. This was as removed from the comforts of New York as one could get, and I feared for her happiness.

We got a drayman to carry Libby's trunks to my log house on Idaho Street, and I walked her uphill to the door.

"This?" she said, looking doubtfully at the small structure.

She entered, shivered at the deep chill, surveyed the shadowed rooms, and bestowed a smile upon me.

"I'll build a fire," I said.

"I guess I should learn," she said.

I crumpled old editions of the *Post,* stuffed them into the potbellied stove, added kindling from a woodbox, then some chopped wood, and scratched a lucifer. Even in the warmth of a bright June day, it took a long time to heat that house. But Libby didn't mind.

"Some governor's mansion," she said.

"Libby, some day we'll be in a real one. Everything's new here. This will be a state soon. We've completed a constitution and shipped it to Congress with a petition. There's a Democrat majority here. They're lined up solidly behind me. We can make a new state. Governor. Senator. Plenty of chances to make money."

I thought again of Peter Townsend and that skepticism in his face whenever the subject of money rose up. I never felt comfortable with him, knowing that I was being judged.

"How?" she asked.

"Franchises. Toll road monopolies, freight companies, bridges." I took both her hands in mine, for what I had to say was important. "Libby, I'm on the very brink of success. This territory will be our bonanza. All these years I've been seeking a means, and here it is. I'm looking into a dozen possibilities, each one brimming with potential. When we return to New York, you'll have a man of substance beside you. This is the place, the moment, the *chance*."

She stared at me gently, and I pursued the matter no further. She shared her father's skepticism, but that only spurred me onward.

I showed Libby the territorial capital, stretching six or seven blocks along Wallace, with streets above and below. She took my arm, drew a lungful of mountain air, and strolled with me. Everywhere, men doffed their slouch hats, amazed at the sight of a lady, or delighted to greet The Acting One, as I was calling myself.

I steered her up the long stairs to the Territorial Offices, and unlocked the door. She stepped into the icy gloom, toured my office, examined the empty conference area, and laughed.

"The capitol exceeds even the governor's mansion," she said.

"Yes, a true splendor."

"How can you stand the cold? It's June, Tom. But this room is numbing."

"I'm an army man."

"Well, it's not a capitol for civilians, then! And you might dust it now and then."

"Some day soon, Libby . . . things will be better. And then you and your father . . ." I stopped.

She followed me out the door, which I locked. Even in summer, a chill settled over the city as dusk fell. We fled to the house, which still lacked warmth. She tossed her straw hat on the bed, and toured the mansion.

"Tom, I think I'll like it here, at least for a while."

That was a grand summer. The legislature gave the territory the property and tax laws it needed, and I signed the bills into law. The militia was forming under Neil Howie, and consisted of seventy colonels, fifty captains and thirty sergeants. One of those days we'd recruit a private, probably by bribing him. The local savages were quiet, but the Sioux were rumbling along John Bozeman's Trail, and I expected trouble from that direction.

I knew that things were stirring beneath the surface; the merchant princes were writing Washington about me. I did too, emphasizing the progress I was making, the new legislation, the new means of collecting fees and putting the territory on a good footing, the new laws resolving disputed claims. I resolved that I would not neglect to explain my every act to Secretary of State Seward and President Johnson, because my pen was my sole defense, and I knew that there would be calumnies.

Then, in July, I learned by wire from Salt Lake that a Union Democrat from Kentucky named Green Clay Smith would be the Territorial Governor, and would arrive early in the fall.

I was denied the position. My smiling friend, my colleague, Andrew Johnson had turned me down.

39

Connell wasn't pouring.

"Fill it!" I said.

"General—"

I smacked the bar with my fist.

He poured, his lips pursed, his eyes sad.

"All I did was keep the Army of the Potomac out of Reb prisoner of war camps. That's where they would be, but for the Irish Brigade. Isn't that enough? Do I have to be born here to hold an office?"

He nodded, wiped the planks with a soiled rag, and turned aside.

The twilight of summer lingered outside. There weren't many in the saloon. There were always some who were staring at me; it was the price of office.

I sipped his good whiskey and stared back. This was an Irish pub. The city's merchants rarely came here. It was where I came, and where Libby knew to find me, among my own, among the poets and ballad-singers, among the hod carriers and road scrapers and woodcutters, not among the businessmen and judges and lawyers who ruled the territory.

But Connell couldn't disapprove for long, and next I knew he was wiping his damp rag closer and closer to me, and soon he would be mopping up the sweat of my tumbler.

I waited, sipped, and shoved the tumbler toward him. He pretended to ignore me. But the rag whirled closer.

"I'm going to resign," I said. "I don't want to be secretary."

"Meagher of the Sword, quitting! I thought you'd dig in."

"The moment Smith steps off the coach, I'm done here."

The barkeep wiped his big black-veined hands on his apron. That was his way of disapproving.

Cashiered again. Here was I, in my forties, without a position, without a prospect, and soon, without money. My father-in-law was peering over my shoulder again, that wry look in his jowly face. I could imagine what he was saying to Libby's mother: "Told you so, saw it all along. The man thinks that dabbling in politics is a living, stirring up revolutions earns him a competence, holding a commission gets him rich—until the war is over. Starting up some opinionated sheet to sell to his cronies will get him a fortune in subscriptions? Pulling some Tammany strings will land him a law business, or a comfortable office?"

"Dan, my protestant father-in-law once asked me: 'Why are the Irish different? They're homesick for Ireland, and all of them plotting to overthrow the British and go home, as if this country's a camping place. Why is that?' he asked, and I said it's because there's signs in the windows, Irish need not apply. I applied for governor, and there was a *sign in the window*."

"Who's this Clay Smith Green?" Connell asked.

"It's Green Clay Smith. I've been asking the same question. He's a Kentuckian, a veteran, both Mexican and Civil wars, a Democrat."

"That's all you know?"

"I know one more goddamned thing. He's not Irish," I said.

Connell mopped unhappily, and then refilled my tumbler,

pouring slowly and reluctantly. "When is this Smith, he's going to get here?"

"In a few weeks. And don't tell me to take it and be the secretary again."

I wandered to my cottage, and am not sure how I got there. I suffer blanks, as if my pocket watch skipped forward. I fell into the rocking chair. Forty-two years old, and still looking for a competence. Forty-two, and waiting for government spoils to keep myself afloat. Why did the chance, the moment, the combination, float just beyond my grasp? How many hundred times had I tried to snatch it, and found only cold air twixt my fingers?

Libby knew enough to leave me alone and busied herself at the stove.

I was homesick, like every other son of Erin I had met on these shores. Sick of this exile. I could never see the hills of my native land imprinted on my soul, or walk into the dark warm pubs and share a sip with brethren, or watch the cold raindrops slide down a mullioned window.

I dreamed of returning to Ireland, dreamed of seeing my son, seeing Father, walking the cobbled streets of Waterford, speaking again to crowds, until I was jolted back to reality by visions of Van Diemen's Land. I could not go back. I was still an exile, and had been since 1849. If I set foot in Erin, I would be arrested and thrown into gaol, and the darker and bleaker and colder, the better they'd like it. I'd be dead in a year.

Green Clay Smith arrived in October. I met the stagecoach at the Overland Agency, now Wells Fargo, having advance knowledge of his long journey which came by wire up from Salt Lake. I found myself shaking hands with a graying, lean, hawk-like man who radiated solidity and good cheer.

"Long trip," he said, after introductions. "Stiff as a board. Where do I stay?"

"The Virginia Hotel, there," I said.

"Have them bring my satchels, General."

Already I was the secretary, the factotum of the governor.

He was a whiskey-sipping man, and that evening we went over the territory's affairs, the work of the legislature, the paper militia, the equally nonexistent finances, the various questions of public safety, the amount of gold being dug out of various gulches, most of which was going down the river each steamboat season, and the disposition of various territorial officers.

He sipped and nodded and looked me over, and did not neglect to compliment me for my achievements as acting governor. Neither did he neglect to tell me the news from Washington. The president was sinking farther and farther into deadlock with the radical congress, where the talk of impeachment was in the air.

"For what?" I asked.

"For being temperate on the southern issues. They're looking for a legal reason, and maybe they'll find one."

"They would have impeached Lincoln, then. He was reaching out to the South. He wanted reconciliation, not revenge."

Smith nodded.

"Will Johnson hold out?"

"I think so."

I helped Smith organize himself in my office overlooking Wallace Street, and put myself at a desk outside of his bailiwick. It was a sorry corner with no window. All the while I was sinking into melancholia. What had I achieved in forty-two years? I had come west determined to snatch my fortune from this land, only to find myself thwarted again, and reduced to sitting in the governor's antechamber answering his beck and call.

Libby eyed me contemplatively those days. "You might come home for dinner when I have it ready," she said, alluding delicately to my sojourns at the saloon.

"I'll eat when I'm ready to eat," I retorted.

She stared at me, wounded but unsurprised.

By November, after weeks in that purgatory, copying out letters, filing documents, excluded from every conference as one by one the notables of the territory slipped into his office and made their wants known to him, I knew I had come to another wall.

The next day I told Smith I was resigning. "I wrote the president today," I said.

"But I want you here, General."

"There is nothing for me."

"Nonetheless, I want you to stay on as secretary, and assume responsibilities, and help me deal with these clamorous people. I can scarcely sort out one faction from another."

I sighed. It was the first time anyone in office had wanted me to perform a duty, for as long as I could remember. I nodded.

"You'll stay?"

"If you insist."

"Good! I'll wire the president asking him to reject your resignation."

And so it was that I stayed on. In December I leaned why:

"General, I've spent weeks discussing the state of affairs here with everyone, and it's clear that the president hasn't the faintest idea what's needed here, his cabinet knows little more, and congress even less. They hear only the agitators. There's a total deadlock. Anarchy. It's not anything that can be handled by correspondence. I need to do some serious palavering with these people, and clear up a few acres of ignorance. And they've been misinformed by various people who've gone back there."

"How well I know."

"I'm leaving after the first of the year, and you'll be acting governor again, Tom. For how long, I don't know. The Territory will be in your good hands. I'll leave a summary of policies I want to maintain in my absence."

So it was that on January 7, 1867, I saw Smith off, and found myself acting governor again. He boarded a Wells Fargo coach, burdened with papers and records, many copied out in my hand, and was soon off for Salt Lake City. In Utah, he would catch another coach east to the railhead in Nebraska.

I moved my papers to the governor's desk. I had one last chance.

40

I had been accumulating ene-
mies ever since I called the legislature into session. Edgerton's
nephew, young Wilbur Sanders, had boarded a coach for the
east in July when the work of the legislature was done, commissioned by the local Republicans and judges to undo everything
that we had achieved. My erstwhile friend had barely spoken to
me for weeks; for him, friendship required my subservience to
his ruling clique, and when I chose an independent course, I
was no longer welcomed to his table.

Something important was happening: these autocrats were
not merely opposing me, they were bent on *ruining* me by fair
means or foul. Now I understood the constant surveillance. A
man could hardly lift a drink in a saloon without it being
noted. This was vendetta, not politics.

When Sanders left, I wrote the president at once, saying
that the most vicious of my enemies was en route to Washington: "That I shall have, everywhere he goes, the worst word he
can utter, I well know. I am convinced he will in the most vul-
gar manner abuse and defame and blacken me." I asked the
president not to heed such talk.

I knew that the territory's United States Marshal George
Pinney was blackening my name as well. But I had my own pen,
and wielded it relentlessly, with letters to Seward and others.

As long as Andrew Johnson remained in office, I supposed I would have a friend and protector. But Sanders was not alone. No sooner had my legislature completed its work, than the seniormost territorial judge, Lyman Munson, proclaimed that the laws of the entire session were a nullity; that the legislature had not legally existed. I responded tartly that I would govern according to my lights. The new laws gave my administration what was needed, including a means to levy imposts.

But I didn't count on the radicals in Washington. Word reached me in April that the Republican congress, led by the Johnson-hating Representative Ashley and Senator Wade, had nullified and voided my legislative sessions. So Wilbur Sanders had done his insidious work back there. The territory was again lost in a morass, without laws, without surveyors or tax collectors, without means to resolve land disputes. All because partisan politics overruled every other consideration.

Then came the Daniels affair, and I was soon to learn that the vigilantes of Montana, though entirely an extralegal organization, still ruled the territory, and were an adjunct of the Republican Party.

About the time I first arrived in the territory, one James Daniels, an Irishman, got into a dispute at cards, near Helena, and had shot another man at the table, one Gaitley, who had died of his wounds. The vigilantes were inclined to hang the gambler, but agreed at the last moment to let civil law prevail, and Daniels was tried on manslaughter charges before Judge Munson, found guilty, and sentenced to three years imprisonment.

I received in due course a petition from various established merchants in Helena, along with some of the jurymen on that case, asking that Daniels be pardoned.

I looked over the petition, found it substantial, and signed by some of the better men of Edgerton County, of which Helena is the seat, and agreed to it. I wrote out a pardon for the man, requiring his release.

Daniels, by all accounts, failed to acquit himself properly upon being freed, and returned to Helena threatening mayhem and revenge against all who were involved in his arrest, conviction and detention. But that was the least of my problems.

Barely was the ink dry on my pardon when Judge Munson pounced. He proclaimed in the prints and to me personally that I had *no authority to pardon*; that the entire process was without legal foundation, and he let it be known that I had performed this act whilst under the influence of strong drink.

I had, in fact, turned to the Organic Act governing the territory, and found ample authority there: the governor, or in this case acting governor, "may grant pardons and respites for offences against the laws of said Territory, and reprieve for offences against the laws of the United States, until the decision of the President of the United States can be made known thereon."

The manslaughter offense was a territorial one, enacted by Edgerton's first legislature, not a federal one, and I had acted within my powers, Judge Munson notwithstanding. I hastened to defend my decision, but Fate intervened.

The vigilantes caught hold of Daniels, strung him up from the nearest tree in Helena. But there was more: a note with a short piece of rope had been appended to the swinging body: "If our acting governor does this again, we will hang him too."

The threat was palpable. I felt the chill of being a marked man. Did it not matter that I was a public official? That my act of pardon was an official process?

Every word of that threat reverberated through my mind and would not go away. I felt a chill of a sort I had never before experienced. I had faced the Queen's executioners, faced the balls and shot of the Rebels, but I had never faced the threat of death at the hands of anonymous and shadowy assassins.

In the seventeenth year of my exile, ruffians were threatening my life and blackening my honor at a pace remarkable for its fury. I had never before seen the face of hatred so plain and bleak and hard.

Munson contributed his own scorn, proclaiming in public that I had issued the pardon while drunk. *Drunk!* He called it "the unfortunate habit." I learned that Lyman Munson himself had close ties to the vigilantes. I knew I faced a formidable foe, and summoned Nathaniel Langford to my chambers. I knew him to be the chief executive of the Virginia City vigilantes as well as an influential businessman, entrepreneur, and pioneer. I confronted him with this threat to my person, as well as the hanging of a pardoned man.

"Is this your work? Is this how your cabal treats a properly appointed public official? What sort of sedition is this, Mr. Langford?"

He smiled smoothly. Langford was the suavest of men, and chose bonhomie and evasion. "General, this was not done by our direction, I assure you. We gave no such command, and I find the matter inexplicable."

"So it just happened! A man's been hanged, and not by the government. I insist that you disband your organization. And turn over the perpetrators to the law."

"It was the Helena branch, general. They aren't under my influence."

"They were your colleagues. They will not hang a citizen or threaten me without paying the price. Bring them to me—or supply me with names."

"Ah . . ."

That long *ahhh* was all I needed to know. There was still a shadow government in the territory, and it was plainly stronger than the federally mandated one. I got no further with him. For all his respectability, Langford was merely a thug, or an apologist for lynching, and I took a sharp look at the man. There were fifty more like him in the territory, outwardly pillars of the frontier, inwardly hangmen.

I must have exuded gloom that night, because Libby questioned me sharply.

"Why do we stay here? Is there nothing we can do? Have you reported this to the marshal?"

"He's among them, Libby. His party is more important to him than seeing to justice."

"Tom, resign!"

I held her tight. "No, I won't run away. I've never done that. I'm the governor. If I call their bluff, they'll back away."

In all our years together, this was really the first time I had seen Libby angry. She had seen me off to war, heard me tell of Antietam and Fredericksburg, heard me tell of having a horse shot from under me, of sewing up my shirt where a ball had torn it. She had absorbed all that with great calm and pride of eye. But now she turned to me, distraught.

"I don't like this place, Tom."

She threw her arms about me, hugged tight, and wept, and I could not stay her tears.

41

The butchery of John Bozeman in mid-April threw the territory into a fright. The trailblazer and Gallatin valley merchant was traveling along the Yellowstone, when just east of the great bend of the river, he and his companion, Tom Cover, encountered five Blackfeet, one of whom shot Bozeman.

I listened in horror as the story whirled from camp to camp. Some said the Crows did it. Others offered different versions. But John Bozeman was dead only hours after leaving Nelson Story's cattle camp at the bend of the river that April morning.

Only a few days earlier, Bozeman had written me:

General: We have reliable reports here that we are in imminent danger of hostile Indians, and if there is not something done to protect this valley soon, there will be but few men and no families left in the Gallatin Valley. Men, women, and children are making preparations to leave at an early day. If you can make any arrangements to protect them, they will stay; if not, the valley will doubtless be evacuated.
J. M. Bozeman

Cover himself wrote me from Gallatin Mills, a letter that swiftly appeared in *The Montana Post*.

Gen. T. F. Meagher, Virginia City:

Sir—On the 16th inst., accompanied by the late J. M. Boze-man, I left here for Forts C. F. Smith and Phil Kearney. After a week or so of arduous travel, we reached the Yellowstone River and journeyed on in safety until the 20th inst, when in our noon camp on the Yellowstone, about seven miles this side of the Bozeman Ferry, we perceived five Indians approaching us on foot, and leading a pony. When, within say 250 yards, I suggested to Mr. Bozeman that we should open fire, to which he made no reply. We stood with our rifles ready until the enemy approached to within 100 yards at which time B. remarked, "Those are Crows. I know one of them. We will let them come to us and learn where the Sioux and Blackfeet camps are, providing they know." The Indians meanwhile walking towards us with their hands up, calling "Ap-sar-ake." (Crow.) They shook hands with B. and proffered the same politeness to me, which I declined by presenting my Henry at them, and at the moment B. remarked, "I am fooled—these are Blackfeet. We may, however, get off without trouble." I then went to our horses (leaving my gun with B.) and saddled mine, when I saw the chief quickly draw the cover from his fusee and as I called to B. to shoot, the Indian fired, the ball taking effect in B.'s right breast, passing completely through him. B. charged on the Indian but did not fire, when another shot taking effect in the left breast, brought poor B. to the ground, a dead man. . . .

Many wondered how a party of Indians with only one smoothbore musket among them could put two balls into Bozeman's chest, while Cover, with a Henry repeater and revolver, failed to stop the assault. Story, upon hearing of the death from Cover, sent a party to pick up Bozeman's body and find out how many Indians were lurking about, but Story was entirely close-mouthed about what he found.

John Bozeman, only thirty-three, lay dead. He had scouted a trail running from the North Platte into Montana Territory, and had numerous business interests in the valley, and was ever alert for ways to improve and settle the territory. He was a dashing man, attractive to the ladies, and always immaculately dressed in a black cutaway, boiled white shirt, and cravat, making a compact, handsome figure on foot or on horse. I grieved his loss.

I accepted Cover's story, coming as it did from a man of unquestioned probity. Cover was a prominent businessman in the Gallatin valley. The Blackfeet had always caused trouble. It all pointed to grave conflict. Bozeman's trail down to Fort Laramie was already besieged by Sioux, who had slaughtered a whole command near Fort Phil Kearny, sending chills through the territory. The Crows could not be trusted, and now the Blackfeet were erupting.

I called in Neil Howie at once.

"Summon the troops, Neil," I said. "We've an Indian war."

"All right. I'll summon the militia, general, but you'll need to fund this war. I'll have men ready to march in ten days."

"Leave the funding to me," I said. "I've wired General Sherman. Once we're outfitted, we'll march, and I'll be at the head of the column. The Blackfeet will feel our sting."

To hasten matters along, I called in the press. Henry Blake of the *Post* responded.

"We're going to patrol the roads and ensure the safety of every man, woman, and child in the territory," I said. "This is just the beginning. The Blackfeet are rising up. The Sioux are menacing. The murder of Bozeman was an outrage by barbaric warriors."

Blake for once treated me with respect, scribbling my words on a pad of newsprint.

RICHARD S. WHEELER

In time, the other papers in the Territory picked up the news. The *Helena Weekly Herald,* on May 2, ran a fine story, headlined in this manner:

KILLING OF CO. BOZEMAN
AND WOUNDING OF THOS.
COVER BY THE BLACK-
FEET INDIANS!

THE PANIC AMONG THE GALLA-
TIN SETTLERS!

THEIR APPREHENSIONS OF
A GENERAL ATTACK UP-
ON THEIR HOMES.

THEIR APPEAL TO GOVERNOR
MEAGHER AND THE PEO-
PLE OF THE TERRITORY!

I was satisfied that the territory was summoning its resources, and was entirely behind my efforts. Except for one or two Indian agents, who professed to be skeptical—one was calling the war "humbug"—I now had everyone marching lockstep toward the deployment of a militia.

I waited impatiently, hour by hour, for word from Sherman, and eventually it did arrive by wire and messenger: I could raise an 800-man militia at federal expense for a two-month campaign, but no federal forces would contribute. To help citizens defend themselves, Sherman would send 2,500 muskets to Fort Benton on the earliest of the river boats ascending the Missouri. I would have them in July; maybe even earlier.

I didn't waste a moment.

"Send word to Howie," I said to the clerk I was employing. "Tell him that we can supply the corps."

I clattered down the stairs and headed along Wallace Street, showing the telegram to the merchants. The federal coffers were open; we could outfit the militia.

Everything had changed: now, as I strode along Wallace Street, I was *General Meagher*, and when I walked into a store, I met with smiling clerks. When I ordered flour and powder and blankets, they let me sign. They let Colonel Howie sign.

Federal dollars made the difference. The territory might be insolvent, but Uncle Sam wasn't. We could spend: flour, Salt Lake City pork, beef, beans, gun powder, blankets, haversacks, canteens, saddles, bridles, gloves, slouch hats, knives, harness, revolvers, tents, freight wagons, ox-teams, hay, oats, barley.

We were enlisting the two-month volunteers, too, not only because they were civic-minded fellows protecting the territory from savages, but because we promised them an equal share of anything we captured: horses, guns, blankets, saddles, muskets, and a mustering bonus as well.

I set up a cantonment at the foot of the Madison Mountains, named Camp Elizabeth Meagher by the boys, and soon had militia learning the ropes, patrolling the roads and trails. We had horse platoons out on the Yellowstone. I had light cavalry swarming the road from Fort Benton to Helena. We didn't find any savages, but we all felt safer, and Uncle Sam was footing the bill. Indeed, the absence of savages was the ensign of my success.

42

At first the boys were itching for a scrap, but that faded, and it was all I could do to keep them riding. Colonel Howie's promises of booty were not enough, so I appealed to their patriotism and sense of duty, reminding them that the safety and purity of the territory's women, as well as its defenseless children, rested upon their manly shoulders. But their army-mandated pay of forty cents a day didn't answer.

Their numbers dwindled as May melded into June. One moment they would be sitting at a campfire spinning yarns and chewing tobacco; the next, they would be gone, often upon sighting a gold prospect. When morning came around, they weren't there for the muster. I called my militia "the Invisibles." A quarter of them were officers, but I didn't mind. If a man required a commission to serve, then he got his commission.

I was often out riding with them: there is nothing like the bivouac, the saddle, the orderly column, the briar pipe before a crackling campfire, to gladden the heart of an old warrior. I learned that Governor Smith would soon be back in Virginia City, and my days as acting governor were numbered, and for that very reason I redoubled my efforts to vanquish the Black-feet and Sioux and Cheyenne menacing the territory. Let them see what a veteran officer could do. I would present him with a safe domain, and that would lead to other emoluments.

Howie had other concerns.

"General, look what those pirates are charging us!" he said, noting that the Buford Grocery had priced fifty-pound sacks of flour at fifty dollars.

"They're afraid they won't be paid," I said.

"They're profiteering, general."

"So they are. That's the way of business in war. Our task is to keep on going; requisition what's needed. Sherman'll pay. I want these brave men paid their forty cents a day, well fed, armed and equipped, and rewarded for the sacrifices they're making for the territory."

"We've already spent half a million dollars. Half a million! Who'll pay?"

"Army. The vouchers go to Sherman. He'll send them to Grant. Grant will grumble and okay them for the War Department."

"What if Congress rejects the cost?"

"Colonel, we'll get what we need to fight a war, and leave the rest to the politicians. Congress won't leave citizens naked in the face of savages."

"We lost another twenty-seven men this week; they just walked out."

Howie just shook his head. He was a fearless man, and if we could keep troops in the field, he was the one to lead them. He had done his turn for the vigilantes, knew hard choices, and wasn't afraid to make them. The reality was, my militia's officers were drawn from the vigilantes. They would not admit it or identify themselves, but I had been in the territory long enough to pick them out.

I wondered, uneasily, which of these captains and majors

had threatened my life over the Daniels pardon. They were watching, waiting, taking my measure, a hundred staring eyes. But if I surrendered to all my apprehensions, I would rate myself a coward. There was a war to prosecute.

In spite of these forays over the roads and trails, I continued to spend most of my time in Virginia City. I had no trouble finding support for the war: even Blake at the *Post,* my most vociferous critic, was bleating for action, arms, men, and victory.

"When are the first steamboats going to reach Fort Benton?" I asked Deputy U.S. Marshal Biedler one day.

"Late June. Water's high this year."

"The muskets will be on one of the first. Ah, that'll be a sight! Put those in the hands of the militia! Tip them with bayonets! Then see the savages run."

I haunted the newspaper for the wire reports that came in by express, there being no direct line of communication between Virginia City and the east. But I learned nothing of the Sioux and Cheyenne, who were expected to block passage on John Bozeman's trail. Fetterman's command was dead. Red Cloud was gathering strength. Thunderclouds hung over the territory.

June heat lay thick and cruel over Montana, making men irritable. I heard prophecies of doom; the red race would exact its toll on every hamlet, every miner, every lone voyager, sweeping through the thinly settled wilds like a fatal scythe.

I ignored these forebodings. Soon we would have muskets, and the waxed cartridges to go with them, and then my ragged militia would march.

I am fey, like most Irish, and felt a strange darkness stretching over the land, as if the red fury would soon dash our civilized shores. The Sioux and Cheyenne were gathering for war,

and only the Crow stood between that mighty force and ourselves. We needed those rifles.

Green Clay Smith arrived overland from Salt Lake, and
glad was I to see him, for I was weary of civil service and wanted
relief from the harangue and clamor of office. Suddenly I was
Secretary Meagher again, no longer occupying that front desk.

"Governor, I'm leaving for Fort Benton to pick up those
rifles," I said. "They're probably waiting for us, and if not,
they'll be arriving on the next steamer or two."

"All right then, General. Take care to count them. I don't
trust the river boat companies."

I approached Libby that evening. "I'm going to Fort Benton to pick up the rifles General Sherman's sending us. I'm
thinking you could wait for me in Helena and see the sights."

"Such as they are," she said. "I suppose you'll want to show
me the tree where they hanged Daniels." She didn't say the
rest: That was where vigilantes had threatened the acting governor the first time. There had been more threats, mostly insin-
uations rather than bald warnings. But now I was secretary
again, not acting governor, and I counted myself safe enough.

She smiled, as she always did. "If you want me, I'll be
there."

And so it was arranged, and my spirits lifted.

The air remained hot and tight and dry, and I would have
welcomed spring storms to relieve the sullen heat. But that was
not to be. I sent my staff ahead, and caught the coach with
Libby, and by the time we reached Last Chance Gulch we were
dehydrated and worn by the brutal swaying of that mud wagon.

I installed her in a room; few were the comforts in Helena,
where everyone had been much too busy gouging gravel out of
the gulch to bother with anything so effete as comfort.

"Wait for me here, my darling," I said, as we gazed out a window overlooking Last Chance Gulch.

"I'll see you soon, love," she said, her hand in mine.

"Libby . . . I'm the most fortunate of men. You make it so. We've been together now for many years, through highs and lows, war and peace, and you've always been there, heart and soul."

"It's because you won me, Tom."

"And you won me, such as I am. If I've failed you in any way, I . . ." I wondered what on earth was impelling me to make such declarations just then, and in a room and city not our own. "Libby, don't go near that tree."

"Tom, they wouldn't even have to tell me what tree it is. I would know."

"Libby, whatever I've been, whatever I am, you've brought me grace and love. I . . . I sometimes wonder how you manage, the times I've dreamed, the times that things go wrong. But there you are, at the end of a day, or the end of a campaign, or the end of a road. There you are, your arms open, making me whole. If I could be half the person you are, I'd count myself favored."

"Tom? Tom?" She clasped me, something eloquent in her hug.

"They're waiting for me, Libby. Adieu for now. If I can't return in a few days, I'll send word."

We hugged. A strange passion infused us and disturbed us both as we parted. I left her at the door of the clapboard hotel.

My staff and I took the wagon road out of town, amid a brutal heat that hung close and sweated the horses. I had with me two officers, and six teamster-privates to load the heavy cases into wagons. Even with that entourage we could not take more than a few hundred of the rifles with us. The rest would await further transportation in Fort Benton, where the old fur-trading post would serve as a secure base.

We struck the Missouri and followed it until we were forced by the terrain and the falls to take the long, dry, dusty arc north of the river across desolate and forbidding grasslands where nothing grew to cheer the heart. I grew unwell, having sipped some bad water, and soon was deviled with the summer complaint, which compelled me to stop frequently for relief, whilst my men waited a polite distance forward. The heat made me giddy. My foreboding increased as I traveled eastward toward the head of navigation.

"You all right, general?" asked Colonel Howie.

"No, the complaint grips my bowels, but let's push on."

The first day of July, 1867, in the eighteenth year of my exile, was a particularly difficult one. I clung to the saddle, let my horse follow the rest without further guidance, and concerned myself only with staying in the saddle and keeping my britches clean. I had become fevered in the brassy afternoon sun, which glared down upon the yellow clay and brought tears to my eyes, until my body lacked the fluids to lubricate them.

Late in that day we descended a long, dusty grade and rode across a denuded flat on the north bank of the Missouri, where the little outpost lay along the river. Miserable it might be, but it had been the entrepôt of the territory, and even now, great merchant empires were springing from its riverfront street.

Over two thousand river miles downstream rose the great city of St. Louis. But here, for the briefest of seasons whilst mountain waters permitted travel, the manufactures that sustain life in the territories arrived on boat after boat, and were heaped along the levee until ox-teams whipped along by blasphemous teamsters carried these iron goods and cloth and grain to the most remote camps in the United States.

We clattered onto Front Street, which was bounded by the levee on one side and mercantile houses on the other, and there encountered the first mortals we had seen for dozens of miles.

"There he is!" yelled one bushy-bearded fellow, and I stared at him, not liking the revolver at his belt.

Was he the very one who had pinned the threat to me upon the jacket of poor Daniels, as he hung lifeless to a tree in Helena?

I took the measure of the man, and decided that Fort Benton was no friendly port for General Meagher.

43

I felt strangely distracted, as if I were out of my body, as we traversed Front Street. Three river steamers bobbed alongside the levee, the *Guidon*, the G. A. *Thompson*, and the *Amelia Poe*. I did not see on the levee what I hoped to see: numerous coffin-like crates containing the Springfields. I did not feel up to making inquiries, and sent my staff to reconnoiter.

These battered, mud-stained steamers were a far cry from the gilded palaces floating the Mississippi, but still an impressive sight at this vast distance from the States. They had fought their way up a treacherous river to this remote corner, consuming twelve or fifteen cords of wood a day, bringing with them adventurers, gold-seekers, as well as mountains of merchandise.

I watched my men spread out to these amazing vessels, but I felt weak and dehydrated, and filled with a dread I could not explain. I was surrounded by crowds of people; nothing would afflict me there, save for the weakness of my bowels, which savaged my peace and comfort. Why did I see menace in every face? Why did I startle whenever anyone said, "Hello, General!"

I could not explain my own malaise, save for the pernicious complaint of my bowels. But nothing would allay my fears; not bright sun, not the comfort of crowds, not a port city where I might find a secure place to rest.

Seeking some shade, I tied my horse to a hitchrail and entered the store and warehouse of I.G. Baker, an acquaintance of mine from my previous trips, and one of the aggressive merchants who was filling the needs of the whole territory. He received me sympathetically and took me past fragrant burlap sacks and crates and heaps of ironwork and barrels to a cheerful back room where the cool and quiet soon assuaged my strange disorders.

"General, you're pale," Isaac said, helping me to a wooden chair.

"It's the stomach complaint," I said. "We've been six days from Sun River, fighting heat, alkali water, and flies and swarms of biting insects at every buffalo wallow. It's taken the starch right out of me."

"Thirsty?"

I nodded. He filled a tin cup with cool water, dipped from a pail, and I sucked it, feeling my bowels protest even the water I needed.

"A little blackberry wine settles the bowels and stops the flux," he said.

"Yes! Please!"

He poured a tumbler-full, and I downed it and another, and felt the wine begin its beneficial work.

Colonel Howie materialized at the door. "General, the rifles aren't here yet."

I nodded. "We'll wait. Billet the men; I'll sign the vouchers."

"Several more boats due in the next three or four days," Isaac said. "One'll have your rifles."

"Let me know where to find you and the men."

"Give them leave tonight?" he asked.

I nodded.

"Where will you be, General?"

I didn't know. "I'll leave word here," I said.

Baker hovered solicitously, though I knew he had business to attend during this, his busiest season.

"Isaac, would you oblige me with some stationery and ink and a pen, please?"

"Certainly," he said. Soon all I needed was at hand, and he offered me his desk.

The blackberry wine had settled my complaint a little, and I was determined to write, sending the mail downriver on the next steamer to leave. I wrote Richard O'Gorman in New York, wanting him to stay abreast of this relic of Young Ireland, governing a land as distant as Timbuktu. The writing quieted my nerves, and I found comfort in my ancient gift of words.

That done, I felt well enough to explore the familiar old town, and strolled into the brassy sun again. This time I drifted along the levee to the old adobe fur post to the east, gazing ever down river, as if my salvation would steam around the bend at any moment. I thought maybe my staff and I should ride further down to one of the staging areas where goods were commonly disembarked during low-water periods. Maybe the rifles had come only as far as Cow Island.

My shaky frame permitted me only the briefest of walks, and on returning I encountered again several fierce-looking men, all wearing revolvers, who pointed at me and whispered.

"Good afternoon," I said tautly.

"General," one said, as they strode past me. Was he wearing an old Confederate shirt? I felt naked, without so much as a pocket pistol.

I stumbled back to Baker's store and retreated to the quiet cool of his back room, feeling distraught again. I found the wine and helped myself. My stomach was perilously close to rebellion.

Baker appeared. "Captain Doran of the *Thompson's* looking for you, General," he said.

There was Irish in that name.

A moment later, a wiry and affable fellow appeared before me.

"Johnny Doran, General," he said, offering a hand. "No, don't get up, sir. 'Tis all my honor, meeting a man I admire, and here of all places on earth. Isaac Baker said you're much distressed with the complaint."

I shook his warm hand, noting the clamminess of my own.

"General Meagher, I've followed your entire life, from the days you spoke up before the Queen's men in behalf of the people, to now, when you govern a vast territory. You've a friend in Captain Doran, sir."

The man's kindness lifted my spirits. "Thank you, Captain. I just may need a friend at the moment."

"How is it that I can help ye?"

"My life is threatened. I'm sure of it. Do you know of a safe place?"

"Threatened? Who's doing the threatening, sir?"

I shook my head. "They're here, watching me."

"It may be the fever, sir."

He didn't believe me. I don't think Baker believed me either. They probably thought I'd been sipping.

"But count on Johnny Doran, General. I'll put you in one of my staterooms if you want. It's a guarded ship, the watch on duty all times."

"Would you? Ah, Captain, you relieve my worries."

"It's a comfortable billet, General, good bunk, cool and safe. You'll be much improved in the morning."

His cheer heartened me. We talked a while more, and my strength returned to me.

THE EXILE

We left Baker's shadowed retreat and strolled the bustling levee, where profane teamsters maneuvered wagons, and stevedores hoisted goods into the wagon-beds. Few women were in sight, and even fewer children. This was a man's town in a man's frontier.

"There, that's the *Thompson*, my little scow. We brought two hundred tons and sixty-eight passengers upriver. Over there's the *Amelia Poe*, brought a hundred eighty-three tons and fifty passengers, and that one, the *Guidon*, brought two hundred twenty-five tons, and fifty seven passengers."

I felt a strange chill. "Long ago I escaped Van Diemen's Land in the *Elizabeth Thompson*."

"Ah, then the *Thompson* will be your salvation again."

"What about the *Louella*? We think our shipment's aboard her."

"She's behind us. Maybe a week."

"How do you know that?"

"We talk to the ones we meet on the water, megaphones. We know the scheduled departures."

"You know them all?"

"Every one, General. I know each one with a glance."

We had reached the end of the levee. "Captain, I'm about done in."

"I'll see you to your stateroom, General, and an honor it is for Johnny Doran to give you a berth."

I followed the captain through the jostling, cursing, grunting toilers, sweating teamsters lifting keg and carton into the wagons, while drooping oxen slumbered in their yokes and stood in heaps of acrid green dung. No one paid any attention to me, or was I mistaken?

We walked up a gangway and I found myself on the boiler deck, where cordwood lay in heaps and a great iron furnace waited cold and mute. I dread boats, especially these monsters, but I welcomed the haven Captain Doran was offering me. We ascended a stair to the cabin deck, and there he showed me into a small, clean private room. A chill ran through me, for no reason at all.

"How's this, General?"

"It looks fine, Captain. Does the door lock?"

"It's not the sturdiest lock, sir." He eyed me. "I tell you what: I'll be back in a while, and we'll have some cigars and brandy, and I'll look after you."

I thanked him, and he vanished. I walked to the rail overlooking the river, which ran cold and fast and mean past these vessels, tugging and sucking and pounding the tethered boats. The Missouri was a cruel river, all snowmelt from the mountains, carrying in its bosom everything it could rip up, from trees to the bones of buffalo. The sun was low, and shimmering off the racing waters.

Night came hard to the north, and temperatures dropped hard, as fast as the sun retreated. A summer's day on the high plains could range from freezing to a hundred degrees. I retreated uneasily to my cabin, tried the door, knew it wouldn't hold out any determined man, and lay uncomfortably on the bunk, feeling a malaise again.

Dusk settled, and Captain Doran returned, this time with a copy of *The Collegians*, a novel that interested him.

"Have a look at it. A fine fiction it is, and I'm halfway through already. Come out to the deck, and we'll take some tea," he said.

That suited not only my mood but my stomach, and in short order a cabin boy brought us some steaming tea. I sipped, having the sense that it would settle my tumultuous stomach. The river raced by us, black and chill, as the light dimmed and the yellow bluffs across the water shrank into the gloom. From our deck chairs we watched the day soften away, and the bleak night close. I felt the old foreboding again.

"Johnny, I'm in danger. I'm sure of it!" I said. "Do you have a revolver?"

"I do."

"May I borrow it tonight?"

"Certainly."

Doran left me for a few moments, and when he returned he placed a Colt Navy in my hands. I checked the nipples and found them all properly capped. It felt cold and heavy in my hand.

"I'm going to leave you, take care of business things. You can lock yourself in. There's a coal-oil lamp hanging in there, if you want to read that novel."

"I will, then, Johnny."

By the time I settled in my room it was full dark, and the scowl of night lay over the ship. A few lamps shown from Front Street. I closed and locked the flimsy door, and set the revolver on a stand beside the bunk. In the dark I pulled off my soiled trousers and shirt, and settled on the hard bunk in my white union suit.

I didn't feel like reading. I missed Libby. Doran reminded me of home, and my exile, and the Ireland I would never see again. Eighteen years had I been adrift. Eighteen years since I had walked the wet cobbled streets of Waterford. Eighteen years since I had raised the sword, escaped the hangman's noose, sailed to the ends of the earth, escaped to New York, married an American rose, fought in the bloodiest of all wars for a people not my own, and now served obscurely in a wilderness province. Was this all there was of Thomas Francis Meagher?

I felt tears rise in my eyes.

The cramps were lifting; tomorrow would be a bright day.

The door crashed open so suddenly I startled. Two men, cloaked entirely in black, burst in and caught hold of me even before I could reach for the revolver.

"Up," said one, yanking me to my feet.

"Go ahead of us. There's a gun in my hand."

I knew that voice.

"You!" I said. "You!"

EPILOGUE

For two months, Libby walked the banks of the Missouri River, but the swift and icy stream kept its secrets. On July 5 Governor Green Clay Smith offered a thousand-dollar reward, supplemented by another thousand dollars pledged by the citizens of Helena, a handsome amount in those days, for the recovery of Meagher, but no one ever claimed it. The Helena citizens' reward had been gathered by Nathaniel Langford, who held high position in the vigilantes.

Libby returned to New York and lived for nearly forty more years in dignified widowhood.

On August 14th, a requiem mass for Thomas Francis Meagher was celebrated in New York's Church of Saint Francis Xavier. The obsequies were conducted by the officers of the Irish Brigade, each wearing a sprig of boxwood to commemorate Fredericksburg. Every seat in the church was occupied, and many more people collected before it.

Following the mass, Richard O'Gorman offered a funeral oration at the Cooper Institute, where the officers of the brigade had again gathered, flanked by Irish and American flags, and before them all, a portrait of Meagher.

"In Ireland, in America, he invited no man to any danger that he was not ready to share," O'Gorman said. "Never forget this : he gave all, lost all, for the land of his birth. He risked all

327

for the land of his adoption, was her true and loyal soldier, and in the end died in her service. For these things, either in Ireland or in America, he will not soon be forgotten, and the grateful instincts of two peoples will do him justice and cherish his memory in their heart of hearts. And so, old friend, farewell."

Historians have treated Meagher harshly, and never more so than in their criticism of his efforts to raise a militia in 1866 and 1867. The cost of that two-month campaign, which never encountered a hostile force, ran over a million dollars, of which Congress eventually paid half. Territorial merchants had grossly overpriced everything Meagher bought, and the territory was stuck with the remaining debt, which wasn't paid off until the middle of the 20th century.

But the judgment of historians has been too severe. Meagher was responding to a clamor for protection that issued from all quarters of the territory, from his friends and enemies alike, upon John Bozeman's death. Avowed enemies, such as the *Post's* editor Henry Blake, hastened to accept commissions in that militia, and praised Meagher in print for his call to arms.

At that time, the Sioux under Red Cloud were engaged in full-scale war against army posts not far east along the Bozeman Trail, and that winter of 1866–67 Captain Fetterman's entire command had been wiped out by fifteen hundred to two thousand Sioux and Cheyenne warriors. The avowed purpose of the Sioux—and they succeeded—was to close the Bozeman Trail, one of the three arteries from the States to the mining camps.

Nothing much stood between the mining camps to the west and the vast military strength of the powerful Sioux in southeastern Montana Territory and what is now Wyoming. The Sioux forced the closure of those forts and the Bozeman

Trail was shut down. As historian Dee Brown put it, "Red Cloud had won his war."

It is no wonder that nearly everyone in the territory fervently wanted either regular army or militia protection. Meagher might be faulted for failing to watch the purse, but not for organizing militia, and indeed, had he failed to do so he would have been accused of gross negligence.

General Meagher lives on in memory, in the name of a Montana county, in the form of a handsome equestrian statue on the grounds of the Montana state capitol and another in the Antietam battlefield. And as an American hero.

The death of Thomas Francis Meagher has been shrouded in mystery, and probably always will be. Upon his death, his fierce critics proclaimed that he was drunk and fell overboard, while his defenders asserted that he was sick and fell overboard. The other possibility was that he was murdered, most likely by Montana's vigilantes, or one branch of them.

According to Thomas Keneally (*The Great Shame*), a letter that Meagher wrote to Richard O'Gorman just before his death is extant, and shows no sign of the sort of sloppy handwriting one might expect from an inebriate. Meagher had enemies, and they were willing to blacken his name by any means, and may even have used the inebriation story as a cover for something darker, a vigilante murder.

The merchant I. G. Baker records that Meagher had dysentery, but was not so sick that he could not stroll the town. If he could navigate around town, he could also navigate the railed deck of a anchored river boat. It seems unlikely to me that either sickness or inebriation led to Meagher's death.

Far more likely is the prospect that he was murdered. He had been repeatedly threatened. He had gravely and repeatedly offended the vigilantes and their political allies. He was in fear of his life and said so to Johnny Doran, the river boat captain.

AUTHOR'S NOTES

Long after his death, an aged vigilante made a deathbed confession that he and others had executed Meagher that night, only to rescind the confession before he died. The sensational confession was immediately ridiculed by surviving vigilantes.

Part of the reason Meagher remains a fascinating subject is his mysterious demise. But he was also a man so loved and hated, so admired and scorned, that I sometimes found myself wondering if the admirers and critics were talking about the same man.

He was certainly complex: bold and courageous and gallant; but a heavy drinker, unable to earn a living, and prone to rely on connections rather than abilities. The most balanced, and I believe accurate, portrait of him was offered by Professor Denis Gwynn as an O'Donnell Lecture at the National University of Ireland. Gwynn describes a gallant, brave, idealistic man who had terrible weaknesses as well, weaknesses that ultimately destroyed him.

I came at last to the belief that Meagher was a greathearted man who gave his all to just causes. He gave voice to the Irish people and even gave them their tricolor flag. And he fought valiantly to save the Union and rid it of the abominable institution. His Irish Brigade may well have saved the Army of the Potomac from disaster more than once.

There are two well-balanced biographies of Meagher, those of Athearn and Keneally, and two books by Lyons and Cavanaugh that are simply hagiographies. I have listed these and other material in the sources.

The librarians at the Montana Historical Society found everything I was looking for, including the Organic Act that established the Territory of Montana, and I wish to acknowledge their great contribution to this novel, and thank them. I also wish to thank Lenore Puhek of Helena, who generously made her research material available to me.

And I am most grateful for the valued counsel and editing of my Forge editor, Dale L. Walker.

—Richard S. Wheeler
May 2002

AN INFORMAL LIST
OF SOURCES

Robert G. Athearn, *Thomas Francis Meagher: An Irish Revolutionary in America*, University of Colorado Press.

Lew L. Callaway, *Montana's Righteous Hangmen*, University of Oklahoma Press.

Thomas J. Dimsdale, *Vigilantes of Montana*, University of Oklahoma Press.

Thomas Flanagan, *TheYear of the French*, Henry Holt (novel).

Denis Gwynn, *Thomas Francis Meagher*, O'Donnell Lecture, National University of Ireland.

Joseph Kinsey Howard, *Montana High, Wide, and Handsome*, Bison Book, University of Nebraska Press.

Robert Hughes, *The Fatal Shore*, Alfred A. Knopf.

Michael Kavanaugh, *Memoirs of Thomas Francis Meagher*, The Messenger Press.

Thomas Keneally, *The Great Shame and the Triumph of the Irish in the English-SpeakingWorld*, Doubleday.

Conrad Kohrs, *An Autobiography*, privately published.

Nathaniel P. Langford, *Vigilante Days and Ways*, American and World Geographic Publishing.

W. F. Lyons, *Brigadier General Thomas Francis Meagher: His Political and Military Career*, D & J Sadlier and Co.

Betty M. Madsen and Brigham D. Madsen, *North to Montana! Jehus, Bullwhackers, and Muleskinners on the Montana Trail*, University of Utah Press.

Michael P. Malone and Richard Roeder, *Montana:A History of Two Centuries*, University of Washington Press.

R. E. Mather and F. E. Boswell, *Hanging the Sheriff*, HMP.

AN INFORMAL LIST OF SOURCES

Robert Ryal Miller, *Shamrock and Sword: The Saint Patrick's Battalion in the U.S.-Mexican War*, University of Oklahoma Press.

Joel Overholser, *Fort Benton: World's Most Innermost Port*, privately published, distributed by Falcon Press.

Carl Sandburg, *Abraham Lincoln: The War Years*, Dell Laurel edition.

Robert M. Utley, *Frontier Regulars: The United States Army and the Indians 1866–1891*, Bison Book, University of Nebraska Press.

David C. Whitney, *The American Presidents*, Doubleday.

Muriel Sibell Wolle, *Montana Pay Dirt*, Sage Books.

MONOGRAPH

Merrill G. Burlingame, *John Bozeman, Montana Trailmaker*, Museum of the Rockies.

SHORT MATERIAL

Organic Act, Territory of Montana, Montana Historical Society library.

"Alder Gulch in 1863," Mollie Sheehan, MHS.

"The Fighting 69th," *The World of Hibernia*, Summer 1995.

"Red and Green: The Irish Brigade at Fredericksburg," James Callaghan, *Civil War Times*.

America Singing: Nineteenth Century Song Sheets, Library of Congress.

Birthplace of Montana, John G. Lepley, Pictorial Histories Publishing Co.

"On Being Found Guilty of Treason," Thomas Francis Meagher, MHS archives.